The Invisible Heiress

KATHLEEN O'DONNELL

 ITALICS

ITALICS PUBLISHING

$\int\!\int$ ITALICS

Italics Publishing Inc.
Cover and interior design by Sam Roman
Editor: Joni Wilson
ISBN: 1-945302-27-5
ISBN-13: 978-1-945302-27-5

Acknowledgments

For my mom,
who probably couldn't have seen the love letter embedded in this
story,

and for my kids,
who will.

For Ed,
always.

      This book would not have been possible without the support and encouragement of many. My sweet Adelia, whose young life has lifted, and broken my heart, at the same time. Who made me realize the importance of legacy and the written word. Marsha Bailey, for her invaluable insight and writing talent, who has faithfully read every single thing I've given her multiple times and made countless useful suggestions. If it weren't for her I probably would never have been brave enough to write. Toni Lopopolo and her writing group who taught me to write a story worth reading. Renni and Ross Browne from the Editorial Department whose encouragement, support, and expertise went way above and beyond the call of duty. Sandy Dillard, and Christine Turner, for cheering me on and reading even the worst drafts. Doctor Carol Hemingway who gave me the skinny on behavioral therapy and ethics, and who is, mercifully, not anything like the therapist in this novel. And finally, Ray Barnds, who I will think of every time I write a word, and who I wish was still here to read them.

*Daniel, Kayla, Kristen, Kenneth, Che Sr., and Paul

Part I

Haven House

Chapter One

Preston

I don't know which scene satisfied me most—my posh parents waiting in the concrete-walled visitors' room or me deposited in front of them by a uniformed guard.

They sat across from me at the Formica-topped table. My father's face was tight, eyes damp. Seeing him distressed kicked a dent in my smug demeanor, so I stopped looking at him, my eyes ping ponged toward my mother. Despite the sordid circumstances, she shone, her beauty ferocious, perhaps highlighted even more by the dour surroundings. Thick hair still a perfect shade of bombshell blonde, skin pale but flawless despite time's march, the blue of her eyes a perpetual shock.

So entranced I forgot to insult her.

Almost.

"My incarceration poses a real problem for you. Doesn't it, Mother? Harrison Blair doesn't sully herself with the downtrodden."

She shifted backward then forward quick.

"You're the problem, Preston. Downtrodden? That's how you think of yourself? You—"

"Harrison, Preston," Dad said. "Please. Let's start right. Preston, your mother and I haven't seen you in so long. Though God knows I've tried. Let's all make a real effort."

He paused, probably to steel himself for objections in stereo. None came.

Dad continued. "You're not incarcerated. You're hospitalized. Your new therapist what's her name." He squeezed his eyes shut like her name had been tattooed inside his lids. "Um, she, Isabel, says you've made some headway, participating in therapy now."

"Might as well," I said.

"That's the spirit. Won't be long until you're back home. You're doing so well considering how difficult, well you're done with that part of the, uh, the rehabilitation."

"You mean the sweating, shaking, puking, padded room part?" I said.

"You're sober. That's all I meant."

My mother's eyes popped like a kidnapper just yanked the hood off her head.

"Sober?" she said. "Doesn't that term apply to alcoholics? Surely they have another term for homicidal, drunken pill add—"

"She's clean, Harrison. That's all that matters."

Dad kept yanking on his tie. I thought he might hang himself with it right before our eyes.

"*All that matters*? Is that your idea of a joke, Todd?"

"Nice dye job, Dad. Only you'd believe those stupid commercials. So natural no one will—"

"*Darling*, stop," he said to Mother. "Of course sobriety's not all but it's a start. I think, *we* think enough time has passed. We should jumpstart our family therapy."

"*We* who?" I said.

The guard took a step forward, disapproving of my elevated tone. My father waved him back.

"Not *Mother*, I'm sure."

"Well, Isabel thought—"

"Just because I'm in the cuckoo's nest doesn't mean I don't have rights," I said. "Isabel shouldn't talk to you at all about me. I'm an adult. She's *my* shrink. Confidentiality too big a word?"

"Shrinks. Therapy," Mother said. "In my day you poured yourself a scotch and got on with it."

"You don't pour yourself anything. You hire that out," I said.

"Family therapy's part of the deal," Dad said. "The judge insisted—"

"*You* own the judge. *We* don't *have* to do anything. Remind him, Mother."

"You should kiss Judge Seward's robed ass," she said, hissing like a stabbed tire. "You'd be someone's bitch if not for his mercy."

"You mean, if not for *your money*. Don't pretend you did shit for me. You did everything for yourself, Mother, to stop the gossip. That's what you do."

With both fists, Dad twisted the tie he'd finally managed to take off.

"Preston, we hoped something good could come out of—"

"Todd, the only good that could possibly come out of this mess is if Preston stays *hospitalized* for the rest of her natural life."

"Harrison, please. We agreed—"

"*You* agreed. With no one but yourself."

"Hate to break up the party but I'm ready to go back to my room," I said more to the guard than my parents.

"Wait, Preston," Dad said, peering around the room, looking for his spine. "It doesn't feel like it now, but here's a chance for you and Mom to, I don't know what, start again, improve your relationship, even a little. That's what we all want, isn't it?"

"Steady on, Dad. The devil comes dressed as everything you want."

I let the guard take my arm, turned in time to see Mom lean her head back enough to dab at the scar under the collar of her ivory silk blouse, a scarlet line cut across her throat, not quite ear to ear, a vicious permanent necklace.

Chapter Two

Isabel

"Isabel, taking on a prisoner from the social register wasn't the best idea." Jonathan held pen and notepad ensconced behind his prized cocobolo desk.

"She's a *patient* in a private psychiatric hospital," I said.

"We both know you're in over your head. You need to ease back into our practice after your, well, your R&R. I'd hoped you'd spend more time here since you're back. I can't keep filling in with your clients while you're hoop-jumping at the asylum for the rich and famous."

I sat in one of his two new club chairs so low to the ground I had to look up to see him. If I'd been any shorter I wouldn't have been able to see over the desk.

"Wife complaining?" I said. "She's painted the place? Vagina pink belongs nowhere, much less on a therapist's office walls."

"Whole thing's horrible but after the fire we needed to remodel. Yes, wife complains. You'd know how it works if you'd manage to get married."

"How long could she take to redo?" I said. "Fire didn't damage *that* much."

"Had to practically gut the place. That's enough about my wife and the office décor. What about your star client?"

"Preston Blair's a hopeless case. I'd refer her on except I promised."

"Promised who?"

"Judge Seward," I said.

"Since when are you chummy with a judge?"

"I'm chummy with a lot of people you know nothing about."

"Oh, well. Excuse me. Didn't realize you were so well connected."

We simmered a bit in an awkward pause. I crossed and uncrossed my legs several times before Jonathan piped up.

"Why on earth would you want to refer a well-paying client out?" he said like he'd thought hard about the possible answers but discarded all of them. "You know your situation here might not last as long as you think. It behooves us both for you to pull your weight."

That rankled.

"Really?" I seriously could not believe the nerve. How stupid was this guy? Time would tell. "I'll keep that in mind. At any rate I try to take on clients who actually want to get better. Preston's too attached to her insanity. She barely speaks except to bark insults. Thinks the whole endeavor's a joke."

"That might explain the involuntary commitment," Jonathan said.

"Thanks, Captain Obvious."

"No charge."

"She's refused to see her father every time he's come to visit," I said. "Because family therapy is court ordered now she doesn't have a choice. It'll be spitting in the wind. The sooner they all cry uncle the better."

"Thought you said the father's sappy where Preston's concerned."

"He is. She's nonresponsive. And that mother, Harrison, no coming back from this for her."

Jonathan pointed at my face. "What's with the fake eyelashes?"

My hand leapt to one eye with a will of its own. "Clearly, you're not on the fashion down-low. False eyelashes have been back in style for a dog's age."

His gaze wandered. I squirmed.

"Stop fidgeting for chrissake," Jonathan said.

"We done barking up the Preston Blair tree?"

"One thought."

"By all means."

"The girl needs help. Don't bail on her. Act like a therapist for a change."

"Got it."

I stood to go, before the lecture started full force, or before I decided to introduce unpleasant topics. I could feel them darken and gather speed all around us like a biblical plague.

"Isabel?"

Shit. Almost made my escape.

"What now?"

"Stop biting your nails. That one's bleeding."

Chapter Three

Preston's Blog

Musings from the Dented Throne

Ain't No Mountain High Enough

Well, my faithful, my royal parents popped 'round to observe me in this unnatural habitat. Thrilled me *no end* to discover the Queen and her Jester confer with my new shrink, whose gourd's on backwards along with her shirt. I'll get a bead on that situation in due time, don't you worry.

Shrinky's behind-my-back treachery tweaks. Family therapy? Bitch, please. A whip and a chair would be more useful. Luckily, the Queen's not falling for that trickery. Jester can't wait. Probably wants to air his marital grievances (of which there are many) behind protective cover. Thinks the Royal She won't throw down in front of a professional. Almost worth talking about my feelings to witness such a spectacle.

Even though the thought of the Queen in close quarters nearly shivered me timbers (vice versa, I'm sure) I felt nothing but happiness to not have to endure Dad's puppy dog devotion unbridled. His drop-ins are a near constant. For all the good it does because I'm not in the mood to humor him with my presence. Ever. Mother can keep him muzzled. Don't give up your day job, Jester.

Never mind that yawning topic. What you really want to know is: what about the Queen?

Royal She's hot under the collar.

Been over a year since I laid eyes on my mother, who wasn't expected to live, I heard. I couldn't help but note her trembling fingers and their white-knuckled grip on one another or how her cool remove jumped ship to be replaced by a jittery rage. Had to give her props for the fuck-you-open-neck shirt she wore that highlighted the startling evidence of my wrath. As I stared at the thin red line dividing the Queen's elegant neck from her collarbone, a weight pushed into my ribcage, a routing pain.

You'll find this hard to swallow, but I forced down an almost uncontrollable urge to climb on the Queen's lap to stop the hurting. My marbles are indeed lost. Once I'd have said I knew the Royal She better than anyone. Then truth hit me like the butt of a gun. I didn't know her at all. Who was this creature whose beauty could still burn down the house? Why did she come to see the one person she should never want to lay eyes on again? Thundered in like a warrior but thundered in just the same.

If you've got an opinion on this debacle, voice one, my faithful.

The simmering hatred I hoard below the surface boiled over when I remembered the source—I'll admit—details are fuzzy. I'm sober but not plugged in. Drugs, drink, and denial (Shrinky's brilliant deduction) sucked up years of my life, like Dorothy's house by the tornado, but I do know one important fact.

The Queen's hands, while bejeweled, are not clean.

My confusion and anger at everything to do with my parents fixes me in its clutches. So three hots and a cot suit me fine for now.

The Invisible Heiress

Go ahead. You know you want to.

Comments

Maggie May

Heiress, your mom coming to visit, pissed or not, means there's hope. She can forgive. Much as she might not want to, she loves you.

Reply: This is your brain on drugs.

Hubba-Hubba

Three hots and a cot? Are you fucking with us? You're on a

five-star vacation. Sounds like first-class problems to me.

Reply: My yacht sank though.

Jill

I can't ever tell if this is a giant snow job. Nevertheless, you've gotta meet my brother. He'll die when he reads your stuff. Big bro's a documentary filmmaker.

Reply: Hopes up.

Chapter Four

Preston

"That's *not* a real baby, you loony toon."

"Preston, don't start again. She's not hurting anyone, loves taking care of her baby," said Nurse Judy. "She knows he's a doll. Don't you, Rosie?"

Rosalie faced the wall like a naughty toddler in time out, bald rubber doll mashed against her chest, murmuring to her invisible friends. I couldn't figure out where the crackpot kept getting new dolls.

"Anyone can take care of a fake baby," I said. "No heroics in that."

I hated the day room—all the nuts in one bowl—talking to themselves, fighting over the remote, shitting their pants. The abrasive shuffle of hospital-issued slippers circling the tiled floor, mumbling in a sedative-laced language understood only by space aliens or the over medicated.

A glimpse of my mother through the barred window diverted my murderous intentions toward Rosalie's doll. She walked with purpose near the parking lot, alone, head held high like those African women with rings around their necks.

Wasn't it only yesterday when Mother and Dad graced me with an audience? Tried to recall the date. No luck.

I checked the wall calendar with its preschool big numbers and sloppy red Xs slashed through the days. Some of the sycophant crazies took turns crossing dates off, but they weren't the most reliable. Looked like it'd been at least two weeks since my parents' last visit. Give or take.

"Judy," I hollered over the squealing from the *Family Feud* contestants on the flat screen. "Did I miss the free-for-all with Isabel and my parents?"

Judy smacked at the computer keyboard with two meaty fingers. "Hmmm. Well, looks like you *were* scheduled for today," she hollered back. "No one called down for you."

"Lucky me."

"I'll go see."

She instructed the orderly to do who-knows-what then lurched out the door.

I scanned the grounds from the barred window. There the old dame stood on the inky pavement in front of Haven House, home to the depressed degenerates, consulting her Cartier.

"Something's fishy in Blairville," I whispered to no one.

Didn't see my father. Super moony over family therapy, didn't make sense he'd miss. My mother. She'd bail. So why was she here? Why didn't I know?

My mother's driver picked her up in the Town Car that never got dirty. Say what you want about Harrison Blair, but she could pick a serf. Chauffeur jumped out from behind the wheel to open her door. God forbid Mother should exert energy on the mundane. She leaned in to fold herself into the backseat, swayed like she might fall but caught herself before buckling under the weight of knowing everything.

Chapter Five

Isabel

"Hey." I stood in Jonathan's office doorway.

He swiveled around in his chair to face me, checked me out from shoes to head. I wanted to cut his wanderings off at the root with a withering comment but didn't. The quiet swelled. I didn't intervene.

"Hey to you too," he finally said.

"Blair Fitzgerald family therapy started today."

I could feel his relief that I'd come to talk shop. The stink of something rotten clung to us.

"Mom arrived solo, District Attorney Dad couldn't make it, or so she said."

"Harrison wears the pants," Jonathan said. "Todd Fitzgerald probably doesn't even own pants. You'd think as DA he'd follow the court order though."

"Judge Seward's their patsy." I leaned against the doorjamb, munched on my fingernail.

"I can't understand you with your fingers in your mouth," Jonathan said.

I jerked them out. My thumb burned where I'd gnawed it to the quick.

"I gave Harrison a stern reminder. She gave no shits." I lowered my chin to growl out my best Harrison Blair imitation. "The court doesn't order me. My father served as the attorney general of this state, my grandfather the governor, Todd's brother the senator—"

"Mom's James Earl Jones?"

"Voice box damage," I said. "Harrison wants Preston committed for life."

"Why'd she bail the kid out in the first place?"

"She didn't. Todd did. Harrison stayed in the hospital for months, thinks Todd's view of the situation is *optimistically skewed*."

"What do you think?"

"I'm inclined to agree. Preston doesn't want help. I can't get excited about treating her. Going through the motions. So far, she talks a lot about another patient. Preston swiped her doll, stepped on its head. The patient with the doll fished a photo out of the trash that Preston had thrown away."

"What's in the picture?"

"Don't know," I said. "Supervising nurse just told me."

"You drive here with all the windows rolled down?"

I smoothed my mussed hair with open palms.

"The Blair girls," Jonathan said. "Big chips on their shoulders, all named for men. Family ran out of boys. Don't change their name when they marry."

"How do you know?"

"How do you *not* know?"

Jonathan loved to show off his endless capacity for trivia.

"Like everyone does?"

"Google them," he said. "They're Virginia's version of the Kennedys. Everything they do is news. Although, Preston's last fandango sprinted through the press, must've cost 'em a load in payoffs."

"I live under a rock," I said.

He whirled around in his chair again, his back to me.

"I wish."

Chapter Six

Preston

"Lots of books," Isabel waved at the floor of my private room.

"Think I'm illiterate?"

"Of course not. I'm just—"

"I went to Harvard, Brown, Yale," I said.

"Three schools. Wow."

"Didn't graduate from any."

Isabel fell silent so I poked at her.

"Only one of us in this room attended community college," I said. "On scholarship."

"Sorry to disappoint," Isabel said. "Paid my way through a top-tier school with loans like the rest of us working-class schmucks."

"Since when is clown college top tier?"

To my surprise, Isabel laughed. Out loud.

"Now *that* was funny," she said.

I didn't see that coming.

She reached in her vinyl bag, scored a notebook, put her therapist look back on and started in again.

"Didn't you want to finish college?" she said. "Learn a profession?"

Caught off guard by Isabel's laugh, a hearty and (if I'm truth telling) kind of sexy one, it took me a bit to answer.

"Yeah," I said. "But not the college or profession my parents chose."

"What'd they choose?"

"Law. Like we need another lawyer."

"What would you have chosen?"

"You don't care about the answer any more than they did," I said.

"Yes, I do."

"Matricidal mania," I said. "I'd have stayed for that class."

There she went again. Laughing. Definitely on the sexy side.

"I know I shouldn't spur you on, but you're a clever girl, Preston. And funny. Fucked up but funny. So why'd you quit?"

"Isn't there some shrink rule about not telling a patient they're fucked up?"

This chick got my attention.

"What were you saying about schools?" she said, her face unreadable.

"Quit one." I'd go along. "Two kicked me out. They don't like you to bring drugs on campus. Or smoke 'em in class." I took a happy trot down memory lane. "Guess I did kick that one wimp's ass but he owed me money."

"Is violence your usual response to unhappiness?" Isabel said.

"Black eye's hardly violent. No one got hurt. Well, not really."

Isabel sat back, stared at me. I'm sure she expected I'd wade right in to the deep end, erupt like Mount Vesuvius, a gush of hair-raising confessions. I took her measure instead.

"Those lashes come with glue or no?" I said.

Apparently made of Teflon, Isabel still stared, mum. I made another run at her.

"A for effort on that combover though, Baby Jane."

She touched the loose lashes, then her hair. No laughing this time.

"Does insulting me make you feel better?"

"No, but it's a start."

"I don't know if I believe that."

"Do you believe your pancake makeup covers those bruises?"

Her fingers bolted to her jawline, lingered a few seconds but she didn't miss a beat.

"Did trying to kill your mother make you feel better?"

"You don't know shit from shinola about me and my mother."

****

Isabel's further attempts to discuss my mother fell flat. She went another way. "Let's talk about something else then. Why do you feel you can't get along with the other patients?

"I thought we agreed. Who gives a shit what I feel?"

"We didn't agree to any such thing," she said. "How you feel determines your behavior."

I almost admired her attempt to propel me back to what happened with my mother. Before anything offensive rolled off my tongue she said, "*Feelings* are not *behaviors*. You don't have to *behave* the way you *feel*."

"Like that's news," I said. "Doesn't take an Einstein to know my *behaving* the way I *feel* got me in quite a pickle."

"Why smash Rosalie's doll?"

"Why not?"

"Because of a picture?"

"Because she's a drooling moron," I said.

"We talked about how to harness your anxiety without lashing out."

"I forgot."

"Why'd you throw the photograph away?"

"What's it to you? It's no one's business what I trash."

"That's it?" With her pen, Isabel pointed out the lone, crinkled photo, a bit worse for the trashing but intact, taped above my bed. "Is that you?" She'd gotten up for a closer look. "Holding a baby?"

"Well, it's not one of the Olsen twins."

"How old were you?"

"Seven or eight, I think."

"Who's the baby?"

"My brother, Cooper."

"How old?"

"I dunno. A year maybe."

Isabel crept closer still. "Thought you were an only child."
"I am now."
"He died?" She touched the photo with her fingertip.
"Yes."
"When?"
"He was dead in that photo. Been dead half that day."

Chapter Seven

Isabel

The dealer threw a jack of diamonds.

"Shit."

I flipped my cards so the table could see my loss, snatched my empty glass off the felt. Thank every god in the universe—club members drank free if they gambled. I passed the tumbler to the cocktail waitress.

"Scotch," I said. Her glittered acrylic nails barely made contact. "Never mind, I'll get it in the bar."

"You in or out?" the dealer said.

"Out." I jumped down from the stool.

Some loudmouthed jackass, whose toupee looked like a squirrel had crawled up his scalp, held court in the lounge. To avoid him and his ilk, I veered toward the slots, sure I could win big before calling it a night. I'd hit a bad patch. *No one* got lucky all the time.

Except, the Blairs.

Unlike me, who scratched and clawed for every single thing, they hit the jackpot every day of their useless *Town & Country* lives. Never worked, married important men, or lived on daddy's largesse, didn't go to jail no matter the crime. Flitted about with their golden spoons, rolling sevens every time they shot the dice. Their only accomplishment was being born to the right family. Their existence bored under my skin like ticks.

I perched the tumbler I'd meant to fill, but forgotten about, atop the first available slot machine, scrounged around my purse. In it to win it, I bet my last two dollars.

Shit. Shit.

The club hummed with losers like me looking to score. Shrill bells, whistles, winning sounds, the whine of the air conditioners, and the onslaught from the 1970s cover band consumed me. I felt sick, trudged for the exit, head hung low like someone snapped my neck. Aimed for the blackened doors, the dark quiet a 180-degree shift to my overstimulated senses.

I drove away broken and broke.

****

"Ms. Warner, we need to discuss a financial matter."

"Call at your earliest convenience to make arrangements."

"This is Frank from Honda leasing. I'm sure it's an oversight."

Skipped through the collectors' threats on my cell, tossed the unopened mail in the trash. More demands for payment.

My near-empty apartment didn't uplift me. My financial priorities didn't include furniture. A few thrift shop essentials did me fine.

I staggered to the bedroom. About to fling myself on the bed in a tantrum of toddler proportions, I remembered the rigid mattress, thought better of it. I fretted at the edge of the bed. Preston Blair posed with her dead brother zipped through my mind, struck me like a slap. How did I not know about that baby? Ghoulish freaks.

I doubted Preston's story was true, but even so, what kind of mother would Harrison Blair have to be to inspire her daughter to tell such a lie? What if it wasn't a lie? Preston's insults came to mind. Rude? Sure, but still funny as hell. Every therapist knows humor is pain's prettier cousin. Jonathan nailed it. Preston did need help. If anyone could understand Preston Blair's mother situation, it was me.

With every intention of calling time on this fresh hell of a day—I didn't.

****

"What are you doing here?"

"Hello to you too."

"My wife—"

"Doesn't live here. Don't you think I know that?" I wriggled around him, forced myself into the foyer. He called it that, a *foyer* in an ugly American, French accent. My heels clacked on the marble floor. I could fit my apartment in the oxblood varnished entry.

"This isn't allowed. There are rules—"

"Don't talk," I said.

A cashmere pullover clung to him with casual elegance. His arms drooped in a lazy, passive, defense move.

Pushed him toward the library, knew right where it was.

"Please," he stumbled backward. "We're supposed to be anonymous. We're not in a real relationship. Stop. I mean it. After last time we promised."

His rambling annoyed me but not enough to stop.

"How did you know I was alone?"

Didn't bother to answer.

"Stop, I mean it. I don't think—"

"Shut up," I didn't need him to think. Didn't fuck him for his brain. Got my own brain, thanks. I *didn't* have my own cock. Pulled his out while he squeaked like a mouse, mumbled about his wife again.

Nothing like the feel of a hard dick in your hand—the universal symbol of power—sleek, smooth, the tip sticky and wet. Ran my hand up and down the stiff shaft. He moaned, collapsed on the desktop, elbowed desk crap out of harm's way. I shoved it all to the ground with a crash. Flat on his back, he yelped something about broken glass and the maid, pants and briefs were already hunkered down mid-thigh. Skirt bunched around my waist, I mounted him. Before he could throw me off or come, I yanked him forward, my mouth against his ear.

"Hit me."

Chapter Eight

Preston's Blog

Musings from the Dented Throne

Ghostbusters

I don't like bringing up the dead. It riles the living.

So, my Dented Throne followers, I'm not sure why I told the new shrink about my brother. I wanted to shock. If you'd seen Shrinky, you'd know why—a hot mess—like someone dragged her to our session on the back of a bumper.

She tried to muscle more info out of me. Regretted my blurt, so I clammed up. Hate to say I drank my mother's therapist Haterade, but this one intrigues. She thinks yours truly is a comedian, actually laughed at some of my nastiest bits. And get this—she cusses at me like a teamster.

I suspect she's one tick away from an explosion.

Unless you've guessed my identity (despite my ingenious blogosphere ruse) and have an ear to the ground, you didn't know about my brother either. If you'd stumbled across a blip on Wikipedia or dredged up dirt on the interwebz, you'd know he'd been born, then died, a long time ago. That's it—but not nearly all of it.

No one ever said for sure how he died, that I can remember, but I suspect perhaps the Royal She committed an unfortunate act. As attached as she was, I wouldn't have been surprised to learn she'd accidentally smothered the poor thing. Afterwards, you couldn't blame me for not asking. The Queen holed up with my brother for a couple of days before he'd expired and hours after, in the Royal suite, door locked. Didn't want anyone, especially her parents, to know the only son born to a Blair in generations died on her watch. You've probably caught the hints I've dropped about my grandparents' peculiarities. In fairness, the Queen didn't want her son to be dead either.

She loved that baby like crazy. (Me too, when I wasn't withered inside with jealousy. I know that now.)

My father banged on their bedroom door.

"Let me in! You've got to let me call someone."

I'd never heard my father raise his voice, much less yell like a madman. I didn't wonder at the time why anyone had to *let* a father call someone when his own son died.

"You keep that man's balls in your purse," my grandmother used to say to my mother. "A change purse."

Police chief hustled in, so Dad must've finally sent up the flares without the Queen's permission. I didn't know he was the chief of police back in the day. He'd always been just an FOD (friend of dad) to me. He came to the *super-festive* Christmas party and the Fourth of July barbecue my parents threw every year with his chain-smoking wife and their freckled yowling brat of a son.

Between the police chief and the Jester they coaxed the Queen into giving up my poor, dead brother. On one condition— she'd get a photo of the two of us together. For the Christmas card.

"Be careful, you'll drop him."

Dad held me down, kneeing me into the wingback chair to keep me from squirming out from under the small corpse. I bit the inside of my cheek until it bled. I remember that like yesterday.

"He stinks," I told them.

"He does not." The Queen rewarded my observation with a hard pinch to the soft part of my arm.

I did my best to keep from bawling my head off or barfing. The Littlest Heir felt icy, unnaturally stiff, a cold dead thing. Chief took the photo but didn't ask me to say cheese. After, he carried my brother away, wrapped in a little blanket embroidered with his own little monogram, of course.

One could argue that offering up this story to a therapist might help me, might give context to my bad behavior but I'd argue back—nothing doing. I already know what she'd say. "No wonder the girl's a head case," or some twaddle like that. Besides, my feelings for my brother belong only to me. Feelings are like dollar bills—the more of them you put out for public circulation, the less valuable they become.

I never stopped missing him. If he'd survived I wouldn't have felt so alone in the unhappiest house in the world, the only living witness to the fossilization of my parent's marriage. One that was once easy (if the honeymoon photos don't lie) but turned hard. Hebrew-slaves-building-the-pyramids hard. Drugs helped me deal later. Without them, now I feel the shock of my brother's death all over again. My gut churns so much I fear it'll turn to butter.

"I don't know how I'll bear the heartbreak," I'd heard Mother say at his funeral.

I think if I could ask, and she was honest, my mother would admit she wasn't referring to my brother dying but to me living.

The Invisible Heiress

The Heiress loves to hear what you have to say so she can ignore any and all good advice. By all means, advise.

Comments

Masked Man

Your life is so sad. Wish I could do something for you. Hey, maybe we could hook up. I've got ten inches of shock therapy with your name on it.

Reply: You wish. Get a life, freak.

Maggie May

Hugs 2 you, Heiress. What a terrible thing 2 live thru. Can't imagine how you coped. You're such an inspiration. Hope you're getting all the help you need.

Reply: All the help I need doesn't exist.

Scribbler

I just stumbled across your blog. After reading this latest offering, I'm relieved to know it's all a fiction. I mean really, you should write a novel. What an imagination. You're not going to keep up the ruse that this is real, are you? I mean, how stupid do you think we are?

Reply: How much time do you have?
Jack
My sister made me read your blog. Super weird. I'd love to talk to you about a film project. Got an email?
Reply: crazybitch@fuckoff.com

Chapter Nine

Preston

"Give me the fucking remote." I yanked the clicker out of Rosalie's hand. "Doesn't your doll need a diaper change?"

Nurse Judy kept her head down, studied the crossword puzzle she struggled over, the tip of her purplish tongue poked out the corner of her mouth. I took liberties during her distractions.

"I want to watch *The Life of Kylie*," Rosalie said. Only a smudge of the marinara we'd eaten for lunch smeared her tunic.

I surfed the channels while Rosalie pouted.

"Hey," she said. "Your dad. Purse Bramson."

"What? Where? Purse Bramson?"

"Double-oh whatchacallit. Spy guy."

"Oh brother. James Bond? Pierce Brosnan? My father is not Pierce Brosnan."

I pressed the back arrow. Rosalie's new drug regimen stirred up whatever brain cells she could still rouse. District Attorney Dad filled the screen, surrounded by aides, reporters, and spectators on the courthouse steps. 007 huh? I guess he was handsome. I squinted. From afar, he did look younger with his new hair and all. Plopped my butt on a folding chair in front of the console, scooted closer to the screen. Dad's charisma leapt off the TV. Female reporters scrambled to get near him. He could work a crowd for sure.

"Can't hear," Rosalie scooted along with me.

I flicked up the sound.

Rosalie banged on her doll's head.

"Mama mia," she said a few decibels louder.

"Huh?" I scanned the gathering around DA Dad. "You really are a nutter, that's a reporter, not my mother," I said.

Rosalie dropped her baby, jumped to the screen, her eyeballs an inch away. "That's your M-O-M." Backed into her chair again.

"Fuck me, that *is* my mom."

Nurse must've upped Rosalie's meds. There she was, in the back, barely caught on screen. Mother never showed up ever, let alone *behind* DA Dad in a non-election year. Her mingling with the great unwashed jarred me into high alert. Something didn't make sense. Mother never did anything nonsensical.

"What's she doing there?" I said out loud.

"Maybe it's a surprise," Rosalie rocked her doll back and forth. "Daddy's birthday."

"No, it's not but you're onto something."

Mom lingered, hair loose, unkempt, not the immaculate coif of norm. *Unkempt* and *Harrison Blair* didn't belong in the same sentence. I sat straighter, leaned closer. "Dad didn't know," I said. "*That* makes sense. Mom showed up unannounced, but for what?"

"It's *her* birthday," Rosalie said. "Duh."

"Hush. No, it's not," I said. "Is she wearing Lilly Pulitzer?"

"No," Rosalie said. "*Larry.*"

"Shut up," I elbowed her. "She didn't know about the press conference. No way."

My mother never wore Lilly Pulitzer outside her garden, to bark loud slow orders to the landscapers. Only the working class wore cheerful prints in public.

"Look out, she's a runner," Rosalie ponged up and down.

Sure enough, Mom bolted stage right, but the surging crowd ensnared her. The camera followed her, not my father, who yammered on and on several rows of people in front of where Mother tried to dodge her way through. Press probably hoped for a sleazy story, but I doubt anyone recognized her in such a state. Probably thought some lunatic was trying to cause a commotion or shoot someone. They'd recognize her later. I felt sure. Payoffs would follow if history held. Suddenly, she froze, like somebody zapped her with a stun gun. I half stood to watch, glued.

Her expression gripped me. So foreign, it took a few seconds before I could name it. Panic. The camera shifted farther into the jostling crowd, giving me a better view. A matador without a cape, she stepped to one side, then the other, forward and back, the pulsating pack didn't stand down, kept growing. With one hand at her serrated throat, she stopped short.

"The constitution prevails in Virginia," DA Dad droned, unaware of the drama at the rear. If he half turned, he'd see, but the camera's siren song kept him fixed. Questions ricocheted, cameras clicked, people shoved—Dad oblivious.

The volume hadn't changed, but I'd gone deaf, stared like a sniper. Mother stared right back. I imagined shooting her between the eyes, dropping her like a peony-covered bag of bricks. She crumpled, staggered back a few steps, as if I'd done the deed for real. Then as quick, before anyone could notice, Mom righted herself, pushed through the morass and ran.

"She's off," Rosalie said, like she'd bet a thousand dollars on the twenty to one at Churchill Downs.

I stretched to my full height to take in the spectacle. District Attorney Fitzgerald, handsome in Armani, charmed whoever held a microphone. In his element, Dad played a flawless statesman, mouthing platitudes on TV. Didn't look sad in the slightest. You'd never know his only child studied him from a place where the fixtures, furniture, and clothing were designed so she couldn't kill herself using any of them. Or that his wife, seconds before, fled the scene like a penitentiary escapee.

"Preston," Nurse Judy called. "Your husband's here."

Chapter Ten

Isabel

"That's the last one for me." Jonathan scratched off the remaining item on his agenda. "Your turn."

Missus Jonathan's assault on the conference room walls still distracted me. Paint fumes mashed up with a hint of ash assailed my senses. Before I could refer to my list, his lips started moving.

"Hope you've given up that home repair nonsense," he said. "Bruises gone."

"Learned my lesson," I said. "No more DIY or shaky ladders for me."

Note to self—use a stronger safe word next time. Yell. Don't whisper the damn thing.

"Got a decent haircut too," Jonathan said. "Don King wasn't a good look on you."

I tucked a coiffed, strategically placed extension behind my ear.

"You need to look professional, Isabel, not like a fugitive. Not a fan of those fashionable lashes, but what do I know about trends?"

"Not that again." I scratched an item off my list to make it shorter.

"Thought it might have something to do with your new man."

"What?" I scratched a second one.

"Saw you and your fella last weekend. Well, you and the back of his head. Didn't see me I guess."

"Where?"

"That dive on Sixty-Eighth Street."

"You're the one not feeling up to snuff," I said. "Haven't been there since we—"

"Coulda swore it—"

"Don't have a fella." I picked up my chopstick to poke inside the carton of almond chicken from the Chinese dump down the street. "What were *you* doing there? Wife out of town?"

A pinkish stain spread up his neck, across his face. "Oh, well, I just—"

"I know *just* what you do. Hope you do it with a condom this time."

"Isabel, come on."

"Never mind. Preston Blair's set to get out of Haven House."

"Already?"

Jonathan tossed his chopsticks in one of the empty takeout containers, his face a study in relief for the subject change.

"Time flies when you're making no progress," I said. "One month left of a twelve-month recommended stint."

"Is she ready? I mean cutting her mother's throat . . ."

"Dad paid for a new wing means she's ready."

Jonathan whistled. "What about Harrison? Thought she set everybody straight on Preston ever getting out."

"She might not know. Harrison spent months in the hospital. Lots of complications, I heard. No memory. She doesn't even remember what happened to her, much less minutia like dates. Like to be a fly on the wall when the old broad hears this spoiler."

"What about family therapy?"

"A bust."

"What's Judge Seward say?"

"Nothing. Never responds to my reports."

"Par." Jonathan made origami with his napkin.

"Preston's voiced no threats," I said. "That's the litmus test. Indulges in the occasional tantrum, nothing that can't be dealt with as an outpatient. The guard Todd hired to dampen Preston's tomfooleries Haven House already got the boot, all systems go."

"So Preston's still a therapeutic zero?"

"She makes listening sounds, still insulting, obnoxious," I said. "Too bad if you want to know the truth. Preston's intelligent, good-looking, witty. She could make a real life for herself if she tried."

"You're getting soft. Sounds like you've warmed to her."

"Calling it like I see it. Preston grew up with everything and nothing all at the same time. Told me about her brother but since then, nothing useful."

"I checked that out," Jonathan said. "You?"

"Better believe it. Cooper Fitzgerald Blair born, then died, sixteen months later. Short illness was all I found. No details."

"Do you really think Mom and Dad forced Preston to hold her dead baby brother for a photo op? It could certainly explain a lot about her." He made a face. "And them."

"I'm certain she's lying," I said. "Actually, I'm on the fence. Humans are capable of all kinds of atrocities."

"Indeed." Jonathan capped his pen, closed his folder, pointed to my list. "Anything?"

"Think we just covered most of mine." I'd scratched through all my items but one. "Before we call it a day—"

"What?"

"I need money."

Jonathan flopped backward in his seat. "Speaking of atrocities. Jesus Christ. I knew you'd do this. I gave you the money we'd agreed on."

"I've got this thing—an emergency."

"What emergency? You get free office space. Pay no expenses—all courtesy of *me*. Your whole life's an emergency you greedy, crazy—"

"I'm sure I can work out alternative arrangements with your wife."

The skin around his mouth tightened. "For a minute there I thought you'd grown a heart. Should've known where this was headed when you brought up condoms. A threat."

"You need threats?"

Too bad our la-di-da meeting turned sour. Didn't intend to piss him off or renege on our deal, but this couldn't be helped. Despite his wandering dick, Jonathan wasn't a bad guy, but too bad for him. I needed more cash. Dodging creditors took up more time than my job. Jonathan beat the conference table with a closed fist.

"You're gonna blackmail me into eternity," he said.

"Probably."

Chapter Eleven

Preston

"How'd you find me, Brendan?"

"Wasn't easy," my husband said. "What kind of place is this? Jesus Christ, what happened?"

"*Now* you want to know?"

Brendan reached for his man bun with delicate, paint-stained hands, held aloft by a skinny paint-by-numbers type paintbrush, uncoiled the long auburn hair, rewound it.

"No phones here? You couldn't call?" he said, after he'd anchored his hair.

"Call where?" I said. "The teepee? No one knew where you'd gone. Besides," I waved an arm around. "Been otherwise engaged."

"I took my cell phone," he said.

"Shoulda used it to call me then. You're the one who left."

That stumped him. We stared across the table at each other a while.

"I know your mom isn't exactly Carol Brady," Brendan said. "But still. Jesus Christ, Preston."

"You know what I'm like."

"Yeah, I do. You were headed for the cliff before I left, but slitting Harrison's throat is over the top even for you."

"Think again."

"Your mom must've pulled one hell of a boner for you to— how nuts are you?"

"Judge said I was exactly nuts enough. So none of it's my fault."

"Of course he did."

"Says the out-of-work artist who used my family's money to fund his year-plus globe trot. Don't try to sell your crazy to me. I got that in spades. What do you want?"

"I want to hear what happened, from you." He flicked lint off his black jeans, torn in that hipster way, too cool to make an effort or money.

"Ask your dad."

"Did already. Big, bad, dad, chief of police said what I'd heard through the rumor mill. You got in yet one more bitch fight with Harrison, but this time slit her throat because you were drunk and high. She should've died but didn't. Your mother doesn't remember a damn thing. Far as he's concerned it's a private family matter. Bless his cold, dead, bought and paid for heart. Not a *real* crime."

Brendan tilted back, balanced on two legs of the four-legged chair.

"He's still pissed at me about the drugs. About everything, but he's forever loyal to your father, fucking lap dog."

"Nothing more to tell," I said. "Same ole, same ole. I got high, drunk, my mother came to the house. We fought."

"You fought over what?"

I felt the room turn upside down. Brendan sounded far away, he'd faded out, the air around his body waved, murky. I blinked for focus. "Something bad for sure. I gave her what she deserved."

He reached across the table to take my hand. I jerked it back. I feared his touch as if his skin would loose my dormant devils. Memories rushed me—good ones, shitty ones, most from our kick-the-hornet-nest early years, huge gaps where more recent ones should've been.

"Leave me alone, Brendan. You need money?" As soon as I asked, I knew I was worried he didn't have any.

"What the hell, Preston? Shit no. I got sober, sold some paintings." He pulled a thick chain out from under his T-shirt with a disc hanging from it. I leaned in to read it—six months.

"Good for you."

I could see his accomplishment meant a lot to him, even though he worked to edit his face so he wouldn't smile. I knew every gesture so well. I'd studied them my whole life.

"I mean that, Bren. Good for you."

"You're sober too. Right?"

"Yes. But by force, not choice."

His deep-as-the-ocean blue eyes stretched bigger. Hopeful.

"Couldn't we try again?"

Yes threatened.

"Why would we do that?" I said.

"Because we—"

"Don't. Please don't say a thing about love."

Weariness settled on me. Our short but difficult marriage had taken the oomph out of both of us. He might not want to remember it that way, but I did.

"You took off in the middle of the night without a word," I said. "I didn't lift a finger to find you. Trying again implies we tried the first time."

"I know but—"

"I'll tell Daddy Warbucks to write you a check."

I lost interest in reminiscing. I pushed away from the table, aimed to leave. Took a few steps to the door. My feet felt trapped in concrete shoes.

"Send me divorce papers," I said. "I'll sign."

I looked back at him sitting there, worry written all over his face. Made me remember why I'd once loved him.

"You should be free of me so you can get on with your life," I said. "Start fresh."

"Who died?"

I stopped, hand on the knob. "What are you talking about?"

He'd followed behind me. I felt his breath. "I know people too, born and bred here, they talk. Somebody died." His words wet my neck.

Rage started a slow march up my spine.

"You don't know shit. No one does," I said, still not facing him.

"Someone's dead, just not your mother."

His voice didn't sound harsh enough for the message he

delivered.

"You should get your delusions checked out while you're here," I said to the door.

"I don't know what's going on Preston, or who did what to who, but I'll find out, that's a promise."

Before he got away from me, I spun, stood eye to eye with him, grabbed his stupid six months chip on a chain and pulled it tight across his Adam's apple. His head jerked back, fingers clawed at mine to break my grip. I held fast. Brendan kicked the door, made gurgling sounds, tried to shake me off before I choked the life out of the bastard.

Chapter Twelve

Isabel

"I suppose you felt certain your poor husband wouldn't press charges," I said.

"Charges?" Preston made a face. "My parents'll shovel up a load of cash to squelch any nonsense like that." She reclined on the bed like Lady Gaga on a litter. "Asshole should thank me for reopening the flood gates. Idiot said he doesn't need money, but no such thing as too much money."

"You'd be a widow if the orderly hadn't intervened."

"Get off the drama train. I would've let him go."

I dragged the one chair away from the wall. She'd been confined to her room until I could sort out the mess.

"Preston, this is serious, a major setback. I can't make a convincing argument for releasing you now."

I waited for Preston to explain herself, forgetting she never felt the need.

"How could he waltz right in?" she said.

"You're not a prisoner. Visitors are welcome. You don't have to agree to see them. Lord knows you've turned your father away often enough."

"I had to see Brendan, at least once more. Old times' sake."

Preston turned her face away, whipped her long hair around in a blonde swoop. Could've sworn I saw tears so I scooted closer.

"What happened?" I said.

"Fucker pissed me off."

"Tell me something I don't know."

"Came to gossip. He doesn't give a monkey's ass about me."

"Do you want him to?"

"He *is* my husband."

"That's not what I asked."

Preston mashed her damp eyes with both fists. "I . . . he . . ." She bit her lip to stop its trembling but couldn't.

I kept my lips sealed, hoped against reason Preston might fill the silence. A real breakthrough might happen, if she'd only allow it. She cried in silence while I fought the urge to care. No good could come of that. Never had. Never would.

I inventoried her room to keep myself in check. Most patients were allowed only the bare minimums. Preston wasn't most patients. She'd arranged her books in neat stacks on the floor. The questionable picture of her and Cooper glared back at me, still taped to the wall. Three artfully arranged watercolors hung over a small desk that I hadn't noticed before, where more books, a laptop, and a spiral notepad covered in doodles waited. Rich brat lived in better digs than me, when she should've rotted in prison. Trying to tally how much Preston's bare minimums cost brought my bitterness out. I beat it back.

To get the ball rolling again, I said, "Preston, talk to me about your husband."

"I don't give a whore's twat," she said.

"Does not giving a whore's twat equal trying to kill him?"

"Kill him? Hell to the no. I wanted to scare the dickhead, put hair on his chest." She laughed. "Should've seen him. Eyes bugged out, face ballooned all purple, screamed like a little girl."

I clenched my teeth so hard I thought they'd break. Took a few breaths as calmly as possible, hoped she wouldn't notice my unintended empathy had been replaced by escalating fury.

"You don't have a criminal record," I said. "You're one month from getting out, starting over."

Preston didn't flinch. "I could die here for all you give a shit."

A film of sweat covered my face. "You were almost free."

"I've never been free."

"You've got all the money in the—" I stopped myself.

"You're one of those *money buys happiness* kind of idiots?"

Something inside me cracked. "Aw, poor little rich girl whose parents' money bought her a free pass out of prison."

Preston laughed. "Geez Shrinky. What's crawled up your ass? Keep talking like that, I'll scratch your snarky ass off my Christmas list."

"I'm not here to make friends," I said to both of us.

"Finally. Something you actually mean."

I couldn't unsay what had rolled off my tongue too easily. Best to say nothing for a few moments. I quietly fantasized about slapping Preston's entitled ass across the room.

"How much longer will they keep me here?" she said.

"With the stunt you pulled, could be six months. Even your parents don't have the stroke to talk the clinic director into signing off on your release."

Of course they had the stroke. Todd's check for the new wing cleared but plenty more where that came from. Judge Seward was in their custom-made pockets, but Harrison would look for any chance to keep her wild child under lock and key.

"You mistake me for someone who gives a shit," Preston said.

"I think you do."

"You think wrong."

"One. Goddamn. Month."

"What?" Preston said. "Can't hear you when you talk to your invisible pals."

I realized I'd once again said out loud what I thought I kept to myself. Shit.

"Look we're stuck together for a few more months," I said fast. "Take the next few days to think about what we can talk about that you might find useful."

"Why?"

"Why not?"

"You're killing time. Think I'm too nuts to notice you don't give a fuck either?"

I managed not to say, *no, unfortunately*.

"Don't you want to get out of this place?" I said instead.

"No."

"You're not serious."

"Serious as a razor blade to the jugular."

"You almost choked your husband to death so you could stay?"

"Yahtzee."

Chapter Thirteen

Isabel

"Christ Almighty," Todd said. "How did this happen? Why are we hearing about it two days after the fact?"

DA Fitzgerald slammed the door of the clinic director's empty office behind him. The VIPs got to use the feng shui decorated office for crisis interventions instead of the institutional green visitors' room.

"I left a voicemail at the number you requested I use for all matters regarding Preston," I said.

"Todd's too busy to listen to his voicemails. Aren't you, dear?" Harrison said. "That's what you tell me anyway."

Todd gave Harrison the evil eye. She returned the favor with a smile usually reserved for the gynecologist who tells jokes during a pelvic exam.

"We checked Preston in here to keep a lid on potential damages, considering her state of mind. This'll cost a fortune. Brendan will milk us dry." Todd pulled his cuffs at the bottom of his jacket sleeves. "Not to mention how far back this sets Preston."

I shifted my gaze back to Harrison, expected her to jump on Todd's use of the words *we* and *us*. She stared out the window instead.

"Unless advised in advance, Haven House doesn't keep visitors out. Preston's husband wouldn't raise any red flags," I said. "They *are* married."

Harrison spoke up. "We should certainly respect the sanctity of marriage."

A muscle in Todd's cheek jumped. "Harrison, can you water down the sarcasm long enough to—"

"So," Harrison turned to me. "She stays at least another six months, barring any additional unfortunate incidents, right?"

"Could be less, or more," I said. "Depends on Preston and the judge. You know she's not really a prisoner, right?"

"I'll call Judge Seward myself," Harrison said. "Well, Todd, good thing you've paid for a new wing. She'll have somewhere to stay."

"Harrison, really I—"

"Imagine my astonishment when the director thanked me for the check ten minutes ago," Harrison said.

She faced her husband full on. I noticed a stain on her pale pink, silk blouse, collar loose, the dreadful scar around her neck showing, hair flattened in the back like she'd just gotten out of bed. Her eyes, normally glacial and clear, had gone murky.

"You've worked up quite a nerve, spending that kind of money behind my back. How much exactly?"

"This isn't the time or place," Todd said.

Ah, the suffering of the rich and pampered. I kept quiet, watched the volley, favored Harrison forty-to-one despite her post-apocalyptic appearance.

"It's a little late to hide our dirty laundry," Harrison said. "What's one more pile of dung on the heap?"

"We're here to talk about our daughter."

"What's to talk about? She's psychotic. Wake up, Todd."

With no preamble, Todd broke. He dropped his head like he'd been cuffed from behind, heaved sobs from somewhere deep. Neither Harrison nor I said a word, more from shock than discomfort.

"Harrison," he croaked out. "I can't imagine what you've gone through. You've lived a nightmare." He looked at his wife full on, face wet. "But this isn't just your nightmare. It's mine too."

"How dare you compare what—"

"I'm not, Harrison. I know there's no comparison. But I'm doing what I think necessary to save our family. If paying for the stupid new wing helps get Preston the best care, then so be it. I'm helpless to do anything else. Can't you understand that even a little?"

"Can't you understand Preston's lost? All the care on the planet won't change her one bit. Now answer my question. How much? I'll find out as soon as I get home anyway. I want to hear you say it out loud."

"Harrison, she asked for a photo of Cooper. I brought her one of the two of them together a few weeks ago, the last one, that Christmas."

Harrison shrank like a dehydrating sponge. If Todd threw that photo out to dissuade his wife's inquiry, he succeeded, at least temporarily.

"What?" she said.

"See? She's feeling homesick, or nostalgic, or whatever you want to call it."

"Todd, you've always been a dunce where Preston's concerned. Jesus. You've got early onset Alzheimer's? Sudden case of amnesia? What's wrong with you?"

He turned to me. "Isabel, don't you think Preston's interest in her brother is a good sign? She misses a sense of family?"

"Well, uh, frankly, I only just heard Preston had a brother." I paused. "That he died."

I'd hoped I'd get a reaction, a clue about what happened that day, or some piece of information that could confirm Preston's lurid story. I should've intervened but couldn't. Or asked more questions about Cooper but didn't. Harrison turned her face toward the opposite wall, silenced. Todd sighed like a man who knew he'd been beat, wiped his face with both hands using broad strokes.

"Well, you've got your car and driver," Todd said. "I suppose I'll see you at home eventually." On his way out, he said over his shoulder, "Isabel, I'll call you later about Preston."

"If he thinks he can continue taking liberties now that I'm not comatose, he's got one hell of a shock coming," Harrison said to the slamming door of the visitors' room.

"Is there anything else you'd like to discuss?" I said. "About what just happened? About Cooper? Preston?"

"Of course not."

"Would you like to see your daughter?"

"You're the worst therapist ever."

****

After Harrison Blair swanned out of the day room, I filled out the necessary forms, made pointless notes, tried to make sense of my tactics and unprofessional behavior. I'd let Harrison and Todd control the session, my tone-deaf indifference unmistakable, lost it with Preston. Big no-nos. Preston's nonchalance about staying on at Haven House felt like a ploy, but for what purpose? I didn't know or care. Well, I didn't want to care. Trying my damnedest not to. What's worse, Preston knew it.

Truth was Preston reminded me a lot of me. If someone, anyone, had shown an interest in me, before it was too late, my life would've turned out differently. There was a lot I didn't know, but I knew that. I needed a drink. I'd learned the hard way that living went down easier with a shot of tequila to keep my feelings trapped below the surface.

Couldn't get a pulse on Harrison. Flawless socialite turned trailer park wreck? Not likely. Something unpleasant brewed. Had no idea what to think about the son who only lived a short time but whose memory could deliver a two-ton wallop.

I gathered my crap, trudged toward the exit, stumbled into a doll-carrying resident in the hallway. Preston's nemesis, I assumed. Couldn't remember her name. Roxie, Rosie, or something.

"Should you be out here?" I said.

"Dunno. I'm here anyways."

"I'll see if I can get the nurse to help—"

"Tow truck took your car." She cradled her doll in the crook of one elbow.

"What are you talking about?"

"The men. Big truck hooked it up."

"How do you know my car? Never mind," I said. "Outta my way."

"Hauled it off. Bye-bye, car."

"You *are* crazy."

She held up her little finger. "Pinky swear."
I pushed past her through the glass doors. "Shit. Fuck. Shit."
The psycho got it right.

Chapter Fourteen

Isabel

I stood in the parking space at Haven House where my heap of a car used to be, punched at the buttons on my phone.

"Mom? It's me. Don't hang up."

I heard her two-packs-a-day breathing, the wet cough that sounded like cancer. Couldn't remember the last time I'd seen her, forever ago, even though she didn't live that far away.

"What do you want, Isabel? Let me guess. Money?"

"I'm in a bind, Mom. I'm desperate or I—"

"Knocked up again?"

"Like you should talk."

"What was I gonna do with another kid? Couldn't keep track of you as it was."

"You didn't give a shit about keeping track of me."

"You want something from me? Better rethink your delivery, drop the smartass history lesson." The top of her Coors can popped in my ear.

"The leasing company took my car."

I should've lied, told her it'd been stolen, but I'd used that one already. Besides my wimp nerves jangled me into truth telling.

"Here's a fix," she said. "Why don't you pay your goddamn bills?"

"I'm getting back on track. Really—"

"You've never been *on* track."

"I'll pay you back."

"Don't start," Mom said. "You won't pay me back. Never have. Never will. Your gimmes are done. I paid for how many abortions? Bought you a new car then you wrecked it. Paid your rent. Then the fancy psych hospital—cost me a fortune. Won't fall for that again. From what I could tell, you got a free holiday at a swank spa. Suffering for your stupidity is *not the same* as a nervous breakdown."

"*I'm sorry*. How many times do I have to say so?"

"Don't bother. Stop blowing up your life, demanding bailouts. Grow up."

"Big talk from the woman who a couple of years ago lived in a single wide, on the government's dime, with her seventh husband, after what? Twenty-seven boyfriends? You act like it's a million of your precious dollars. It's not that much. You can afford it."

"Nothing spends faster, or is sooner forgotten, than other people's money. Consider this cash cow dry."

Fucking Christ. No one brought on a crying jag like my mother.

"Mom, I really need your help. I've got creditors threatening me. I can't keep my job if I can't get to it."

"You need to get your life right."

"I will this time. Seriously," My fingers hurt from gripping the phone so hard. "I need about ten thousand. I know you've got it. Mom? Are you there? Hello?"

Hypocrite bitch hung up.

I felt that certain catch in my chest. The one that always gave away the hope I nursed that my mother would care what happened to me. No matter how far I fell, no matter how dire my circumstances, she never budged, never met me halfway. She only paid for shit so I'd go back under the bridge I crawled out from under. I let myself cry for one more minute. I timed myself. Sixty seconds' worth was all the sadness I'd allow. Right on time, I shrugged my feelings off the best I could, flung my phone back in my purse.

Now what?

Groped for my compact, snuck a look. Not too bad. Did some quick preening and fluffing. Phone back in hand, I poked at a few digits, stopped. I'd promised not to call him again.

"We never should've taken off the masks," he'd said last time. "I think about you too much, never meant to get attached. We're playing with fire."

Sorry, Sherman. Gotta pour some gas on the flame.

About to stab out the last number, I saw a long, black car in my periphery. Curious, I watched it roll closer, veer past me in the middle of the parking lot. Slow enough to catch a glimpse of the passenger.

Harrison Blair in her Town Car plus driver. What the hell? Checked my Timex again. She'd left my Haven House office almost an hour before.

Chapter Fifteen

Preston's Blog

Musings from the Dented Throne

Shizzleosity

Something's stinky with Shrinky.

The wreck popped in a few days ago to remind me of house rules (I broke one. Big whoop. So my stay got extended). Stevie Wonder could've seen the change in her, all spruced up. No more *Walking Dead*. Wouldn't say *Vogue* material exactly but definitely somewhere between *Sex and the City* and *Sons of Anarchy*. New haircut, extensions filling in the bald spots, designer stilettos, eyelashes on straight, eyebrows drawn on just right, fake nails to hide her stubs.

Changing up your shizzle is the universal sign for—*new man on the radar*. Am I right, girls?

You're wondering—who'd date that freak? Who wouldn't? Take it from me—men love crazy pussy—probably a line out the bathroom stall for a Shrinky hummer. Whatever loser she's lassoed slaps her around. Bruises healed from before but I know she's hiding more. Long sleeves, pants, neck covered. Before you get sucker sympathetic, don't. I'd bet the estate the skank likes it.

Another thing—Shrinky's got it in for me—can't hide it anymore. She's never liked me, but who can blame her? No one's ever accused me of being likable. Anyway, she got a little gangsta on me. Seemed too invested in my expiration date. Can't wait to get rid of my unruly ass. I think I'm too much work for her. She's getting easier to bait. One more sideways glance from the Heiress, and she'll go blitzo. You wait and see. Already gets this astonished look on her face like I've suddenly gone naked and have three tits. Riddle me that if you can.

By contrast—the Queen. Saw the old darling on TV. She looked a fright. *Fright* is not in my mother's MO unless she's instilling it in someone else. The world has spun off its axis if the Queen looks like something fished out of a drain and Shrinky like a *Project Runway* contestant. They've traded places. *That* boggles even my sick brain. Renders me sleepless. I toss and turn, mull things over, ponder possibilities.

Enough about the Queen. What about me?

Someone stole my journal.

Same day Shrinky pranced in to put the fear of God in me about rule breaking, my journal disappeared. Shrinky didn't take it. I know I saw it in its usual spot after she left. I'd hustled to the day room to rattle Rosalie's cage. No cray-cray Rosalie to be found. Schlepped back to my room, no fucking journal. Glad I reserved my spot here for a bit longer, mysteries on top of mysteries. Got my work cut out for me.

My previously MIA spouse (you remember him) showed up on my doorstep. As you'd imagine, he left our not-real-warm reunion much worse for the wear. After, I realized he reminded me of my brother. Or would if my brother had lived. Creative, smart, beautiful, just what baby brother would've been, as odd as that is to write (you'd expect no less than odd from the Heiress) considering I only knew bro as a toddler. Don't know why, after all the years I've known my husband, I'm only now realizing I'd married the grown-up version of the Littlest Heir. Can't decide if the notion gives me the incestuous creeps or fills me with joy. Nor am I quite sure why the doppelganger situation pissed me off.

The real kicker—Hubby says someone died, in addition to the near mortal injuries inflicted on the Queen by you-know-who. Swore he got intel from a reliable source.

Did I kill someone? I don't think so. The Irishman didn't accuse me either. My head's an attic full of cobwebs. In due time I'm sure the whole nasty event will gallop back to me like a barn-soured horse. I'll tell you first. Until then I'm better off here.

Nevertheless, my husband's on-the-down-low info set me off. I reminded him quick. When it comes to me—love hurts.

The Invisible Heiress

The Heiress loves to hear what you have to say so she can ignore any and all good advice, but by all means have at it.

Comments

Scribbler

You're a car crash I can't look away from. Meant what I said in my last comment. You should write a book. Do you have an email? I'm a literary agent. Let's talk.

Reply: Let's not.

Norma B.

I've never read a blog before. Don't know why I'm reading yours. Should I hate or feel for you? Forced to hold a dead baby? Trying to kill your own mother? Is that really your life? Whether it is or isn't, something about you fills me with sadness. Maybe it's your battered heart, the one you think you've toughened up enough to withstand any onslaught.

Reply: Morphine's a fix for that.

Jack

I'm with you, Norma. The Heiress, for all her bravado, is a sorrowful girl. The public would love you, Heiress. I could get it all on film. Documentary style.

Reply: You and Norma should work for Hallmark. I'm gagging here.

Hannibal2

We're kindred spirits—if you know what I mean. Love to compare notes. Mine are finger lickin' good.

Reply: Tempting. But I'll pass.

Chapter Sixteen

Isabel

"Think I've got permanent dents," I said.

"Thought you got off with the handcuffs. *We* got off with cuffs."

Sherman dropped the cuffs to the thick-carpeted, hotel room floor.

"Yeah, well, I don't need scars. Christ. Can you unchain yourself from my collar?" I said. "You're choking me, flapping your arm around."

He unhooked. "We should never've left the club scene. We broke the rules, shared personal information, took the masks off. Now it might not be as fun or exciting."

"Don't be an idiot." I rubbed my neck. "That club's depressing anyway."

"We're too far in. It's like *real* dating. You've got to quit calling me at all hours. It's too risky."

"If you're complaining, I could find an available guy like that." I snapped my fingers.

"At the club?"

"I'm out of the club scene for a while. Can't pay the dues anymore." The heat of humiliation spread across my face.

"Well, where else would you meet someone with the same, you know, tastes? You love a hard-on up your bum and you know it. Besides you can see me for free because we're using hotels now. I'm paying. Remember?"

"You're missing my point."

"Which is?"

"How blank are you?"

I untangled myself from the slimy, sex-toy, leather-crap mess on the bed. I rolled over to my side. He followed. We spooned like we liked each other.

"I'm broke," I said. "Why do you think I needed you to send a taxi today? My car's gone. Repossessed."

"How can that be? You must make a good living. You're getting lots of clients."

"Never mind. This is too much personal information. You said yourself—we've got nowhere to go but down in deep, stinky shit. Let's call it good."

"That's drastic, isn't it?"

"Is it? I can't see you if I can't get anywhere."

He pushed himself against my back. I could feel him, still wet, getting hard. "You're a naughty girl talking nonsense."

"I'm serious. This isn't a game."

"What do you want from me? You know I'm married."

"I don't want to have to tell you what I need. I'm drowning. Isn't that obvious?" His erection wilted. I squirmed out of his embrace to sit up.

"I guess." He rearranged himself on the mangled sheets, the lube tube slid off the bedspread. "You're a therapist. Don't you all have weird issues for chrissake?"

"That line'd pull a bigger punch if you didn't have a plug hanging out your ass." I bolted out of bed. "By the way, you don't have to stay married. No one's forcing you."

"Are you insane? Did you think I'd get divorced?"

"I don't know what I thought."

I felt hot shame spread up my chest and neck. Sometimes mortification didn't settle with me. Checked the top of my head, my lashes. All hair systems still a go. Now I'd committed the gambler's greatest sin—showed my hand. Where'd I drop my clothes? I felt exposed, raw. I picked the cat-o-nine off the floor.

"How about I rent you a car until you get things straightened out. For a week or two? I'll pay for it."

That struck me as hilarious. I cackled like a chicken. My

shame dissipated to make room for disgust.

"You can do better than that, and you know it," I said.

I'd stopped taking birth control months ago—hedged my bets. The possibilities made me bold as brass.

Sherman sat upright, appealed to the ceiling for inspiration.

"What? You expect me to *buy* you a car? You can't be serious."

The whip across his bare legs let him know just how serious I was. Didn't hurt that I nicked his flaccid little Sherman too. His screams filled me with happiness. I kept the whip raised just in case he didn't get it. When he quieted to the whimper stage, and I was satisfied he knew I meant business, I dropped my weapon, pulled on my skirt.

Sherman sniffed. "You know, you're not a very good submissive."

Chapter Seventeen

Preston

"Call for you, Preston," Nurse Judy said. "In the phone room. Senator Fitzgerald?"

"Huh? Dad's brother?"

Nurse shrugged. "Don't have to take it."

As if. I stomped to the tiny closet that passed for a room, snatched the phone off the small desk.

"Hello?"

"It's me."

"Good Christ, Brendan. I haven't talked to Uncle Thomas since I was, like, ten. He might be dead for all I know."

"Don't have to tell me twice."

"Apparently, I do," I said.

"You could hang up."

"Could, but I gotta ask—what mouth breather would call someone who tried to kill them?"

"You didn't try to kill me. *That* I know."

"Gotta admit, one hell of a good imitation."

"Preston, stop. You're talking to the one person you can't fool."

"What do you want?"

"An explanation. Harrison and you clash like Titans. Always have. I get that, but good lord—cutting her throat? Jesus, Preston. I can't wrap my head around it. If someone else died that night I don't think you've got it in you to kill someone. Except your mother? You did that quick enough. What the fuck? I don't know what to think." Brendan's voice raised an octave with every sentence. "Well, even if it's true that someone died, it doesn't mean they got murdered. I mean people do die without help, right?"

"It's your story, dude. You're talking to yourself."

"But who? Who died? Why? Riding off the reservation is your thing, Preston, but slice and dice? Murder? I can't stop thinking about it."

"Not your fucking problem. You should kiss my ring I didn't slice, dice, or murder *you*."

"Drop the bad-ass act. It's me you're bullshitting. We grew up together. None of this feels right."

"All that sap sentiment for what? A fucking Boy Scout badge?"

The guard posted outside the door again, peeked in. I smiled, waved like a person with their faculties intact.

"I owe you," Brendan said. "I hightailed it out. Left you alone to fend for yourself when you were your worst."

"Get real, Brendan. You couldn't keep your own ass afloat, much less mine."

"Nothing like you were, Preston. You can't say different. It's not the same shit or the same day. I want to help you."

"Didn't you get your payoff?"

"What?"

"My parents paid you off."

"Yeah, got a million dollars and a nondisclosure agreement."

"Get lost then, Superman. Lois Lane ain't interested."

"I sent it all back. Not taking their money or shutting up. You *do* need my help. No one else can do it. You won't let them."

"So you're deaf *and* dumb."

"Stop, Preston. Jesus. I can't believe you killed someone. If you did, tell me. Was it an accident? Another man, a boyfriend, or something? Some low life druggie threaten you?"

"Pfft. You mean a lower life than you? You're gonna take that tactic now? No matter, can't breathe a word. On the advice of counsel—"

"Really? That's still how you want to play it? How about this?

The house on Nottingham Lane belongs to someone else now. Drove all the way up to it yesterday. Saw Allied trucks and the Stepfords moving in. Mommy, Daddy, two kids, and a stupid, yapping dog."

I stood to attention so fast the phone dropped, moved quick to catch it. "Our house?"

"No. The other house."

"Now you're fucking pulling my chain. That place has been in my family since—"

"I know."

"Aunt James lived there. Before, well, Mom worshipped her. She'd—"

"Never sell it."

"What's your game, Brendan? I don't believe a word."

"No game. Looks like someone's living in our house too."

"Times up, Preston." Nurse Judy's big head jutted through the door.

"You can't be right."

"Drove up there too. Got all the way up the lane, right near the fountain, thought about getting out, but someone was watching me out the window."

"Who?"

"Beats me. Didn't get a good look. Backed outta there fast."

"Think my parents sold it too? Could they, since I've been committed? I don't think I'm actually committed, though. What the fuck do I know? It can't be true."

"Might be true. No clue."

"You're no help. Zippo."

"I'm gonna find out," he said.

"Come on, Preston." Nurse Judy propped the door open with her fat ass.

"Don't take advantage."

"Just a sec," I said to Der Führer Judy. Then to Brendan, "Can you get in?"

"Is the extra key still where we kept it?"

"Under the gargoyle to the right of the front doors. My mother—she can't know about Aunt James's house. Could she? Maybe she changed her mind about Nottingham. My mother isn't—she's not the same since—maybe the old gal's cutting me off, unloading historical shit."

"Oh yeah, that sounds right. Have *you* been in a coma?"

"Okay, got me, but what does any of it have to do with the price of Prozac at the nut farm?"

"I don't know. Maybe nothing. It just doesn't pass the smell test."

I reminded myself to breathe, my mouth filled with drool. Wished I could punch Brendan in the mouth to shut him up, keep him from messing with my head. I imagined my Irishman, my rescuer, calling from Christ knows where, squirming with Catholic guilt over his crazy-ass wife. The dumb mick thought I could be saved, tried to do it for as long as I could remember.

Brendan cut through the quiet. "I asked you before if you remembered what happened that night. You really *don't* know, do you?"

I started to say something but felt like an invisible hand covered my mouth. Whatever truth wormed its way up for a split second vanished. I couldn't retrieve it.

"Oh, I remember plenty. Like the box cutter in my hand."

Chapter Eighteen

Preston's Blog

Musings from the Dented Throne

Space Invaded

Hell might've frozen over my Dented Throne devotees. My Irishman rang me up. Fuck on a raft, right? His devotion to delivering roof-rattling news overrode what should've been his distaste for his batty wife. Rattle me he did with this flash—

Squatters invaded my dead auntie's mansion.

BFD you say? Well, hear this—pre-Royal We—the Queen's sister and only sibling reclined on her velvet settee, gulped a handful of pills then tied off a plastic hood at the neck. Her suicide about ruined the Queen who sought solace in the Jester's arms, but she rallied when Grandfather gave the newly engaged couple Auntie's empty castle. The Queen refused to cross *that* moat. Instead, she kitted out the shrine with all things Auntie, pulled up the drawbridge for good, refused to sell. Her beloved sister's abode has *never* been open to tourists.

I never knew Auntie but the Queen's devotion to her memory stirred me. I'll admit the story felt like urban myth, as oft-repeated familial history often does. So why does my chest feel hollow when I think of how my mother's heart must be truly broken to resort to a measure such as parting with Auntie's house after all this time? I don't believe she'd do anything of the sort—not in her right mind anyway. So her mind is obviously all kinds of wrong.

Thanks to me.

Irishman still pushes his murderous theories. Insists on investigating Auntie's improbable real estate transaction and its possible relation to my current situation. I believe his disappointment will reign supreme. For reasons unknown to me, I feel a good puke coming on whenever I think of what my situation might really be, a splinter of something sinister works its way up my cauliflower brain.

Can't believe he'd go out on the limb after I cleaned his clock last time he popped his head up like Punxsutawney Phil. Could his heart still beat true for the Heiress? We'll see.

A bit of business—since my last post went viral faster than genital warts, I don't have time to make smart-ass responses to most of your fucked-up comments. Okay, I have all the time in the world. Still no.

Stay tuned and strap in, Dented Throne devotees. We're getting to the juicy stuff.

The Invisible Heiress

If what you're saying tickles me, I'll reply. If not, know I'm still feelin' it but not showin' it.

Comments

Love Rules

So exciting! Your Irishman loves you! I can feel it. You're so lucky! I think a knight in shining armor is riding your way!

Reply: What's your address? I'll send you something you can use to slit your wrists! Seriously! Get a fucking grip!

4 Christ R Lord

Follow the Blessed Redeemer who will forgive u and show u the way. You must ask yourself—What would Jesus do?

Reply: Aim better.

Christa L.

You're a sick freak. What kind of a psycho does the things you do and writes about it? You're either a serial killer or a chronic liar.

Reply: I wondered why they kept me in a padded room. Thanks for clearing that up.

Jack

Almost dying has a way of reorganizing your priorities. The Queen might not want one more sad memory in her already bulging portfolio. Maybe participation in a documentary could help get to the bottom of everything. Besides, I could make you famous.

Reply: I could make you disappear.

Norma B.

Jack's got a point. If it's not fame you're chasing, rehashing the whole mess might help, as would help from an objective party. Another thought—Irishman could be dead on, everything's probably related. No such thing as coincidence.

Reply: Despite your disconcerting cliché you might have a point. Not about Jack the nag but the Irishman. At the risk of using another tired phrase—time will tell.

Chapter Nineteen

Isabel

I couldn't believe the elusive family therapy session stayed on the books after the last cockup, but here we were. We'd sat in my cramped Haven House office for twenty minutes. Harrison stared at Todd in a dreamlike state. Drugged? Hair-of-the-dog? Looked like she rolled out of bed in her thousand-dollar smashup of an outfit. After that creepy, hour-long, still-unexplained stretch with her driver in the parking lot last time, I expected chaos not hypnotics.

I glanced at the clock on the visitors' room wall, waited. Preston seemed to take her cues from Harrison, not amped like normal. I needed to jumpstart a dialogue.

"As you're all together we can talk about goals," I said.

"Is this a hockey game?" Preston said.

Harrison gurgled out what sounded like a chuckle.

"Mommy's grown a sense of humor." Preston looked oddly pleased to have amused her mother. For once, Harrison didn't seem infuriated at her daughter.

Todd said, "We need to move this process forward."

"I'm not a process, Dad."

"No, Preston I meant—"

"Preston, let's try to keep all comments constructive, okay?" I said. "I'd like to know what each of you would like to accomplish in therapy."

"We want Preston home," Todd said.

"My goal is to stop pretending this is a family," Harrison said in a low, quiet warble. Her absent rage more nerve-racking than its presence.

"Harrison, that's ridiculous. We—"

"Todd," I said. "Let Harrison say what she wants. No censure."

"Like she wasn't gonna say what she wants." Preston leaned forward ready for a skirmish now.

Harrison's heavy lids dropped. After several seconds I thought I saw watery eyes. Crying? That'd be the day.

I said, "Harrison, is there—?"

She reached for Todd's hand, turned it over, caressed its skin.

Just when I thought this whole exchange couldn't get more awkward. The whole room felt like it was holding its breath. Harrison stopped her trancelike massage to stare at the long scar snaking down the back of Todd's hand. He yanked his hand back. I thought for a second we'd have a repeat performance of last time's meltdown.

"Harrison, please," he said.

"Do you remember what you said the night you proposed?" Harrison broke the spell.

"What does that have to do with the crisis at hand?"

Harrison looked at her husband like only the two of them existed. "You said you didn't think you'd live to marry me, because every time I walked into the room your heart stopped." She got to her feet, weary. "Yet here you are, still alive, and I'm the one almost dead."

She shut the door behind her with a quiet click.

****

I escorted Preston back toward her room. She didn't give an inch. Stayed silent while we walked through the day room. "Preston, I know the session didn't go well but—"

"If you thought it would you're thick as a plank."

"I'd hoped—"

Before I could finish my sentence, Preston lunged. It took a couple of seconds for me to realize she'd jumped another patient, the one who'd seen my car get towed.

"Give it back you thieving bitch. Where is—"

"Don't. Don't. Don't," Rosalie yelled over and over while Preston pummeled her.

Before I could stop them Nurse Judy barreled over.

"Rosalie, Preston. Stop this instant."

She divided them with her bulk while I stood inert on the sidelines.

Rosalie used both hands to cover her face. Blood dripped down her lips and chin. Seeing she was really hurt got me moving. I dug a tissue out of my bag, pressed it against Rosalie's nose. She leaned into me, shaking. In those few moments I felt her weakness and frailty. I knew without concrete evidence she'd been abandoned here, no one loved her. Before I could make a fool of myself by bursting into tears Judy took her injured patient by the hand.

"I'll deal with you when I get back from the infirmary," Judy said to Preston. "Take her to her room, and make sure she stays there," she said to me.

I grabbed Preston's elbow. She yanked it back. I grabbed it again harder, rushed us both to her room. I threw my bag on the floor, slammed her door behind us.

"What on God's earth was that about?"

"Why was she following us? Mongoloid nosy freak. You know she eavesdrops. Anyway, didn't mean to do anything. I ran into her. Ever heard the word *accident*?"

"That was no accident. You jumped her like a thug."

"Bitch stole my journal." Preston plopped on her bed.

"What?"

"Rosalie stole my stuff."

"How do you know?"

"Seriously? Get your degree in dumbass? Who else?"

"Rosalie has the mind of a five-year-old. Why would she want your journal?"

I could tell Preston hadn't considered the inconvenient facts.

"She likes to fuck with me," she said. "That's all."

The something inside that cracked the other day cracked bigger.

"Of course she does," I said. "You're easy to fuck with. Ever thought of that? Dependable as the goddamn post office. Want to get under some bitch's skin? Preston Blair's your bitch."

"You're a fucking shrink. Aren't you supposed to *not* get mad?"

"Who told you that bullshit? You—"

Todd plowed through the door startling us both. I tried to quickly put on my calmer face—more caring therapist, less raving bitch.

"Todd, you know Preston doesn't have to see you outside family therapy. I really must insist you—"

"Let it go, Shrinky," Preston said. "What's up, Dad?"

Chapter Twenty

Preston

Shrinky packed up her crap and scurried out pronto. Leaving my father and me alone for the first time since, well, before *that night*. While Dad acted as my most staunch ally where my mother was concerned, he was more reactive than proactive, intervening if called on. Not like we indulged in any Daddy/daughter lovefests or cozy, fireside chats. He golfed, went to the spa, asserted his influence to fight crime for paybacks, and avoided my mother. I got married and stoned. Whatcha gonna do? We were busy.

I could think of nothing, at this late date, that I wanted to say to him. So I didn't. No one was more surprised than me that I'd let him in my room. He stayed standing until I motioned toward the chair usually reserved for Isabel. He sat.

"Thought you made a clean getaway, Daddy-O."

For some reason, that did him in. He cried, head bowed, noiseless—silent tears for a daughter who had committed a loud crime. His shoulders sagged and shook. Custom-made suit jacket bunched up as he leaned forward to rest his elbows on his knees. I'd seen Dad get teary the couple of times he'd come with Mother but nothing like this. This was full blown. I scooted farther down my mattress to get closer.

To do what?

I wanted to comfort him but knew the outlandishness of that idea. I couldn't be the cause *and* the cure, so I watched him (in increasing discomfort) sob. He straightened up, gulped a few breaths. I thought he'd managed to shore it up. Then he wrapped both arms around his own body, to hold himself together, as if he had to keep his insides from falling out and cried in earnest. He held on so hard the blood left his hands leaving them ghost white.

Except for that red scar.

The one he got trying to keep my blade from slicing my mother's throat.

Seeing that again jacked me up. A sharp pain hit my chest like my heart had been slammed in a car door. I almost pitched forward.

For the first time, I felt the gravity of what I'd done. My arrest didn't do it, rehab didn't do it, confinement in a psych ward didn't do it, witnessing my mother's wound didn't do it. My father surrendering completely to what must've been unendurable pain and grief—that did it. What can a man do whose family has spiraled so out of control that his only surviving child would try to kill her own mother? Who does he see about that? I realized my father felt responsible. Who is to blame for such a disastrous violent failure if not him?

Me.

"Dad, come on, it's gonna be . . ." I couldn't say it would be okay with a straight face. Nothing would be okay again. I knew it now for sure.

Before I could think of something else inane, he stopped. I heard his deep sigh, saw his back square. He lifted his head up, wiped at his face with impatient fingers, like trying to get a horsefly to leave him alone.

"Preston, please, please tell me what's going on in that head of yours. Just once."

"Dad, I—"

"You weren't right in your mind when you—when your mother—" He searched and stumbled for a way to say the unsayable but couldn't. "I'm convinced you didn't know what you were doing then. But today, with that poor woman in the day room, well you, she—" His face turned red, his anguish turned to anger. "You attacked that sick woman for no reason. Why? For god's sake why?"

"She took my journal!" I sat up justified.

His right hand shot up like a crossing guard. "No. Not good enough. Now tell me what you're thinking. What goes through your head all day, every day, here? Are there things that make you mad?"

"What things?"

"I don't know. Thoughts." He got up, sat next to me, put his arm around my shoulders. I felt like crying but held it in.

"What thoughts?" I said. "You mean like hallucinations or something? Voices?"

"You tell me."

"Nothing to tell. Rosalie pissed me off. End of story."

"That can't be all. Don't you think about that night? What made you so angry? What makes you so angry still?"

"You were there weren't you? What do you think?"

His chin dropped to his collarbone. "By the time I got there whatever words you'd exchanged with your mother had already been said. I could only try to get between you two. Too late." He grabbed my shoulders. "What happened?"

Something. Something big. Something I couldn't grasp.

"I don't know."

Dad's arm fell off me in defeat. He stared ahead, quiet for several seconds. I didn't want to sneak a peek at him, but from the sniffling I thought he'd started crying again.

"Mercifully, your mother remembers nothing of that. When that, well, what happened. I hope to Christ it stays that way. If she could recall it I think it'd be the end of all of us."

"From what I saw, Mother looks like she's been dipping into my old stash."

"What do you expect, Preston?" he said, as if he thought I should answer.

"I dunno." I examined my hands.

"If you're worried about her, which despite every horrible thing you've done, I suspect you are, she's getting the best care at home. She'll rally."

"Right. Whatever."

"Preston, your mother and I have carried your expenses all this time." He spoke fast, all the words meshed together. "It's time you finally grew up and paid your own freight."

"What?"

That was a big leap from my mother's care to my leeching.

"Your house. The upkeep is tremendous. This hospital. Outrageous."

I jumped up, pissed, to think I felt sorry for him. "So you're gonna sell it like you did Aunt James's place?"

"What do you know about that?"

Almost blurted out everything I knew but kept my big trap shut for once. The last thing I wanted was for my father to know Brendan was out there snooping. My father's affection for the Finneys stopped at my father-in-law, Marv, whose position as chief of police often served our family well.

"I heard," I said.

He got up, brushed off his pants, but didn't press me for my source. He blinked fast. Now that I wasn't feeling quite as generous toward him I couldn't help but wonder if he flexed his eyelids periodically to see if he still could, what with all the shit he'd had injected in his face.

"We sold it to help you. As usual," he said.

"How did selling Aunt James's house help me?"

I decided not to stray from the topic at hand to comment on his vanity.

"Never mind. It doesn't matter. From now on we're going to pay your expenses out of your trust. We spoiled you. Now we're all paying the price. No more."

I almost laughed. Only in the rarefied world I'd grown up in would *paying your own freight* mean paying my bills with the shit ton of money earned by my ancestors and given to me when I'd turned twenty-one.

He pulled a folded piece of paper out of the inside of his jacket.

"You need to sign this."

I grabbed the paper. "What is it?"

"A power of attorney. I'll need it to access your funds."

So my psych ward stay *didn't* strip me of everything. I handed the paper back.

"No can do."

Chapter Twenty-One

Preston's Blog

Musings from the Dented Throne

Don't Hate Him because He's Hip and Other Exhortations
After months and months of denying the Jester private access, I finally relented. That led me to some self-examination, which as you know, I welcome like Stooge fingers to the eyes. I realized it wasn't really that I didn't want to see my father, per se. After all he's the only one who could ever stand me. What I couldn't abide was seeing him seeing *me,* just the two of us. Because I knew I'd get that look. The one I knew he'd give me if the Queen's absence encouraged him to drop his armor.

Boy was I right. He didn't disappoint. Only it was worse than I feared.

The death of whatever hopes he'd had for my life played out across his face accompanied by the horror of who I'd actually become. In the pools of his eyes I saw the urge to recoil wrestling with his need to rescue. The way he clenched and unclenched his hands gave away his struggle to either hold me close or hit me. But as it happened, just as I started to feel for him, he pissed me off. So that was that. Whatever good could've come of our visit didn't.

When, in the name of George Herbert Bush, did the Jester turn hipster? I believe I've mentioned his ever-darkening hair? Now it's stylishly mussed. With gel. He wore a *windowpane* checked suit and a *paisley* tie. Jester thinks Rag & Bone's a pet store. Rich, white, republican dads don't dress like MR PORTER millennials unless? Unless what?

You tell me if you can think of a reason.

If his wardrobe malfunction wasn't enough fool got snippy with the Queen during therapy. Drum roll—she *allowed* it. First time I've laid eyes on her since she made that impromptu appearance on TV.

The Royal She's not well.

I choked up a little at the sight. I felt nostalgia for the Queen of old—the take-no-prisoners, badass bitch with a wicked razor tongue. Now she's rumpled. Glided out of family therapy in an almost invisible huff, but she's boiling under the surface. While never in my memory would I say they were happily wed, it's nothing like now, hostilities out in the open. While the pairing of their incompatible personalities seems nonsensical, nevertheless, they fit—the rich socialite and the penniless blueblood. I'm positive their engagement photo looked smashing on the society page. What I don't get now is why the Queen's downtrodden yet the Jester looks invigorated.

If anything, I'd expect the opposite.

Queen controls the clan's cash, so rocking her Majesty's barge could strike a blow to Jester's luxurious lifestyle, which should scare the shit out of him. Yet he prances about like a Tom Ford-clad village idiot, and she's as oblivious as I've ever witnessed.

Does that defy reason to you, devotees?

Wish my head would stop its spinning, so off I go before I send love and hugs like the rest of the blogosphere buffoons. You'd never recover from such a Dented Throne faux pas.

The Invisible Heiress

Speak free. It's your right.

Comments

Maria N.

Perhaps the Jester is trying to woo the Queen. Pulling out all the stops to make her feel better—other than the snippiness or whatever—maybe the Queen is ill. Dementia? When my grandma got dementia she drank enchilada sauce, took her underwear off during confession, and offered to blow Father Juarez.

Reply: Our sort doesn't woo. We pay lawyers for that. But yo' granny's my kinda gal.

Dr. Frank

I've nothing to offer on the subject of your unfortunate parents, but from what I've read in your posts your therapist sounds a bit off. Also, the police might be interested in your *very* disturbing blog.

Reply: Please, by all means alert the authorities, especially the ones on my parents' payroll. Then try reading this blog with your fucking glasses on, *bozo*.

Well Hung Jung

You pissed off at the Jester? For what, pray tell?

Reply: Jester wants to take over the Heiress's moola to cover expenses.

Well Hung Jung

If they're your expenses, he's right. Get in line, girl. Everybody's got to pay their own way. Signing over your dough is a slippery slope, if you ask me, but if you're in need of financial aid I've got some surefire moneymaking ideas. First, you get a pole . . .

Reply: You're a saint, Jung. Jester's fooling. He'll pay.

Norma B.

Jung is right. Certainly, you can write checks, can't you? Doesn't sound like anyone's keeping you from that. As far as your mother and father are concerned perhaps the Jester's got a chick on the side.

Reply: I just threw up in my mouth.

Norma B.

Women aren't the only ones who change up their shizzle when they've got a new flame on the horizon.

Reply: What da fuck?

Chapter Twenty-Two

Isabel

"Jonathan, let's make the best of it and not fight. I'm in a better place. Not perfect but promising," I said.

"Sit down. I won't bite no matter how enticing the prospect." Jonathan shuffled papers at his desk.

"Isabel, I—" He repositioned more crap, avoided meeting my eyes. "I'm sorry, really. I've never taken full responsibility for what, well, for what happened. I never imagined you'd think we'd ride off into the sunset with a baby but—"

"What's done is done."

"Obviously not or you wouldn't bring it up all the time. So . . ."

"So what?"

"I didn't think the whole thing would push you over the edge like it did. The abortion, the breakdown. I'm sorry for all of it."

"As long as the checks clear and I have my space here, we're good. I'll hold up my end. You hold up yours."

I didn't want to give him an inch. I needed to take care of myself. No one else would.

After a few-second stare into the abyss, Jonathan said, "What's your caseload look like?"

"Growing. Several referrals. My stint at Haven House is generating business."

"Who's referring you?"

"Word spreads," I said. "I've got an infamous client. But if you must know, Judge Seward throws his delinquents my way."

"Because you've done such a bang-up job with Preston?"

"All I know is I've got more business. Be happy."

"How's the new beau?"

"That again? I'm impressed. You slid that right in."

Jonathan hoped another man could take me off his hands. His optimism, despite years of wrangling the out-on-the-ledge unhinged, astonished me.

"Actually," I said, "There *is* a man, but I might break it off."

"*Knew* there was a man. Why dump him?"

"Why not? Nothing special."

Of course, I'd never tell Jonathan about new man's wife or the club. He'd turn judgy—big fat hypocrite.

"Define nothing special," Jonathan said.

"Not that it's your concern, but he's, well, let's just say he's not what I thought."

"Are they ever?"

"Touché."

"You'll raise him right. He'll be what you thought in no time."

"Gotta get your digs in. You give me too much credit."

"You're a behavioral therapist, aren't you? Work your magic. Can't get him to modify his behavior? Modify yours. He'll adjust. Never know what hit him. Trust me, he'll fall in line, but quick."

"Out of the mouths of psychoanalysts. Anything else? Work related?"

Jonathan dug around in his front pocket, lay down a wad of cash, a few aspirin, a plastic-wrapped, peppermint hard candy. "Damn it. Thought your new keys were in my pocket. Hang on." He hurried out to his waiting room. I heard him rustle through the receptionist's desk drawer and, just like that, I plucked half the cash off his desk, stuffed it in my purse on the floor. Planned to go to the club later. I'd replace the dough when I won.

"One for your private entrance." Jonathan handed me a single, loose key. "You probably noticed the construction on our separate parking lots is finished."

"Right, good. No end to the wife's ideas. Six o'clock already. You heading out too?"

"Can't. New client coming in at six-thirty."

I bent over to pick up my purse, ready to go. "Okay, well. See you—"

"Are you pulling your hair out again?"

Chapter Twenty-Three

Preston

"Hope to Christ you're not waiting on me." I stretched out with a bored nonchalance like a cat on the couch she wasn't allowed on.

"Well, I thought you might've come up with things to talk about," Isabel said.

"I'm sure you didn't think that at all."

"Well, I've got something."

"You go, girl," I said.

"We've got things in common."

"Like?" I fluffed my pillow behind me, got comfy.

"My mother's rich too."

"Is that right?" I eyed her up and down. "Why're you working then?"

"Unlike yours, mine won't part with a buck," she said.

"Don't shrinks make a good living?"

"Don't make me laugh."

"If she's loaded why won't she share? Aren't kids of rich parents like owed or something? I think it's an unwritten law."

"Not one she's ever heard of." Isabel warmed to the topic. "Well, she did pay for a few things for me. Got me a car once. Paid my rent for a year, or was it two? Some small stuff here and there. But, so what? Not like she earned it anyway."

"Dad's money?"

"She won the lottery."

"*Get out.*" I straightened up, surprised. "No one wins the

lottery."

"She did—a few years ago. Sole owner of the winning numbers—three hundred and twenty-seven million bucks—biggest in history at the time."

"That was your mom? I remember that for some weird reason."

"Big story around here for a while. In the paper, made the news. My loving mother says it'd be over her dead body before she'd give me a cent."

Isabel's glossed lips pinched together, heavy-lashed eyes flickered, stuck together a little with every blink. She tapped one stiletto to a beat I couldn't hear.

"I don't hire out to kill mothers, sorry Shrinky. Obviously not my skill set."

"Wouldn't matter anyway. The old battle-ax got another husband. He'll get whatever's left. I'm SOL every which way."

"Stop yanking on your hair," I said. "Making me nervous with that crap."

"Well, anyway, I'm telling you because I think we might feel the same way about our mothers."

"That's a fucking stretch. How *do* I feel, Shrinky?"

"Like killing your mother," Isabel said. "Wish I had the nerve."

"Wish in one hand, shit in the other. Guess which one fills up faster?"

"Harrison might let loose with the cash but she—anyone who'd make her daughter pose with a dead baby needs—"

I sprang up. "Shut your flapping mouth. Cooper is off limits."

Chapter Twenty-Four

Preston

I plopped my ass in the only chair in the small room intended to give a modicum of privacy for phone calls. I missed having my own cell phone.

"Hope you've got some straight dope this time, Brendan."

"Some," he said. "Don't think you'll be disappointed."

"Holding my breath."

I yawned, hoped he could hear me though the phone.

"Did you get in our house?" I said.

"Yes. Well, sort of."

"Which is it, Brendan?"

"I got in, but the alarm went off. Code's changed."

"Fuck. Shit. Why didn't we think of that?"

Even though the news so far exasperated me, I liked hearing Brendan's voice.

"Yeah, that's what I thought. Someone's definitely living there. Papers and shit all over the place. Dirty dishes, a mess."

"Who?" I said.

"I don't know."

"Now what?"

"I'll get back in."

"Now you're a decoding whiz?" I said.

Brendan couldn't even work our TV remote.

"No, but I know a guy."

"Oh my God. Of course you do."

I'd forgotten how creative my scrappy Irishman could get. Buying and selling hard drugs made useful bedfellows. For a second our vibe felt like old times—my Irishman and me against the world. I listened to him breathe, the steady rhythm familiar, sensual.

As if he'd read my mind, Brendan said, "Remember when we'd dine and dash that stupid Jewish deli on Eighth Street? The bagels and lox. What the fuck's a lox anyway?"

The sound of Brendan's laugh could soothe the devil.

"Shoulda let 'em haul your ass to the hoosegow," he said.

"Fuck you, you big dumb mick."

"My knees go weak when you go lovey dovey," Brendan said, then quieter, "I wish they'd let me see you." Then he laughed again. "They've got a strict policy about not letting people visit that you've tried to kill."

"They've let my mother in."

"That's messed up, Preston."

Hearing my own laughter startled me. It'd been so long since anything struck me funny.

"We should not laugh about that," Brendan said.

"Too soon?"

"You're never more beautiful than when you're in bad taste," he said.

His voice could move me if I let it. Kicked up my insides. We stopped talking, lost in nostalgia.

"Anyway," Brendan said, all business again. "I asked my mom about your aunt's house."

"Already got the skinny from my dad."

"And?"

"Nothing earth-shattering. From some other shit he laid on me I think they sold it to cover my expenses. Like they're broke now."

"Well, my mom had more to say than that. Cops' wives know everything worth knowing."

True. I'd been in Brendan's family long enough to know that.

"Like?"

"Mom said there's lots of buzz about the sale—closed up all these years—new owners paid millions for that pile. She didn't think your mother knew a thing about it."

"How could my dad sell without Mother's consent? It's not possible."

"That's what my mom wondered. But that's not the weirdest part."

"Go on."

"She said something like, 'Poor James, Todd threw her over for Harrison then killed herself.' That's the gist of—"

"My dad dumped *Aunt James*? They *dated*? Stop fucking with me."

"I know, right? Guess it's true," Brendan said.

"What dunce would date my doofy dad—other than my mother?"

"James, apparently. Mom said, 'Poor sap dodged a bullet to throw himself on a scud missile.'"

"Your mom's a funny broad," I said.

Colleen could tell an off-color joke better than any cop.

"Word is Harrison's in a bad way."

"I could've told you that."

"Other than amnesia or whatever memory stuff, she seemed okay when she got home from the hospital, at first. Well, not *okay*, but okay considering. Anyway, now she roams around in a daze. Mom thinks she's drugged."

"What else?"

"Alicia retired."

"What the fuck?" I said.

What bizarre corner had this conversation turned?

"Yeah, Mom ran into her at the grocery store. Alicia told her she retired while Harrison was still hospitalized. Todd encouraged her, because she didn't have much to do, and Harrison was expected to die."

"My father just told me she was taking care of my mother."

I thought a few seconds about my thorny conversation with my father.

"Well, what he actually said was she was getting the best care," I said.

"Just not from Alicia, I guess."

"Alicia's been my mother's slave since after college."

"Maybe she knows something," Brendan said.

"What's to know?"

"Something inconvenient. Like maybe Todd sold James's house for some underhanded reason."

"I told you my dad couldn't unload anything without Mother's writ of consent. Jesus, Brendan, all these years and you still don't know how my parents work? No way."

"He's drugging her I'll bet."

"What the fuck for?" I said.

"Have you met her?"

Chapter Twenty-Five

Preston

"What's wrong with you, ding-a-ling? Why are you here?"

"You're funny, Preston," Rosalie said.

Rosalie sat next to me on the ratty sofa in front of the TV in the day room, used her plastic doll for a footstool.

"Come on, tell me. Run out in traffic? Dingo ate your baby? Stab Daddy's forehead with a barbecue fork?"

"Dingo ate your baby. Dingo ate your baby."

"Stop that repeat shit."

"Okay."

She yanked the doll out from under her feet to stick it in my face.

"Look," she said.

"So what? A doll." I pushed it back.

"Mom gave it to me," Rosalie said.

"Your mother was here?"

"Your mother was here, your mother was here, your mother was here." Rosalie started mimicking me when all her other annoying habits failed to incite me. Now she just skipped the run-up and went right to it. "Your mother was here, your mother was here, your—"

"Goddammit. Shut the fuck up." I shoved her backward, hard. She sprang right back up.

"Your mother was here, your mother was here," Rosalie whispered to herself, then got up with her stupid doll and walked away still murmuring.

"Preston," Nurse Judy padded into the day room. "Package for you."

She lobbed a package to me covered in wrinkled, brown wrapper, torn with a mishmash of tape in weird places. Some Johnny-on-the-spot aide probably unwrapped, then rewrapped the thing checking for any shit on the no-no list. With an uncanny nose for goings-on that didn't concern her, Rosalie stumbled back over, doll pressed to her chest.

"It's your birthday," Rosalie yelled. "Happy birthday."

"Where'd this come from?" I said.

"Where'd this come from?" Rosalie mimicked. "Where'd this come from?"

Before I could smack her sideways, Judy said, "Hush Rosalie. I've asked you several times to stop repeating what people say. It's not nice."

"Well?" I said.

"No idea," Nurse Judy said. "Dropped at the front desk."

"By who?"

"Didn't see."

I ripped the tattered paper off.

"Yay," Rosalie jumped up and down. "Your thingy. Your journal thingy."

Chapter Twenty-Six

Preston's Blog

Musings from the Dented Throne

Not in Kansas Anymore

I'll level with you, my Dented Throne devotees. My recent love-fest with the Jester got me thinking. A lot. My tussle with the Queen (you know the one) prickles my brain but not to any clear result. We circled, lunged, parried. Seems I gave killing her my best shot. Details? None. No police reports list the facts, thanks to the Blair Fitzgerald stranglehold on my father-in-law lawman. The Royal She doesn't cop to shit either. She's a blank. No hard evidence exists. If it weren't for the ring around the Queen's collar I'd say I dreamt the whole nasty affair.

I keep suspicions buried. But if you, hand to Buddha, promise not to tell, I'll whisper them in your ear.

One: Fuzzy on the details, I feel sure the Royal She tried to take what belonged to me. The Heiress spun around fast as a bullet train. An enthusiastic tug-o-war ensued. Which is when I must've slashed her. I've always been hard to get along with, a real solid pain in the ass but armed and dangerous? No. Why I brought a box cutter to the circle jerk is yet one more mystery. When I dwell on Mother's attempted thievery I feel a murderous rage overtake me—again. A sweat breaks.

Two: Killing a so far unknown person isn't on the Heiress's menu. Is it? How monstrous am I? Wouldn't I recall that dastardly deed? Besides living humans fill space. If their orbit comes up empty, doesn't anyone cry foul? Who's missing? I've heard nothing, read nothing in the online newspapers I devour daily searching for answers.

Three: Ever since the Irishman surfaced, my long-gone brother haunts my dreams. His cries sound fresh in my nightmares. Images plague me to consciousness, sheets soaked. Why does the Littlest Heir disturb my reflections now, when most of my life I've spent undeterred? Is it my sobriety? I'm no longer numb? Perhaps. What's my husband got to do with any of it? Like me, he was a child when my brother died.

I should let my investigating husband know what's on my splintered mind, no?

Take a minute before you plunge in with an answer. Know this—danger lurks. Calamitous foreboding covers me like a second skin. My finely honed intuition promises the only thing between me and sure peril is my current refuge. It should go without saying, but I know it doesn't. I'm worried for the Irishman too. I'm protected in here. He isn't.

FYI: As I predicted, Shrinky's off the deep end. I'm *her* therapist now.

So sorry, fiends and followers, any revelations run contrary to my outlaw status. I'd respect your decision to unsubscribe but hope you rethink. Can't help but wonder if you all hold the keys, know which end is fucking up. If you do, enlighten me.

The Invisible Heiress

Count to ten before you opine. The Heiress won't consider any comments off the cuff.

Comments

Well Hung Jung

Tell the Irishman every suspicion. The jerkoff needs more to do. And 'cause I'm an all-around good guy, I'll pass on the advice my own dear departed dad gave me when I started chasing tail—follow the money.

Reply: What nonsense shoots out your piehole? Money follows me. Besides, what's cash got to do with any fucking thing?

Well Hung Jung

Money has to do with *every* fucking thing—money and pussy.

Amy W.

The Irishman probably doesn't have anything to do with the Littlest Heir. Dreams are unreliable. They never mean what they appear to. BTW, what could the Queen possibly steal from you that she doesn't already own?

Reply: Good question. The Heiress isn't clear, but visions come to me. I can feel it zooming clearer.

Norma B.

Smart to stay confined until more information comes to light. Let the Irishman help. I'm from a fairly small town. Rumors catch like fire. It's a good bet you didn't kill anyone. Since you got your journal back write down what you remember right away. Writing seems to spur you on.

Reply: I'm with you on the baseless rumors. You're smarter than I first thought. I could give haiku a go, but if you haven't noticed, you all are my new journal. Don't need the old one.

Norma B.

FYI: You know shrinks often become shrinks because they're nuts.

Scribbler

Let's email. Seriously. You've got a book in you. I'll help get it out.

Reply: You've got your head in your ass. I can't help get it out.

Chapter Twenty-Seven

Preston

"Heads a muddled mess, but I'm fucking sure I didn't manage to kill anyone. I mean wouldn't a murdered person make news or be missed?"

I drew invisible circles on the wall of the phone room with my index finger.

"I assume," Brendan said. "Probably lies. Bitter people jumping on the bandwagon."

"But I can't shake the feeling. Death plagues me."

"What? We just agreed it's only gossip."

"Gone Helen Keller on me? Said it was a *feeling*. No evidence."

"Well, Harrison might say otherwise."

"It's not that. Well, not *just* that. I dream about something else. Dark, scary. I can't get a handle on. I dream about Cooper a lot."

"Cooper's been dead forever."

"Be that as it may, whatever the Queen and I bitch-fought over," I felt wobbly, the walls tilted around me, "involved Cooper."

"I'm stumped."

"Fucked up, I know but I feel it in my bones."

I closed my eyes to stop the spinning. We stayed quiet a few seconds. I knew Brendan so well I could tell by the prolonged silence and his breathing he had something to say he thought I might not like.

"What's up, Brendan?"

"I found Harrison's maid, Alicia. Talked to her a couple days ago."

"What the hell? Why didn't you tell me that first?"

My husband could still get on my last nerve.

"I'm telling you now," Brendan said.

"How'd you track her down?"

"Talked to Herberto."

"Who?"

"Christ, Preston. Your parents' gardener for thirty-odd years."

"Oh right," I said like I knew but forgot.

I sat with my feet up on the desk. Leaned the fuck in, like a boss.

"Anyway, Herberto told me where to find Alicia."

"How would he know? How would *you know* what he even said?"

"I speak Spanish, Preston. Jesus, don't you remember anything about me?"

"Crispy Christ, I forgot. No end to your mad skills, Brenny."

"Can't deal drugs out of Mexico if you can't speak the language."

"Right, right. Still. Why would Herberto know anything about Alicia?"

"You rich girls. Everyone knows the help sticks together. My dad could tell you the kids' names of most cops still on the force."

"Falling asleep here."

"Turns out, Alicia's got a new condo," Brendan said. "Primo real estate. Clock Tower building."

"Stop *it*."

"Slammed the custom-made door in my face when she caught my drift."

"What drift?"

"I asked why she left. If your folks paid for her place."

This was like getting blood out of a turnip. "What'd she say?"

"Um, did you hear the part where she slammed the door?" Brendan's tone turned impatient. "I'm sure she knows about my past. Thinks I'm up to something fishy."

"Damn it, we needed more. Now what?"

"Well, it could mean nothing."

"What? You thought she knew something before," I said.

"I did at first. Maybe Alicia was straight up with my mom. Harrison stayed in the hospital for so long. Seemed like as good a time as any for Alicia to retire. No telling when, or if, your mom would need her again. Your parents paying for her new apartment doesn't necessarily point to anything bad. Maybe it's Alicia's golden parachute."

"I hate it when you sound so reasonable. So, another waste?"

"Maybe not. While I *hablado español* with Alicia, I saw Marcella sitting on the couch, pretty as you please. Thought she got her ass slapped in jail a long time ago."

"Who?"

"Alicia's daughter. You know, the nurse? Christ, your mother paid for her to go to college."

"What? How? What?"

"Marcella's our age. How can you not know her?"

"Better question, how can you?"

"Dunno. Probably met at your parents' summer barbecue or something. Gonna meet her for coffee."

Holy fucking guacamole. A whole world I didn't know about revolved outside my mansion while I'd shopped Net-a-Porter online loaded. "You talked to her already?"

"Yeah. Not *talk*, talk. Made arrangements. She stopped me before I could drive off. Didn't want Mamacita to see us."

My feet hit the floor. I didn't want to hear more but doubled down. "Why would she go out of her way for *you*?"

"How do you think I made all those connections back in college? She's related to a bunch of guys in the drug biz, plus she's a nurse, peddles prescriptions. Think she got caught though. Anyway, me and Marcella, before. Before you and I got together, well, *officially* together."

So that's why he didn't rush to tell me. Why Brendan's veiled confession coldcocked me I didn't know. What'd I give a rooster's dick who he fucked?

"That it?" I said. "You done?"

"Not even close."

"Speed it up then."

"Look, Preston—get serious. Marcella doesn't mean anything. You and I weren't together then. You're not seeing the forest for the trees. She can help us." I could feel Brendan sweat through the receiver. "You're pissed?"

"Don't flatter yourself."

"I'll take that as a yes. Well, you'll like this. I got in our house this morning."

"You're just now telling me jackwad?" I screeched in the mouthpiece like one of the *Real Housewives of New Jersey* during sweeps. "What's with you today?"

"Guess I felt bad about the Marcella thing. It's all I could think about. I knew you'd get—"

"Move it along. Nothing to be done about the past."

Except stew in jealousy and resentment then hold it over Brendan's head forever.

"Right, okay, well, I didn't stay long. Something happened. The alarm went off again. Scared the shit outta me. My guy fucked up, gotta set his ass straight."

"Find anything?"

"Looks like whoever lives there is a woman. Lacy panties and stuff."

"Lying around on the first floor?"

"Well, folded. On the couch."

"Weird. Go on."

"Must be your mom."

"My mother's *panties*? Lay off the hookah, Brendan. Can't imagine her chin-huggin' drawers flung around anywhere, much less the couch. Plus, as great as our house is, she's got her own nicer one. Not to mention she can barely get herself across the room."

"Yeah, true. Well, here's the best part. After I sped outta there I no more than got on the main road when I saw a car turn into our lane coming from the opposite direction. Just happened to look in my rearview in time to catch it."

"Could you see the driver? What kind of car?"

"I barely saw the thing. Darker colored, I think. A bunch of cop cars swarmed in behind because of the alarm going off so long," Brendan said.

"Why does this feel dangerous? I'm the one everyone's supposed to fear but something . . . someone—"

"I feel it too," Brendan said. "Makes no sense. You did a bad thing. You're locked up. Despite the rumors I'm certain you didn't kill anyone. That's supposed to be the end of the story."

"Not a chance," I said.

"None at all."

Chapter Twenty-Eight

Preston's Blog

Musings from the Dented Throne

Besa Mi Culo, Puta

Much as conformity bores the shit out of me, the Heiress must follow the crowd. You, Dented Throne devotees, might cheat on me (Mon Dieu!) with younger, prettier bloggers. If you do indulge in the occasional dalliance you've noticed those dullard bimbos love lists. So here's one. I've decided the best way to sort out my thoughts are to make like a lemming.

1. Shit just got real. While the Heiress finds herself strapped to the rack in the dungeon, her Irishman's sweating up the sheets with a hot tamale nurse he swears we've both known for years—a relative of the Queen's entourage. Sure, he denies such an unholy alliance in the present day, says it's all behind him, but I know the real deal. "Senorita can help our cause," he told me. "Chica knows things."

"I'll tell you what Chica knows—how to horizontal mambo like the rent's due.

Despite the Irishman's assurances that his dalliance meant nothing, he played hide the chorizo during one of our many relationship breaks back in the day. I felt betrayed. How could his jumping-bean collusion go on under my nose with the help's spawn?

Ay, caramba!

2. There's room at the inn. Some unknown woman has ingratiated herself right into my vacant house. Where she apparently drops it like it's hot in my living room. The thought of this mystery tramp prancing to and fro in her pimped-up lingerie is almost too much to take. It's my *fucking* house. How did I discover this crime?

My husband managed to find time in his own floozy-fucking schedule to make another recon mission to our place where he spied La Perla-type evidence, on my custom-made couch, no less. If my parents sold the mansion they paid for and gave to me, to someone else, I might need to bust outta here and find another weapon.

The nerve.

3. Royal She sat on her daddy's lap until he died. So discomfited by this ick-inducing habit, I've never breathed a word. Every Christmas we'd gather 'round Grandfather and Grandmother's big show-off tree with color-coordinated, ribbon-festooned décor. While the royal relations feigned surprise when fake Santa (Grandfather's valet) hauled his fat ass in, carrying blue Tiffany boxes and loot from FAO Schwarz, the Queen, and Grandfather crept off to the library. Holiday after holiday I observed the Queen cuddled up on Granddad behind his antique mahogany desk.

Ho fucking ho.

4. She won't touch or be touched. As much as I dread thinking about the Royal We *in flagrante delicto,* I can't help but wonder how they managed not one, but two, offspring. If my brother and I hadn't looked so much like them, I'd say we'd been adopted. The Queen has never been keen to have anyone's hands on her or to bestow hers on them. Except with her beloved son. She couldn't keep her hands off him. As for me? Not so much as a peck on the cheek or a hand to a feverish forehead.

I've half a mind to bust out of this juke joint to try to find out what in Slim Shady is going on.

The Invisible Heiress

If you've got the gift of gab, use it. I might join in.

Comments

Jack

How awesome would it be to get both you and the Queen on film? Now that's a star-making documentary.

Reply: Have you read one word on this blog? Queen's already a star.

Monica L.

The Irishman's giving you the run around to distract you from his goings on. Maybe it's all a hoax. It's probably his girlfriend's lingerie. You don't know what he's doing in that house. You should get out so you can cut his throat too. Don't trust him.

Reply: Why would he tell me about the underwear, you asshat? Even he's not that stupid. Thanks for playing. If you haven't noticed, I'm an idiot savant when it comes to throat slitting.

Masked Man

Of course your husband's got a side gig. You're in the booby hatch. When u breaking out? Some group action with you, your MILF, and me would go far toward repairing your rift. From the sounds of it, your mother goes for older men.

Reply: You've almost got a threesome, if you can find two more.

Scribbler

Obviously, the Queen's daddy was a perv. Don't be hard on her about it. Not the Royal She's fault. BTW, seen Twitter lately? Check out #whoisinvisibleheiress #bloggerkiller

Reply: Amateur hour's on Tuesdays. Queen wasn't a child Dumbo but a grown-ass woman. Tweets are for twats. #whogivesafuck

Norma B.

Scribbler's got the right idea, sounds like inappropriate funny business. Doubt the Queen sat on Grandpa happy as Rebecca of Sunnybrook Farm. Probably why she doesn't like physical contact.

Reply: Delusions, Norma. Grandpa babied her. Get your head out of the smut. Besides, no one makes the Queen do squat, at least not without body armor.

Norma B.

Don't underestimate the power a parent holds over a child, even a grown one. Seems to me your own mother's power over you isn't the healthiest, now is it? As far as the Irishman goes, cut him some slack. He's trying to help you. Stay put until he finds more.

Reply: I don't want to admit you're right. So I won't.

Well Hung Jung

I'm with Norma on this one Heiress. You've clearly got an anger management problem. You're too hard on everyone who loves you. Speaking of hard . . .

Chapter Twenty-Nine

Isabel

No lights brightened the front office. I checked the time. It wasn't *that* late. I flicked on the overheads for a look-see in the common zone. Receptionist Rhonda's desk sat empty. Whole place looked shut down. I veered to my side of the office, new key in hand, to unlock my private area. A note pressed to my door greeted me.

Fired sticky fingered Rhonda. Voicemail will catch all calls. J.

Crap. Collateral damage.

Why didn't I think that through? I needed the money. What could I do? The cash box beckoned on a regular basis. Jonathan never paid attention to details, and Rhonda seemed dense as a bag of dirt. I intended to pay it back when the cards fell in my favor. How much could I owe? Twenty here, forty there. *Que será, será.* Rhonda could get another shit job. Couldn't she? My stomach gurgled with discomfort. As far as I knew, she'd never done anything wrong, didn't deserve to get fired. Tried to remember if she had a husband, one with a job. That'd make me feel a little better.

Nothing to do about it now, was there?

I could admit I'd taken the cash and not Rhonda.

That's what I'd do. On the twelfth. Of never.

I couldn't concern myself. Dropped my bag on the floor, heard the jangle of the keys to my new sedan. I stared at the paperwork on my desk. Shoved the whole lot aside. Did Jonathan stash any more loot in his office? Would I even find his space unlocked? New wheels are nice and all, but I couldn't spend my new car at the grocery store or the casino. Plus, Jonathan would assume Rhonda pilfered any cash in there, if he noticed.

I strolled toward Jonathan's side of the building and found his side wide open, marched right through his waiting room. At the end of the long hall, a beam of light lit the floor from under his office door. Goddammit. No mining for treasure there now. Interested to hear Jonathan's version of the idiot receptionist's drama, I went forward anyway until I heard murmurs. Like all therapists, Jonathan took late clients to accommodate their work schedules. So much for that, I turned around.

On my way back through his waiting room, a bright white something on one of the chairs caught my eye. I grabbed a neatly folded piece of paper halfway stuck between the cushions. Scurried to my office, where I smoothed the creased surface, scanned the scribbled contents. I sped to the copy machine to make a duplicate, raced to return the original to the chair cushions, and beat a swift retreat to my office, paper in hand.

I took a quick look. No date, no identifying info, only a short handful of sentences. What was this? A note? I read—*Someone's trying to get in. I can hear them.* Breathlessly intrigued, I kicked off my Manolos to read more when I heard a bustle from beyond my closed door. I cocked my head. Two voices. One was Jonathan. The other was too low to make out even when I pressed my ear to the wall. No idea why they'd have ventured out of their way to my side of the building or stopped right in front of my office. After a second or two, their voices waned. I waited several long minutes then poked my head out. They'd gone. I finished reading.

I killed my baby. They will take him away from me.

****

The delicious new-car smell thrilled me. Couldn't help but wear what I felt sure was a smug smile while I oh-so-carefully swung out to the street. Intoxicated by my plush, fresh-from-the-dealer new car, I didn't give Jonathan's personal parking lot a thought when I drove by, except the light at the corner turned red, so I idled, glanced around to kill time. Jonathan's Mercedes mini-van (a phrase that shouldn't exist if you ask me) sat in its reserved spot, as usual, the car parked next to it was dark and so long that it jutted out well past the rear end of Jonathan's van. Looked like a limo. Huh. He and his client must've gone back to his office after chatting in front of mine. I'd assumed they'd both left. Weird.

I rolled down my tinted window to get a better look in the dusk, jumped when the obnoxious Range Rover driver behind me laid on his horn. Green light. I zipped back into Jonathan's parking lot. Limo looked like Harrison Blair's Town Car. *Jesus Christ Almighty.* Came *this close* to ramming through the tail end of the big mystery car. Harrison's loyal driver stood outside it, smoking. He bolted sideways, so I'd miss plowing his uniformed ass to the concrete.

Chapter Thirty

Isabel

"Preston, wake up." I shoved her shoulder. She shot up like I'd cattle prodded her.

"Don't get grabby, Shrinky, or I'll knock your scrawny ass to the floor."

"Bad habit you've got, knocking scrawny asses to the floor." I jerked the chair toward Preston's bed. "A miracle you didn't do permanent damage to Rosalie this time. Nurse says she had to sedate her. What exactly is your issue with that poor, defenseless woman?" I looked above Preston's head. "Your photo's still there, couldn't be that crap again." Skimmed her desk. "See you found your journal too, so what?"

"Go home. Not in the mood for another heart-to-heart."

"You gotta have one first," I said.

"Geez, Shrinky. You finally slip off the slope? Gone full crazy at last?"

"Look, you're not the only one with problems. I'd much rather be home than in this bin with you. Imagine my disappointment when Nurse Judy called, frantic, 'Preston's on a tear again.'"

I'd just gotten comfy on my new velvet sofa to drink, come up with reasons to justify Rhonda's firing, digest Harrison's visit to Jonathan and the paper I'd found in his waiting room, when Judy's phone call terminated my scheming.

"You and Nurse Judy can jump off a bridge singing 'Kumbaya' for all I give a donkey's dong," Preston said.

"Rosalie can bring assault charges against you, or her family can. Don't you get that?"

"Rosalie's *family* won't do shit. Wanna know why?" Preston scooted to the edge of her bed, faced me full on, cheeks on fire, eyes wet.

"I'll bite. Why?"

"Family pretends she doesn't exist, especially Rosalie's husband. Yeah, nut job's got a husband, if you can believe *that* crime against nature. Hubs never drops in to visit. Never. Ever. Why? Loon-of-a-wife drove her car in the lake with their two-year-old kid strapped in his car seat. Jesus told her to do it. Rippin' Rosie's a fucking *baby killer*. She almost died herself but, of course, didn't. Only deprived of oxygen long enough to make her an idiot and a total burden to her family."

I'd known Rosalie was a pariah. I felt it the day Preston jumped her. Took one to know one.

"Who delivered this headline-making news?" I said.

"Rosie the Reaper told me herself. Kept asking her. Bitch finally purged."

"Rosalie might not be the most reliable source."

"Like you'd know. I could tell she spoke truth, Shrinky. Like it or not."

"That's why you punched her?"

"*Somebody* needed to kick her crazy ass."

"Oh, I see. Somebody who slit her mother's throat?"

"My mother isn't a baby."

"No, but—"

"What you know about me and *Mommy Dearest* would fit in a flea's butthole."

"So you keep saying. Well, I see Rosalie's eccentricities got under your skin in a big way. Why the tears? What's your deal with babies anyway?"

She didn't answer, which didn't surprise me. Cooper Blair wasn't a topic I intended to take up tonight, particularly when I knew what Preston's reaction would be. Why go there when I knew we'd never *really* go there? Besides, a bottle of Don Julio Real waited for me at home.

"You're wasting your rage, you know," I said.

"Oh, am I? Cause you know everything about my rage? This I gotta hear."

"Well, if you're using it against me or Rosalie, it's sure as hell a waste."

"That so? Gotta better idea?"

Harrison's car and driver in the parking lot of my office and what I'd read scribbled on that one explosive page came to my mind.

"You think I don't know squat about your mother. Well, I know a hell of a lot more than you."

"Like?"

"Like, if anyone deserves a hard punch in the face girly, it's your mother."

"Preston," Nurse Judy pushed Preston's door open without so much as a by-your-leave. She looked back and forth at the both of us. "Much as I hate to interrupt your dressing down, Preston, your father's here."

"Tattle tale much?" Preston said to Judy.

"You can bet I will, but your father came of his own accord," Nurse said.

"How many times do I have to remind you? Preston doesn't want to see her father outside of therapy," I said.

"Well, she let him in last time so—"

Preston's wicked-nuts girl cackle cleaved Judy's explanations.

"Tell Daddy-O to come on in," Preston said. "Say g'night, Shrinky."

****

She finally did it to me. I'd lost it for real.

Already rattled by everything that had already transpired, Preston's spoiled, maniacal behavior finished me. The self-control I'd held a tenuous grasp over vaporized. I knew I'd crossed over to the other side again. No reining it in now. Who cared anyway? My address was about to change to 1234 Easy Street. Fuck 'em all. My forefinger throbbed where I'd bit the nail down to the bloody quick. My neckline burned where I'd torn out strands of hair.

I snickered to myself behind the wheel of my new car. The

times they were a changing. Which is why I stopped taking my meds.

Well, that and the baby.

Three tests turned pink, so I'd probably need to give up my evening glass or two of calm-the-fuck-down. I snickered some more. Then I remembered.

Cashwise, I was almost back to zero. Fast too.

I'd paid off most of my debts with Sherman's dough. Like an idiot, I'd gone too conservative when I gave him a number, not sure how much he'd agree to. I'd indulged in some retail therapy but couldn't stop once I started. I got a few additions to my wardrobe, furniture for my apartment, some knickknacks. But a girl couldn't live on shoes and tchotchkes alone. Of course I used a few bucks tempting fate at the casino here and there. Damned if Lady Luck didn't turn on me almost every time. When I did win, I took it as a sign, double or nothing. Now there's nothing. Casino sucked up all my remaining money. If finding myself in the poor house again wasn't tragedy enough, Harrison Blair had shown up on my turf.

Then, like a Batista Bomb from a WWE fighter, it hit me. I'd wavered back and forth on what exactly to do with the damning missive I'd found in Jonathan's waiting room. It all made sense. Now I knew the right course.

Mama wasn't the only lottery winner.

Chapter Thirty-One

Preston

"Weren't you just here?" I said somewhat distracted by Dad's cobalt-colored contacts. "I think you're frowning. Botox much? Jesus, Madame Tussaud could take lessons."

"Enough, Preston," Dad said in his most serious tone.

For a second there, I thought he actually bristled, or maybe gas?

"I've come to discuss a serious matter. Your—"

"What's going on with my house?" I said. I was ready for him this time. No way he'd get out of here without answering some of my questions for a change.

"What? What about your house?"

He sat in the chair next to my bed. The one Shrinky had vacated several minutes before. His beautifully tailored worsted wool, heather gray suit looked in stark contrast to my dreary, oatmeal-colored scrubs. He'd no more than set his briefcase down when I said, "Who's living in it?"

"Living? Oh, right. Your mother certainly didn't tell you anything about that, did she?"

That stung. He knew my mother didn't tell me anything.

"She knows someone's living in my house?"

"Of course she knows. She's the one who offered it up."

"To?"

He shifted in the chair, blew out a huffy sigh. "Oh, what's her name? You know, um, uh, Alicia's daughter. You remember her. The one who—"

"Marcella?" My shriek surprised the shit outta my father, who jerked backward like I'd slapped him. Why did everyone think I knew her?

"Preston, calm down. It was only temporary. But yes, Marcella, Maria, whatever."

I'd jumped to my feet. "How dare Mother give my house to that—"

"First of all, no one *gave* your house to anyone. Second, I think she's gone already." Dad gripped my hand in both of his. "Now please, sit. Your house is yours, no one's taking it away from you, which is why the upkeep needs to get paid, which leads me to why I've come here again—"

I snatched my hand back, dropped back down on the bed, fuming.

"Why was that slut living in my house?"

"Slut? Christ, Preston. Who cares?" He threw his head back, covered his eyes with both hands. "Look, I don't know the whole story. God knows your mother and I, we, suffice it to say, we're not exactly exchanging chitchat at the dinner table these days. Your mother is not at all well."

"Well enough to fuck me over," I said, even though I knew she teetered on the brink these days.

I started to demand more answers, but Dad leaned forward again, pressed a finger to his lips. The universal sign for shut the fuck up. So I did.

"All I know is Maria—"

"Marcella," I said through clenched molars.

"She got into some trouble and needed a place to stay until it could get sorted out. Apparently, it's sorted out, and she's moved on. Months ago, I think. Your mother and Alicia worked it out without my input." He sighed a weight-of-the-world kind of huff. "I'm usually the last one to know what the women in my house do."

"Mother's in no shape to do anything for anyone. You said yourself. Which is it?"

"This was before," Dad's eyes welled up, "before she took a turn for the worse."

I looked away. Hoped he'd get himself together.

"Why didn't Marcella stay with Alicia? Her own mother for Jesus' sake," I said after a few seconds.

"Maybe they don't get along. Can you imagine?"

I'd let that go. Brendan said he'd seen Marcella at Alicia's swank new condo. They got along well enough for that tête-à-tête. I'd already said too much by even asking about the goings on at my place. I wouldn't ask about Alicia's retirement either, even though I really wanted to.

"What kind of trouble?" I said, because I wanted to know. Drugs?

"No idea. I don't care. Who's giving you all these updates? You're supposed to be protected from the outside world in here until you get better. James's estate sale, now this? Is Brendan your town crier?"

Call me puckered. Shit. Me and my big mouth. Why couldn't I just let Brendan find out this crap? He would've. Wait. He probably already knew, that lying, rutting pig.

"I never want to see Brendan again," I said.

"That makes all of us then," Dad pulled some papers out of his briefcase, handed me that stupid power of attorney. "Back to why I came—from now on your household expenses, this cushy hospital, everything's going to get paid out of your trust fund."

I flung the papers at him.

"Good luck finding it, Daddy-O."

Chapter Thirty-Two

Preston

"You won't believe what happened," Brendan said.

I twirled around in slow circles behind the desk chair in the phone closet. "Don't tell me. Marcella gave you the clap."

"I'm fucking sick of snide remarks, Preston. Ever since I told you about me and Marcella—"

"That *puta?* She can suck your dick until the stub turns to *frijoles.*"

"Why should I keep risking my ass to help you? You're an ungrateful, spoiled baby. You treat me like an enemy. Especially now your father thinks I'm telling you shit. Shit he doesn't want you to know."

"Get off the cross."

"Get off the bitch bus."

"Since when do you whine about my defects?"

"Since someone's ransacked my apartment, killed Jesse Pinkman, and left him there for me to find. Like some fucking mafia hit."

"Your apartment? What? Who's Jesse Pinkman?"

"My dog."

"Shit. Oh no, that's terrible," I said. "You owned a dog?" The idea of Brendan brokenhearted over a dog made me feel like crying. Then Marcella, the Mexican mantrap, came to mind again. "Well, my dad wouldn't resort to animal killing."

"No, it doesn't seem like his style. But he'd hire someone quick enough."

"My father? No. My mother? Yes."

"That's true. She's in no shape to do that, is she?"

"Don't underestimate my mother." I thought about the possibility. "Not her style either though. She'd want you to see her coming. Maybe Marcella's peeps don't like you. They're all druggies like she is, aren't they?"

"Marcella?" Brendan said." What are you talking about?"

"Maybe she's cheating on someone too and he got pissed."

"Too? I'm not cheating. Fuck that. I'm done making stupid explanations. I'll be dead as Jesse Pinkman before you know it."

"No one's gonna kill you. Stop hyperventilating." He might be right, but I didn't want to admit it to him or myself. The worse I felt for Brendan, the worse I treated him.

"You really are a piece of work. You're not out here. I am," he said.

"My life is in the shithole right now, if you've forgotten."

"Step off, Preston. My life's not exactly a day at Coachella either."

That got me. I dialed it down.

"Well, what about our house?"

"Fingers crossed," Brendan said. "I'm going tomorrow."

I wondered what he'd say if all traces of Marcella's occupation had really disappeared. Maybe I could glean the truth after I heard whatever he had to say about his observations.

"I'm gonna check it out after I meet up with Marcella," he said.

"Still Marcella?"

Hearing her name hurt my ears. Why did she keep coming up? Felt like *Groundhog Day*. Did he not hear a word I said? So much for dialing it back.

"Look, I'm gonna pretend we didn't even have most of this conversation. Marcella knows something. I know it." He paused. For a second I thought he'd hung up. "After that, well, we'll see."

"We'll see what?"

Panic shot through me.

"Getting to the bottom of whatever shit sinkhole you're neck deep in isn't worth my life. You don't appreciate anything anyway. I'll pass on whatever she knows, and then I should bow out. I'm a moron to keep this up."

I let his slur on my character pass. I knew I'd gone too far.

"You dealt drugs, Brendan, armed to your capped teeth. Now you're scared of some chickenshit who kills innocent dogs? *Come on.*"

I meant that as a kind of pep talk.

"Drug dealers I can deal with. You know exactly what you're getting. Not like you and yours. Shifty rich hoodlums shielded under their shit-don't-stink, blue blood."

"Speaking of drug dealers. Not everything's always my parents' fault."

If Brendan was in bed with Marcella, odds were he was still in the business. The business might be hunting him down. I could tell by the quiet he hadn't thought his own lifestyle choices might be responsible for his plight.

"Maybe. At any rate, I don't know why I can't let go of you."

"I don't either," I said before I could stop. Truth pained me. "I couldn't blame you. I don't know why you married me in the first place."

"I thought you were the world's greatest adventure," he said. "A wild thing, the two of us breaking bad. Brendan Finney— stupid, gringo fake."

"To think for these past few weeks I thought it might've been love."

"You're immune to love."

That hurt.

"Brendan?"

"Now what?"

"I'm sorry about your dog."

Chapter Thirty-Three

Isabel

"When were you gonna tell me, Jonathan?"

"Tell you what? I'm a mind reader now?"

"You know what I'm talking about." I dropped into a chair in front of his desk, sat in it. This might take a while.

Jonathan tossed his bifocals aside. "Harrison specifically told me not to tell you. You know how that works. Or should."

"*Now* you're hiding behind patient confidentiality."

"Harrison insisted. No choice, you know that."

"Doesn't stop you from butting into Preston's therapy."

"You didn't tell me Preston's identity, I figured it out."

"Nitpicking," I said.

"Case-by-case basis."

"Harrison knows we're partners?"

"Yes."

"You didn't see a conflict?"

"Nope. Look, she came in once. Twice, but the second time to get something she'd dropped here. So one session."

"What'd she drop?"

"Can't say," he said.

"Won't say."

"Nothing to do with her session. Honestly, wish I hadn't seen it."

"Must've been bad," I said.

"Well, I'd bet the farm she won't come back, because I'm sure she figured I read whatever it was."

"Intriguing."

"Put the whole business out of your mind, Isabel, like I've done."

"Throw me a bone, Jonathan. Whatever issues Harrison brought to therapy with you might help with Preston."

"Good try." He settled his glasses back on his nose. "I'll say this: I don't know why she bothered. Didn't talk much. Perplexing. Got the feeling she didn't come for therapy."

"What'd she come for then?"

"Never figured that out. Kept wandering around the office, preoccupied. I wondered if she hoped to run into you."

"Doubt it. She could run into me whenever she wanted. They're paying me. Preoccupied or drugged?"

"Now that you mention it, I'm not sure."

"Did she look just-rolled-out-of-bed?"

"Heavens, no. Why?"

"Last couple of sessions at Haven House she looked trashed."

"Hmm. Nope. She looked beautiful, perfect. First time I'd seen her in person, not on the tube or newspaper. Intelligent, well-kept, stylish."

"Still the ladies' man, aren't you? Well, sounds like she's experienced quite the turnaround then."

"Speaking of—you look a little, well, under the weather?"

I tucked my gnarled fingernails into my palms.

"You know me," I said. "I ebb and flow."

"Mostly ebb. Noticed your steady stream of clients slowed."

"They'll pick up again," I said.

"Judge Seward run out of delinquents?"

"They come and go."

"Your fella still around? Or did he run screaming?"

"Fella's around in a big way. Getting serious. Who knows? White picket fence might hover in my future."

"From your lips to God's ears." I headed for his office door. "I'll keep you apprised."

With my due date and resignation, sucker.

****

"It's a global economy," they said. "Whole world's connected," they said. Well, they've never tried to blackmail someone with no landline, no email, no access to their fucking front door. Try to get to a rich person in this day and age. If Harrison Blair owned a cell, I had no idea what the number was. I couldn't very well call the number they gave me exclusively to report on Preston. Besides, cell phones were out, too easily tracked, seemed dicey.

If I tried to find any contact information online, the search might come back to kick me in the ass. That shit's traceable too, unless I did it from Jonathan's computer. No. Still too close for comfort.

Snail mail was my only option. The address had to be somewhere. They got billed, didn't they? With Rhonda gone, I'd have to dig around, because she'd handled all that. Rhonda's old desk still had a computer on it. I could use that. Any hinky search would get blamed on her. My stomach gurgled again. How much could I pile on poor Rhonda? Even if I used her computer, then what would I do, type out a letter? Probably not a good idea either. I toyed with cutting various words and letters out of magazines and newspapers, but that seemed quaint. Amusing, but quaint. Nah. Too much work.

Wearing those thin plastic gloves I'd swiped from Haven House, I spelled out on a plain piece of paper what I wanted, made another copy of the stolen info, popped the discreet-looking envelope into a mailbox at a post office across town. Easy peasy. I couldn't squash my giggles.

Clowns to the left of me, jokers to the right, here I am, stuck in the middle with an impending ass load of cash.

Chapter Thirty-Four

Preston's Blog

Musings from the Dented Throne

Frankly My Dear, I Don't Give a Fuck

My Irishman's throwing shade.

I believe *bitch* held the top spot as his favored description of the Heiress. So stern a rebuke almost toppled my tiara. I fear he's gone Rhett Butler, and now I'm abandoned to save the plantation alone.

Funny how I didn't think I gave a single fuck. Spent most our married life stoned, not concerned with my husband's comings or goings, other than his steady drug supply. I considered the Queen and the Jester's hysteria over my betrothal, to one of the dirty masses, reward enough. Didn't need a happily-ever-after ending. When he stepped out one night to buy a pack of crack but didn't return, I toked up, carried on.

But my Irishman *did* return, to save me. Hang tight for this, my faithful. *I love him for trying.* I'd never tell anyone but you. Like a silly schoolgirl, I imagined a future for him and me better than our past.

We'd turn geezer together. I'd clip the hairs in his nose. We'd wear matching "I'm with Stupid" T-shirts to all-you-can-eat-buffets. We'd laugh, wax nostalgic about that time I got sent to the pokey for trying to kill my mother.

'Til death do us part. Lock, stock, and two smokin' barrels.

If the Irishman votes me off the island, my safety net's gone, no Sherlock to do my snooping. I'm afraid the Heiress might've shot herself with her own derringer.

He promised one last poke at the piñata on *the Heiress's* behalf, *if* I zip my potty mouth. I'm sure he meant one more poke at his senorita. Nothing I can do about that. Yet. Don't know if I'll get the chance to show off any behavior modifications to my husband. Or if I even want to, considering my nagging qualms about his truthfulness.

If you can indulge my sap a moment longer, I feel I must tell the truth. I'm scared shitless, for my husband, for myself. He's in too far. They're after him. *They* who, you ask? I don't know, or maybe I don't want to know. It's anyone's guess at this point. Neither of us have exactly been model citizens. No end to our list of enemies, I'm sure.

Here's a turd in the punchbowl fact: Jester let me know Chica had *insinuated herself into my house.* Chica and her pimped-up lingerie.

I'll wait while you read that again.

The Queen, as a favor to her devoted servant who, I think I told you, happens to be Chica's *madre*, gave her the keys to *my* castle for a brief, but Jester says, necessary sojourn. "Chica's got troubles," he said. Don't we fucking all? Swears she's over it and gone. Another thing gone? My trust fund, thank you very much. Jester's got no idea where all my money went, which cheers me no end.

Boom shakalaka.

You, my followers, comfort me from distant shores. You can't know the half of it. I feel your consoling presence despite my constant irritability and your periodic annoyances. The only thing that won't leave me alone is loneliness. To add piss to the vinegar—I'm motherless. The woman I thought I'd never miss, I do. There's a hole in my life where my mother should be.

The Invisible Heiress

Whatever you say, I'll think about it tomorrow. After all, tomorrow is another day.

Comments
Well Hung Jung

L is for loser Irishman husband. You can clip my nose hairs anytime. Up for a ride on the Jungster? Hey, what about the money? Where's your trust?

Reply: WHJ, you romantic fool, you. Much as nostril cleanup and a giddy-up in your saddle excites, I must pass on yet more of your enticing offers. But know this—my money's safe. I'm not as dense as I once imagined.

Jack

Wish you'd contact me. I'll make you a star, the Irishman too. Protect you both. Hook you two up with an agent. Queen too.

Reply: You again, Jack? Hook yourself up to a potassium chloride drip. Pretty please. (See, the Heiress is warm and fuzzy already).

Norma B.

Good job, getting smarter about your own money. It's high time, sounds like. The Irishman will forgive you if you treat him right. Look at all he's done for you even though you're mean to him. Imagine what he'd do if you weren't. He obviously wants to be in your life whether he realizes it or not. Who cares about Chica? He doesn't.

Reply: Fingers crossed, Norma B.

Norma B.

The Irishman loves you. You do know that, right?

Reply: Here I thought you were the smart one.

Scribbler

Jack's probably a scammer. I'm the real deal. Anyone with an iPhone can call themselves a documentarian. Would a six-figure book advance sweeten the deal?

Reply: Wouldn't get out of bed for less than seven. BTW, any dimwit who can type can publish a book. You, for instance. I mean, *super handsome* dimwit. (Touchy feely, that's the new Heiress.)

Amy W.

Jung, Jack, Scribbler—shut up. Your idiotic comments aren't the advice the Heiress needs. I'm with Norma. Chica means nothing to anyone. All it means is your mother was trying to do something nice. That's good, right? If you've got control of your money and you're worried about the Irishman, why stay locked up? You could help him, couldn't you? What are you waiting for?

Reply: Think I've been unruly too many times. Not sure if I could leave if I wanted to.

Chapter Thirty-Five

Preston

"Geez Shrinky, been hitting Mickey D's pretty hard or what?"

I hadn't noticed her gut until she sat down in my room and it splayed out onto her lap.

Isabel smiled. Not the least bit perturbed.

So, I said, "Valium kicked in?"

I could tell she was trying not to laugh, which made me realize she hadn't in quite a while. That bothered me. The fact that it bothered me, bothered me. I'd need to up my game.

"You've behaved yourself for quite a stretch now. Good for you," Isabel said.

I took a few minutes to comb over her appearance while trying to muster up some smarty-pants retorts. All these months her looks vacillated between loony crone and Banana Republic working girl. Today she was somewhere in the middle. Dress too tight (the gut) but not horrible to look at. Hair neat but styled in a swooshy combover. Something about her struck me as definitely different. Catlike, smug.

"What's going on with you, Shrinky? You're glowing. Run over an old lady on your way here?"

Before Isabel could open her mouth to laugh or talk, Nurse Judy barged in. "Preston, there's a detective here to see you."

****

"Sure you don't want your therapist with you?" Detective Smiley said. "Not a problem if you do or if you don't."

Nurse Judy opened the visitors' room. I sat in one hard chair. He sat on the table's ledge—already a cop cliché.

"Are you kidding me?" I said. "Your name's Smiley?"

Detective Smiley smirked but didn't give an answer. "Therapist?"

"Not even a consideration." I felt the front of my hospital-issued tunic twerk in rhythm with my heart. "Do I need a lawyer?"

"For what? You're already . . ." He looked around.

"I'll take that as a no."

I cased the detective with the weird name, felt a twinge. "Do I know you?"

"Probably not."

"You an FOM?"

"Excuse me?"

"Slow witted for a detective. Friend of Marv? Finney? Police chief?" I said.

"Oh, right. Well, friend is a stretch. Of course I know him. He's my boss."

Told me all I needed to know.

"Recognize this?"

He handed me a folded piece of paper plucked from the inside pocket of his cheap suit jacket. I scanned what looked like a copy of a handwritten document. My eyes stuck on *I killed my baby*. I felt a weight lower itself on the top of my head. It started to hurt.

"What is this?" I dropped the aberrant paper on the table.

"Your mother *is* Harrison Blair?"

"First-class detective work."

"Does the handwriting look like your mother's?"

"Where'd you get this?"

"Does it look like your mother's handwriting?"

He picked up the missive, held it out to me for another, perhaps better, look at the obvious copy of an original. I didn't indulge him.

"Are you a fucking parrot?" I knocked the paper away.

"So, yes?"

"I'm not answering anything 'til you tell me where the fuck

you got this."

"From your mother."

"What?"

"Someone tried to blackmail her with it."

"Who?"

"That's what I'm trying to find out."

"What's she say about it?"

"Says she didn't write it."

"Whoever tried to pull this over on my mother is either brain dead or swings porn-star sized balls. I'd love to shake the moron's hand."

"Any idea who that brain-dead, big-balled person would be?"

"Our family brings out the nuts. You must know that already."

Smiley smoothed back his dark hair, flecks of silver at the temple. Glanced around the asylum, scanned my scrubs. "Obviously."

"Why isn't Marv here himself? He never delegates my family."

"I caught the case. That's all I know."

A missing Marv meant, well, not sure what his absence meant, but it sure as Christ meant something.

"So we're done now?" I said.

I wondered how mashed up I looked, hated myself for caring what this new, suspiciously mysterious cop thought. I didn't even know the jerk. Handsome jerk, though.

"Ms. Blair, what do you remember about the circumstances surrounding your brother Cooper's death? Anything?"

"I remember he died."

"How?"

"Crib death."

"You're sure?"

"Sure as an eight-year-old."

"Did someone tell you he died of crib death?"

"I don't remember," I said.

I felt lines of sweat snake down my sides.

"Didn't Marv tell you anything before he paraded you down here with your *caught case*?"

"You're here at Haven House because you tried to kill her. Your mother?"

Guess no interesting Marv info was coming my way from this guy.

"Can't get anything past you," I said.

"Were you defending yourself?"

A knot pushed at my waistband, felt like kicking the handsome, meddlesome dick.

"Why do you want to know?"

"You look frightened," Smiley said. "Does that question make you uncomfortable?"

"No. Yes. I don't know."

"You don't know if the question makes you uncomfortable, or you don't know if you had to defend yourself against your mother?"

"I don't remember much about that night. What difference does it make?"

"A lot, perhaps."

I kept quiet, couldn't grasp any words that felt right.

Detective Smiley nodded toward the paper lying on the table.

"Do you think you're holding Harrison's confession? Did she kill your brother?"

I could hear my father arguing with Isabel outside my door, their voices more and more agitated. Picked up the page to read the first sentence again.

"Can't answer that."

"Can't or won't?"

"End result's the same."

Chapter Thirty-Six

Isabel

"Mom, you'll never guess."

"Don't tell me. You need money. I'll hang up this instant if—"

I shifted my cell from one shoulder to the other. "No, no, nothing like that this time."

"What else could you want?"

"I'm getting married."

Her coughing fit hacked at my eardrums like an ax.

"To what?" She collected herself.

"I'll wait while you scrape up your lungs," I said.

"Not in the mood."

I heard the flick of her lighter, the catch of flame, her sharp inhale.

"I'm serious this time," I said.

I slurped down the dregs of my booze. Last one. I promised myself.

"When's this miraculous event taking place?"

"Not sure yet. I'll let you know as soon as we set the date."

"Who? Hope he's better than that guy who wouldn't step on cracks or the dope with the harelip. I—"

"Mother, stop. Listen, I've gotta go. Just wanted to tell you my good news."

I'd intended to tell her about the pregnancy but didn't. She could slam me all she wanted but not my baby.

"Don't come crying to me when he dumps you. They always

do."

"Can't you just be happy for me?"

"I'll be happy when I hear your new mark say *I do*."

****

Got comfy in front of my TV, patted my baby pooch, poured a fresh Scotch. *Last* one, for sure. I'd need a bracer to figure out what to do since my plot petered out. That detective showing up at Haven House was a real downer. I could only imagine what Preston told him. I drank, mulled over my epic fail.

Who let the dogs out? Jonathan? Did he read that note and alert the authorities? Doubtful. He couldn't break privilege. He might screw his patients, and his partner, but he wouldn't kiss and tell. Too much to lose for loose lips.

Wait.

Who's to say Preston didn't send the blackmail letter? Maybe that's why the cop showed up. He suspected her. That had to be it. Preston was the obvious choice. It'd never been clear to any of us what pissed her off enough to try to kill her mother. That photo in her room of her and her dead baby brother—if it was true—who wouldn't want at least *some* revenge for that twisted shit? Preston had nothing but time on her hands. Any detective with a pulse would make the leap.

What about the chief of police? Why didn't Marv Finney come riding in on his white horse to pull the plug on Preston's interrogation? Todd Fitzgerald sailed in quick enough. Why not Marv? Could the blush finally be off the Blair Fitzgerald rose?

I'd bet. Didn't I always?

Convinced I'd get away with my failed extortion attempt while the blowback landed on Preston, I felt a kind of peace. My letter might not've done the damage I'd intended, but it'd wreak a bit of havoc for the Blair Fitzgeralds. Who knew what else might turn up? I drained my Tiffany glass in one swig, hit speed dial.

"Hello?" Sherman said.

"It's me."

"Didn't we just talk? I left my wife already. Isn't that what you wanted?" His voice lowered.

"Why are you whispering?"

I heard Sherman's heavy breathing and something else.

"Is that a woman I hear?" Muffled noises in the background. "I know you're covering the mouthpiece with your hand. I'm not a complete simpleton."

"What are you ranting about?" he said louder. "Listen, why don't you come over, see my new place? We could get in a little slap and tickle if you hurry."

I couldn't figure Sherman out. He either jumped all over me like a liberal on sanctimony or shunned me like I'd goosestepped my way through Yom Kippur.

"What? Really?"

"I'm already hard thinking about it." He clicked off.

I realized he didn't give me the new address, then laughed. Of course he assumed I found it myself.

He assumed right.

Chapter Thirty-Seven

Preston's Blog

Musings from the Dented Throne

The Heiress, Interrupted

Tsunami's hit the beach.

Been a dog's age since my last post. The Heiress needed time to gird her loins. I promised details. You know moi, eager to please as that snatch Mother Teresa. I remembered some snippets from *that night*—dreamt it—but know I'm on the road to truth. I keep rerunning my visions like a film behind my eyes. I see clear.

So loud. An unbearable shrill clanging, like an air raid alert, made me want to cover my ears. The Queen burst in. Must've set off the alarm. Thinking about the look on her face blasts me, skin alabaster, sweaty, eyes rolled wild. She lunged. I parried. Fury overrode reason. The Jester, out of nowhere, jumped in the middle of the fray.

So much blood. The Queen's hands grasped at the gash at her neck, her life spurting out. She crumpled, a Chanel heap soaked in vermillion. The box cutter clattered to the wood floor. Would I have used it that day to . . . to what? Open a package? I think I remember doing that or something like that. I was high. It's all a haze now. But why'd I have it then? Did I think I'd need it to defend myself later? Who knows?

The Queen garbled choked sounds. I tried to lip-read. She clawed in my direction with one blood-soaked hand, the other clutched her gushing wound. The last thing my mother saw before losing consciousness? Me. To the grave I'll carry the message she relayed by the only means left—her eyes. *I'm sorry. I failed.*

Sirens screamed. I covered my ears, trailed blood through my hair. I know because later my strands dried stiff as uncooked spaghetti. The Jester paced. A madman, muttering nonsense, his wounded hand streamed blood of its own. My lawman father-in-law showed up, who knows when, kept up alongside.

What preceded such a bloodied skirmish?

No one recalls. But now I think I might.

Maybe I found the Queen's written revelation—but this is where the waters get murky. Yes, my faithful, the Royal She kept notes, admitted she *killed my brother, her own son.* Knowing my predilection for controversy, I'm sure I baited her with her own words, proof on paper. I realize this interpretation of events might be a stretch, but for some reason it's bored into my brain.

Anyway, father-in-law dragged my ass to a squad car. Grabbed furniture to anchor in. Felt desperate to take Mom's admission with me along with the long-gone Littlest Heir's favorite blanket that might've hidden the Queen's memoir. I remember his tiny monogram—three petite initials in a subtle, tasteful font. Both stayed behind. Kicked, yelled, railed to the universe all the way to the state hospital detox ward.

Hand to Bible—I *am* guilty—because I thought the Queen deserved it. But I didn't kill anyone. *She did.* What zapped the Heiress's memory? A strange, unfamiliar detective powered in to my abode today, not my father-in-law, to my shock and awe. He waved the old, familiar words under my upturned nose. Soon as I held the copy of the powder-keg confession, I knew I'd read those words before.

No statute of limitations on murder.

Here's a real humdinger for you, did you note I said an *unfamiliar* detective came to paw around my space? My father-in-law chief of police sent a flunky. Why? In all the years I've lived on planet Royal We, no one but the head honcho wrangled our indiscretions. Now, all of a sudden, we're treated like we live in a rental or ride the bus? If you know the meaning, cough it up.

Even so, no way any dick, new or old, no matter their brawn, would slap the silver bracelets on the Royal She. We're talkin' generations of police favoritism. Don't need to look any further than my own cozy setup for proof. Queen would rather take a lethal injection than suffer public embarrassment. Can't figure why the police would go through ultimately useless motions. Can you?

If you want more . . .

After so many weeks of hellish silence, I finally got a note from my Irishman. So feeble with relief, I almost face planted. *I'm alive but not safe. On to something big. Talk soon. Hang tight.*

Is there any other way to hang?

The Invisible Heiress

Talk is cheap. Thank God, because I've got to shell out for my own lifestyle.

Comments

Jack

That's big, big news, Heiress. Maybe the old guard's dead. Cops don't see the humor in coverups these days. If I were you I wouldn't count on anyone in your family getting away with murder anymore.

Reply: Still. What new could've developed to throw our get-out-of-jail-free-card guy off the payroll?

Jack

Friendships don't always last forever. Maybe they fell out? Could be as simple as that. Maybe the stooge father-in-law got tired of covering up shit.

Maggie May

Forget about father-in-law for now. What's Shrinky say about your recollections? You might not be able to trust what you remember, right? Sounds unreliable all the way around.

Reply: Shrinky who?

Well Hung Jung

Father-in-law probably assumes no wrong doing on the Queen's part. No intrigue there, so why waste his time and handcuffs? I don't think anyone got murdered. What you describe only exists in fiction. A classic example of *mixed the fuck up*. A booty call could clear out the cobwebs. I'd do you for free.

Reply: Priceless, I'm sure.

Norma B.

You should get out.

Chapter Thirty-Eight

Isabel

"Preston's gone," Judy said from the reception station. Not her usual spot.

"What?"

"She barreled out of her room carrying her laptop, some papers. I no more than stepped in front of this desk when a car pulled up out front. Preston hopped in. Off they drove."

"What car?

"Um, no idea," Nurse Judy said. "Nondescript. Beige, I think."

"You let a criminal waltz out?"

Why did my legs feel full of sand?

"Preston's not a criminal. You should know that. She's free to walk."

"Since when? Judge Seward—"

"Sent over a signed order—Preston met all agreed conditions, which were really no conditions at all. Wimp. All the crap Preston's pulled but she's still free to—"

"Anyone think to tell me?"

"Ever look in your inbox? What's wrong with you lately, Isabel? Not like you to neglect your patients."

"You didn't think to call me when Preston rode off into the sunset with a stranger in a car? I *am* Preston's therapist."

I gripped the ledge of the reception counter. Felt my stack getting ready to blow.

"You don't know for sure it was a stranger. Besides you

didn't answer. Left a voicemail. You don't listen to those either anymore."

"Do her parents know?"

"Left a message with her father. Been told Harrison's in no shape. As you know, all things Preston go to Todd. Or did you forget that too?"

Shit. I got exactly what I wanted. So why did I feel like I'd swallowed an anvil?

"Dodged out of here so fast she didn't take all her crap. Now I'll need to box it up," Judy said. "You know, Isabel, you're not yourself. I've been worried about you for weeks. Are you—"

I sped to Preston's room, hackles up, leaving Judy to talk to the air.

The door stood open, nothing to hide. Preston's books covered most of the floor space, shelf too. The creepy photo of Preston holding Cooper in God knows what stage of rigor mortis, gone. On her desk nothing but a small pad of Post-it notes still in the cellophane. Even though I'd wanted her entitled bullying ass out of what was left of my hair, I wanted her out on my terms. How dare she just *decide* on her own to leave? I resented the element of surprise. She'd done it. Like that, she'd split.

Sneaky bitch called my bluff.

Part II

Nottingham Lane

Chapter Thirty-Nine

Preston's Blog

Musings from the Dented Throne

Now You See Me

The Heiress shawshanked herself out of the bin.

Took Norma B.'s sound-bite advice—made my breathtaking great escape. Never mind I could've strolled out unimpeded way before now. Okay, *escape* might be an overstatement. A nail file chiseled breakout makes a better story than an email to Uber. I decided to cut my dependence on everyone else to save me.

That's right my faithful.

The Heiress is trying to assimilate on the outside.

The Irishman's not yet aware of my address change. Not sure how to apprise him of this new situation. My amateur detective husband will figure out my whereabouts when he next calls the loony bin or maybe he might even make a personal appearance there since he found out something *big*. I hope he doesn't tarry. Don't even know where my own husband lives. Soon as my wits are about me, I'll figure that out if I have to.

My rush to live free feels like less of a relief than I imagined. I expected my house to look like Miley Cyrus rode her wrecking ball through, but instead it's spotless. Chica's left no footprint. Nevertheless, there's a presence here I'm not sure I can abide—a blackened, haunting aura met me at the front door. Felt like strings connected my legs to my heart, every step delivered a sharp yank to my breastbone, yet here I stay.

I wait, on pins and needles, to hear of the Queen's arrest for offing her own child. Though I know that's a long shot. Considering my own run in with the Royal She you'd think unbridled joy would run wild through my veins at the thought of her capture. I'm full of sorrow instead.

Should I call? Visit? Check in on her well-being? Ironic, I know. Can't help but wonder how the Queen zoomed from barking insults and orders during visits to me at the psych ward, to crazed harridan, swooning in public on TV, to food-stained zombie in such short order. Then she vanished from my sight. Family therapy tanked months ago, and she's flown under my radar since. I'll admit curiosity as much as anything might motivate me to go a-calling.

What do you say to the mother whose throat you cut?

I beg your forgiveness?

Why does that phrase keep coming to mind? Do I want her to forgive me? Whatever I want feels much more than that.

No Irishman. No Mother. No drugs. Yet somehow, I'm hopeful. No reason. Better bust a move. Lots of nitpicky household crap to do. Like hire a new maid. Woe is me, right? Then I've gotta plan next steps.

The Invisible Heiress

If you've anything to add, do.

Comments

Well Hung Jung

Why the rush to springboard out? Whoever's got it in for the Irishman will add you to the list, no? Aren't you scared?

Reply: Shitless, WHJ. Shitless.

Well Hung Jung

I'm at the ready. Happy to hand out a beating to anyone who needs one with my hard, pulsating bat.

Reply: I'd never send a boy to do a man's job.

Amy W.

Wow. Fingers crossed for you and the Queen. Somewhere there's a happy ending. I can feel it. What do you have to lose by visiting her? The worst's happened already.

Reply: I'll stuff that thought in my bong and smoke it. As soon as I find it.

Jack

Now that you're out I can really help you. Seriously. A cameraman following you around tends to keep evildoers away. Plus, you'd make a ton.

Reply: I already have a ton. They don't call me the Heiress for nothing.

Norma B.

Good job on the break out. You seem intelligent. Use your head. Stay safe. Make no promises. Follow no one's rules. Call me naïve, but I think the questions surrounding the Queen will straighten themselves out in due time. Give that unpleasant train of thought a rest. Tread lightly. Find your husband.

Chapter Forty

Preston

Detective Smiley loitered on my steps. "Can I come in?"

"Can I stop you?"

"Yes," he said.

"Maybe you'll entertain me."

I motioned the dreamy detective through the doors, blasé as all get out. Chica had camped out in my home. My mother might have killed my brother. Marv Finney pawned me off. A dangerous, delicious detective with hazy motives stalked me. Got my game face on though. It's never a good idea to let a cop catch you with your skirt over your head.

"Your driveway's longer than my street," Smiley said.

"All the houses on Nottingham Lane have long *lanes*. It's a thing." Nervy dick started toward the back of the house without so much as a by-your-leave. I followed.

"Beautiful house." Smiley snaked through the entry hall to the great room/kitchen area. "Can I sit?"

He didn't wait for permission before sitting in a shabby chic, dining table chair, too comfortable for my taste. Not sure what to do with my hands, or anything else, I poured two steaming mugs of the French roast I'd made right before his infringement.

Smiley considered the view behind the wall of windows at the back of my kitchen, engrossed for a few moments. Even I admired the perfect pastoral splendor of Virginia's rolling hills. Money did buy happiness or at least a great place to live while you searched for it.

"Your aunt lived on Nottingham Lane, didn't she? Before she killed herself?" Smiley finally said.

My coffee caught in my throat. "Um, yes, a few houses down. Aunt James, my mother's sister."

"Mental illness runs in the family?"

"Why don't you tell me what you really think?"

"Some kind of crazy shit runs amok in your family."

"Checkmate." I stirred the sugar around in my coffee.

"So you pretty much absconded out of Haven House?"

"Well, I've always been free to leave. More or less."

He blew on the top of his mug like the brew was too hot, but it might've been nervous fiddling. I wondered if he felt as jittery as me.

"What do your folks say about that?" he said.

"My mother doesn't say anything to me. My father, well, he's sad, mad, scared for me, all of the above. I had to call him to let me in my house, unfortunately. Gave me an earful. Which reminds me I've got to change the damn locks and alarm code. Dad's got court today or he'd be here already saying all kinds of bullshit."

"Ah, right. You're Daddy's girl."

That would've set me off except he sounded sincere, almost sweet. I studied him. Smiley looked a sad lot. Hollowed. His clothes looked like they used to fit before a hunger strike. If I could peel back his drawn skin I might find only air. Nevertheless, there was something familiar about this new, gloomy detective. Well, new to me. What exactly?

"You ever wade through one of my parent's parties? What with all your years on their paid-for-police department?" I said.

"No. Not a partying, or paid-for, kind of guy."

"Did you work my case?" I cleared my throat. "You know. Before."

"Not much of a case to work, I heard. But no, I wasn't around that night."

I stopped mid-sip. *That night.* Those two small words sounded like a twenty-one-gun salute to shame flush with my ears. I felt myself die a little on the inside. Silly, I know. Not like everyone and the horse they rode in on didn't know. He referred to it the same way I did. *That night.* Why I minded Smiley's exacting reference, I couldn't say. But here he reclined, poking old wounds. My shit-don't-stink façade dissolved.

"You obviously know the deal." I stared at the table like the Shroud of Turin could be found there.

"Pretty much," Smiley took a dainty nip of his coffee.

"Why are you here? What do you want?"

"Do you think Harrison killed Cooper? Maybe by accident?"

"You're still on that?" I said. "Does it matter what I think? I mean I was hardly old enough to form an opinion, gut or otherwise. Some might say I'm biased, not in my mother's favor, considering what I did. Anyway—"

"Hey," he touched my arm. "Slow down. It's okay."

"No. I don't think she killed Cooper, accident or otherwise," I lied.

"Really?"

"You don't believe me?"

"You're pissed off at her for something big, aren't you?"

My thoughts exactly. He'd connected my rage with that confession just like I did. Maybe he wasn't just a pretty face after all. Need to bring my A game to deal with this guy.

"Who do you think sent me Harrison's confession?"

"Alleged confession."

I needed more than a nanosecond before I'd offer up my mother to Dudley Do-Right. She might be a blue-blooded bitch, but she was my blue-blooded bitch.

"All right," he said. "Alleged."

"Like I know? Been holed up at Whackadoodle Inn."

"Who would want to stir up trouble for your mother?"

"Besides me?"

He traced the edge of the mug with his finger.

"Fuck all," I said. "You think I sent that?"

"Did you?" He took another pull on his coffee. "More than one way to get rid of your mother."

"Sending anonymous letters isn't my style. Too subtle."

"I'm getting a subpoena for Cooper's medical records. They should tell us what we need to know."

"Like those can't be doctored." I really needed to stop thinking out loud, but still. I couldn't believe how naïve this guy was.

"You really think your parents are god-like, don't you? There's nothing they can't fix? Well, it's hard to hide much in the information age. This isn't the fifties."

I didn't bother to dignify that with a response. Said too much already. Clearly, Smiley didn't know, or pretended not to know, just who the Blair Fitzgeralds were and what they were capable of. We played chicken across my kitchen table. A clanging phone cut the silence.

"Don't look at *me*. Your phone." Smiley pointed at my new cell phone on the marble breakfast bar. I scrambled to answer.

"You at home or what? Haven House said you'd left. Can't believe your old cell number still works," Brendan said in my ear.

"Oh my God. Where are you?" I said. "Yes, of course. I'm here."

"I'm on my way up the lane right now."

I dropped the receiver back in its cradle. "Brendan's on his way," I said to Smiley with what I'm sure was a doofus smile.

I ran out, left Smiley to his own devices, stumbled through the cavernous entry hall, shoved open the front doors. Brendan's Tesla zipped up the lane, slowed to avoid taking the circular driveway on two wheels, slammed to a stop several yards away, like the cable guy not sure how close to the grand manse he could park. I flew out the front doors sprinted across the wraparound porch, started down the steps. Got a split-second glimpse of the chopstick-anchored man bun on Brendan's head, when a battering mass of air knocked me to the ground. I almost missed seeing the world go up in flames before my head hit the concrete.

Chapter Forty-One

Isabel

"Hope you're not dragging your feet," I said, "*more.*"

"No, no. I'm straightening things out so we can, well, we can start clean," Sherman said.

"You've been saying that for weeks." I fought the urge to either beg or hang up. "I'm starting to look pregnant, not just fat."

I'd changed into sweatpants as soon as I got home—only things that fit, barely. "You still haven't given me any reasonable explanation as to why I heard a woman's voice the last time I called," I said. "You live alone now."

"How many times can I say there's no other woman—only your overworked imagination? I've moved out. I'm getting divorced. Patience. You know what's—"

A second call rang through. I held up my phone so I could see the screen. "Gotta take this call." I couldn't bear Sherman's host of new, or old, excuses.

"Jonathan? What?"

"Whole place is bugged. Bugs all over the place."

"What? What place?"

"Our offices."

"How do you know?" I felt nauseous. Not the pregnancy kind either.

"I stooped down to pick my pen up off the floor and I saw a weird, a microphone-type thingy stuck under the conference table."

The problem with being me is when something bad is going

on, I can always assume it has to do with me. I looked around the room for something to barf in, just in case.

"Now what?" I hate to ask.

"Tricky. Cops want a client list. Can't give them one."

"You called the cops?"

"Of course," Jonathan said. "What else could I do?"

Try to find out what's going on yourself first, jackass?

"Right. So we're gonna do what then?"

"They'll investigate, but no one's sent threats, or made blackmail calls, or anything of the sort, right?"

"You think I wouldn't tell you if someone did?"

Of course I wouldn't.

"Honestly, who knows with you?" he said. "Knew I should've fired sticky fingered Rhonda a lot sooner."

"The old receptionist? Thought you hired her for her boobs, not her brain. Rhonda couldn't pull off anything more complicated than her lip wax."

"Cops said whoever installed the devices was no genius. The more sophisticated would've tapped the phones too."

"Seems over the top for someone like Rhonda to do."

"Probably. I passed on her name nonetheless. Gave them the security cameras tapes too."

"Security cameras?"

"Only hooked up in the parking lots, thanks to all the interior decorating the ones inside aren't up anymore. Whoever planted the bugs probably drove here."

Now I felt faint. I needed to get off the phone.

"Well, keep me posted," I said. "Not much we can do but wait." I tried to sound like an innocent, reasonable person.

"Wait, Jesus, with the bugs I almost forgot," Jonathan said. "Have you seen the local news?"

"No." Like I had time for that.

"Brendan Finney got blown up. Murdered."

****

Brendan Finney was out of his league when he married into the clan. Even though I'd only seen him for a few minutes, I knew he didn't have a prayer in that family. Whatever shitstorm arose, the Blair Fitzgerald machine would handle it. Already plagued by scandal, they wouldn't want to associate with more. But how far would they go? Not this far. Much as they might've delighted in Brendan's absence, his spectacular death would only stir up more unwanted attention.

Oh well, the hullabaloo would die down quick enough if they paid the right people—and they always did.

Preston might actually feel something about her husband dying. My hand went to my bulging belly, a reflex I didn't know I had. No matter how heartless Preston could be she'd take Brendan's death hard. If I let myself I'd feel a little sad for her.

No time for that. I needed to think about those bugs. I put Brendan Finney out of my head like yesterday's trash.

Didn't think it'd take an overpriced psychologist to figure out the most likely perp. Jonathan wasn't always quick on the uptake. Always suspected his wife (what *was* that woman's name?) wasn't as dumb as he wished. I drummed my memory for any incriminating conversations I might've undertaken in my office. Thank God I hadn't spent much time there over the past several months. Still. When's a bugged office not a sign of big trouble?

Why didn't I know about the security cameras? The moisture collecting under my arms wasn't nausea related. Shitting bricks broke me into a sweat. Poured myself a few measly fingers of Jameson, mulled over my dud strategy, which paid out as well as last night's losing spin of the roulette wheel.

Security cameras. Goddammit. I'd never committed any questionable acts in the parking lots, had I? If they'd been on in the office that might be a different story. I forced that unpleasant idea down. My scotch sloshed up the back of my throat. Who cared anyway? Jonathan's old lady knew the worst about Jonathan and me if she'd listened in. That's all she'd care about. If she knew, my cash flow would suffer big time. I could feel the pulse at my neck jolt.

"Don't borrow trouble," my mother always said.

Tapped out numbers on my phone. The ancient clang of my mother's landline jangled in my ear. No answer. A voice-mail-is-full message was all I'd gotten for days. No wedding date to gloat over anyway. Well, I'd show her. Tightwad lush thought I'd never bag Mister Big.

Sherman better step the fuck up. If the fop thought I'd idly dawdle while he *straightened things out,* he didn't know me very well. In fairness, he didn't know me for crap, how could he? Kept my schemes secret.

Obviously, I knew Sherman's sex perversions, which didn't alarm me. But everything else I knew about him certainly wasn't good. Well, my mama didn't raise no fool, especially not a deaf one. I know I heard a woman at his new place. I poured myself a hair more scotch, mulled over what might be afoot. Maybe he'd dump me. That'd always been a possibility, in fact a likelihood. I wouldn't have cared before. Before I invested so much, got preggers. Now, what?

I bolted up like I'd gotten a cattle prod to the ass.

I'd felt completely dialed in where my masked man was concerned, but I really didn't know him any better than he knew me.

Chapter Forty-Two

Preston

"You look better than the last time I saw you." Smiley settled at the edge of my ginormous canopied bed, new housekeeper shut the door behind her. "Skipped out of the hospital already?"

"No more hospitals. Can't sleep there."

"Construction workers humping out front. Can you sleep through that?"

"At least they go home before nightfall. Gotta fix the damage. I can't stand looking at the rubble. Thank God the house is brick."

I touched the swollen, painful, stitched-up cut across my forehead. Gabfest ran out of steam. We sat, me simmering in guilt and grief, not sure what Smiley simmered in.

"Bodies heal pretty quick, hearts not so much."

He broke through the quiet. Smiley's lack of guile brought me to tears. He let me cry for a few long moments.

"I wrote out everything we talked about at the hospital, everything I could remember, like you asked." I wiped my face, steeled myself.

"Great, thanks."

I remembered all right. Spewed like a blender with the top off soon as I regained consciousness. I might've told Detective Smiley *everything*.

"Listen—about that blackmail letter sent to your mother— you were right. Nothing came of it, obviously a crank. No truth to it."

"How do you know?" I said.

"Cooper's medical records. Subpoenaed them, remember? Your brother died of a rare form of childhood leukemia."

"What?"

All the blood rushed to my head wound. Pounded the crap out of it. *I killed my baby. I killed my baby.* Mother said so herself. I saw those very words.

"You've got to be joking."

"I normally don't joke about babies with cancer."

"I don't believe you. Why, she, I . . . ."

For the first time in my verbally incontinent life, I couldn't think of a thing to say. I knew the truth, I could've sworn. That confession. We'd fought about it almost to the death. *Didn't we?* No disease felled my brother. Did it?

"Frankly, I'm surprised you didn't know. Certainly, your parents would've talked to you about it?"

I tried to bring up memories of the day my brother died, the short time he'd lived. My forehead felt like it might explode. I couldn't recall a thing about any disease.

"You'd be surprised what we don't talk about in my family," I finally said.

"So whatever Brendan knew, if he knew anything seedy at all, probably didn't involve Cooper," Smiley said.

"Right. Uh-huh." Medical records or not, I wasn't ready to let go of what I'd thought was true about my mother and brother. I wasn't sure I could trust Smiley. Not yet.

"So now what?"

"The investigation goes forward in one direction," he said. "Brendan's murder."

My fist went to my mouth. I knew that's exactly what happened, but hearing it clocked me. I felt the searing blast, heard the sky-splitting roar, saw the crime-scene photos. But the tiny part of my brain where I allowed myself a sliver of hope clung to denial. How could Brendan die before we got the chance to get to know each other, minus all our bullshit? Maybe we'd have fallen in love for real. Maybe we—I squeezed my eyes shut to stop the waterworks.

"Brendan must've found someone, something, proof," I said

to myself, but Smiley heard.

"Proof of what?"

"I don't know. Something someone didn't like."

My stitches throbbed so hard I thought they'd pop. Smiley had never seen that horrible photo of Cooper and me. Illness or not, that postmortem picture was all sorts of wrong, perhaps criminal in itself. I'd consider unveiling it only if Smiley proved himself. What proving himself would look like, I hadn't decided.

"They're hiding something," I said.

"Who?"

"My parents. Brendan found stuff about them. He's dead."

"I didn't want to tell you this today, but our search of Brendan's apartment turned up a cornucopia of pharmaceuticals. Looked like he was dealing again."

I didn't know anything about Brendan's apartment, just that he'd had one, thought he'd stopped with the drugs. But that was *before* I knew about Marcella. A vision of his sober chip on a chain, me pulling the damned thing hard as I could around his delicate neck, clouded my already clotted thoughts. I knew selling didn't mean he used. My husband's dealing could've finally got the better of him though. I couldn't deny that. In fact, I suspected it while I was still confined. Now that he'd died, I didn't want to feel that way about him, and I sure as hell didn't want this interloper cop to either.

Smiley kept swinging. "Marv thinks drugs were involved in his death, if that means anything,"

"He's been wrong about him before, could be again," I said.

Actually, I couldn't think of a time Marv had been wrong.

"Have the Finneys been to see you?" Smiley looked concerned. Like he worried no one would visit the psychotic mother killer in her hour of need.

"No. They hate me. Always have. Marv loves my father, can't stand me, or my mother."

Smiley's hand covered mine for a nanosecond before he pulled it away, as if he'd momentarily forgotten his role in my life. In cop mode again he turned up a photo he must've kept in his coat with the bottomless pockets.

"Seen her before?"

There sat Brendan, with a Shakira-type hottie, thigh to thigh on what looked like a park bench. Chatting it up over Starbucks. Who could've blamed him? Even in a grainy picture Chica looked easy to love.

"Where'd you get this?"

"Security camera from the café across from Brendan's place. You know her?"

"No," I said, satisfied I wasn't exactly lying. If I'd ever seen Marcella I didn't remember. Didn't need to recognize her face to know she was Alicia's daughter. Who else could she be?

"Marcella Montoya—a nurse," Smiley said. "Been investigated for prescription improprieties, but nothing stuck. Got an uncle in the drug trade, couple of cousins too." He pulled another pic out of his bag of tricks. Bitch looked hunka-hunka-burnin' love even in her mug shot. "Rumored gang ties. We're trying to locate Ms. Montoya. So far no luck."

I could still feel Smiley's hand on mine even though it'd been there so briefly. His knee-jerk reaction to comfort me went a long way toward proving himself trustworthy.

"Brendan thought she knew something," I said. "I think he was on his way to tell me what he'd found out when he, you know, when, well, you were there."

Smiley didn't comment. He sat close to me, relaxed, like he had all day to sit on my bed—the best listener ever.

"I think Brendan and Marcella were dealing together. Like the old days," I said. "Much as I hate to admit it that's what probably killed him." Then, in a quieter tone, "Doesn't mean he didn't find out something, I don't know—sinister—about my family."

"Interesting." Smiley wrote something in his little notepad. "Certainly not a stretch that Brendan's death was the result of a drug deal gone wrong. But you're right. He might've looked under the wrong rock. More than one thing can be true at a time. Drug dealing's only one theory."

"You've got another?"

"Let's just say I'm open-minded. We'll go where the evidence leads us."

I wondered. Marv might be hands-off on my end, but he'd

never let anything untoward go down around my parents. Or would he? His only son died. If that didn't break the mold nothing would.

"I posted a cop at the end of your lane, plus one near the front door, until the investigation's concluded," Smiley said.

"Why? Thought I wasn't a target."

"Don't think you were, but from what I can tell, if anyone could benefit from a little supervision, it's you."

"Whatever blows your whistle."

"Some free advice—fix the gate at the end of the lane, pronto. Hire a twenty-four-hour guard service. The guardhouse is already there. Most of your neighbors have them. I'll recommend a private security company, retired cops, so you can hire guards. Hell, I'll hire them for you if you'd like. Media's all over out there." Smiley stood, brushed off the front of his pants, like he'd eaten something crumbly.

"Seen your parents?" he said.

"Does it matter?"

"To the investigation? No. To you? I'd say yes."

Another reason I left the hospital. Despite whatever tenderness I'd felt for him, off and on in the past, I couldn't stand Dad's fawning or his insistence I set aside my differences with Mom, like she'd be willing (as if attempted murder was on par with borrowing her sweater without asking) and move home for a while. To my shock, Mother had come too, later, without Dad, of course. She smoothed my bandaged brow, pulled up my covers. We didn't speak. I faked sleep until she trundled out again, borne up by her faithful driver.

"Oh, did you check the security camera film from my house?"

"No cameras," Smiley said. "Looked like there used to be some. What happened to them? Do you know?"

"I don't know anything anymore. Probably never did."

"Well, if you think of anything." Smiley tossed a key on my lap. "CSI's finished working Brendan's apartment. If there's anything there you want, landlord said place is all yours 'til the rent's due."

Chapter Forty-Three

Preston

Against doctor's orders, I decided to drive into town, determined to make funeral arrangements for Brendan. A scandalous amount of time had passed since his death. Whatever etiquette applied to date of death and the consequential burial, I'd spurned. Surprised I didn't hear from his parents about any of it but not a peep. I could've called them but didn't.

Devil may care, I rolled by the cop parked near my front door, the winding-down construction crew, putt-putted down the lane until I reached the newly occupied guardhouse. Got a quick look at the milling press stationed across the road when a string of vehicles sped by, blocked the view.

I lowered the driver's side window to introduce myself to the uniformed guard, to keep him apprised of my comings and goings like Smiley instructed. Big mistake. Soon as the road cleared the media swarmed my Range Rover like a SWAT team.

Microphones crammed through the open window paralyzed me. Cameras clicked a crazed tune, a symphonic assault. Questions in stereo ricocheted around the SUV's interior. The security guard pushed and shoved, yelled at everyone to get back. He was outnumbered.

"Why'd you cut your mother's throat?"

"How'd you get away with it?"

"Did Harrison Blair really kill her baby?"

"Is Brendan Finney's death connected to your attack on your mother?"

"Did you kill your husband?"

I couldn't tell which mouths the words gushed from, the squawking buzzards circled me like roadkill. The guard yelled something unintelligible, snuffed by the din. The collective rattle and hum churned, scrapped, jockeyed. I rolled the electronic window up, an arm kept it from closing. I pinched the intruding limb hard with one hand, worked the window down a smidge with the other. The reporter attached to the arm jumped back, yelping.

I stepped on the gas, screeched away from the melee just in time to almost collide with a car turning onto my property. We both slammed to a stop. My neck snapped forward then back, but my seatbelt kept me in place, safe but probably sore. I straightened myself out, couldn't really see the driver through the tinted window but what little I glimpsed pricked something in my swirling brain. Then the trespasser (a woman?) hit the gas, squealed in reverse to a stop long enough to throw the car back into drive, peeled out, tires spitting up gravel like a chainsaw.

****

The first real grownup thing I'd ever done—burial arrangements for my husband. I felt outside myself as the director droned on about casket quality, cremation, graveside service, church, or both. I let the morbid, pale, little man shamelessly talk me into the most expensive everything. My endgame wasn't to do a funeral on a shoestring but to get the whole unbelievable event behind me, no matter the price. Besides, Brendan paid with his life. How much would I need to spend to even the score?

The choreography of death finally done, I intended to answer my stomach's call with a Big Mac on the way home from the funeral home. Not too familiar with this area of town I spied the golden arches a few blocks down in one of the countless strip malls I'd passed.

Of course, in my fervor to find it, I missed it. I hung a sharp U-turn through the nearest parking lot surrounded by shops and restaurants. Maybe one of the more upscale places would suit me better. After all, I hadn't been to a restaurant in who knew how long? True, my appearance left a lot to be desired. Hard to make a bandaged forehead look chic, so I didn't try. I planned to find a secluded quiet spot to eat and think. Especially about that car almost crashing into me earlier. Smiley must've been wrong. I am a target. Perhaps I am *the* target.

I slowed to a crawl so I could get a good look at the various food offerings. That's when I saw them. So intent on each other, they didn't notice me come to a full stop, their heads together mid-coo at a cute, little, alfresco, bistro table like newlyweds in the Poconos.

Chapter Forty-Four

Preston's Blog

Musings from the Dented Throne

My Own Private Hiroshima

So many bombshells dropped, my followers. Pop a Xanax, throw back a stiffie, whatever trick gets you through trauma. Here find the facts only the facts. I must recite them fast or trigger my own downward spiral.

The Irishman is dead. Murdered.

You read right.

My husband martyred himself for my cause, a modern-day Jesus. No sign of the killer. Contrary to rumor mill gist, the Heiress didn't do it. In fact, I'd give anything, *everything* if it hadn't happened.

At this moment only smartass wants to come off the end of my keyboarding fingers. If I give in to the bottomless sorrow, it'll be the end. But know my world is blackened. I don't know if I'll ever see in anything other than deep shades of gray again.

I think I'm being followed. A car with an unknown driver nearly slammed into my chariot. I believe they were turning into the Heiress's drive. Something I can't name agitates my memory about whoever sat behind that blackened window. Her (yes, *her*, but do I really know?) quick escape kept me from seeing enough to know for sure.

Will my funeral follow soon behind the Irishman's?

New Dick in town absolved the Queen of the Littlest Heir's

death. No murder most foul but mundane illness instead. At least that's the story for public consumption, which doesn't feel right. Something happened to my brother, something bad, besides his illness. I feel it but can't prove a thing.

Jester and the Irishman made themselves a hot tamale sandwich with the Chica.

Yes, it's true.

I bore witness with my own orbs. Hubby's Chica and my dad cuddled up for all to see over cappuccino. I think I blacked out for a few seconds. You don't know this, my faithful, but I thought we'd come to an understanding, the Jester and me. I thought he wanted, more than anything, to fix our family. How could I fall for that claptrap?

As you know, if you're a faithful follower, Norma B. hit the bullseye when she said another woman was responsible for Jester's camera-ready beauty routine and snappy suit choices. The reason his face looked like he'd been flung through the sound barrier—a girlfriend the same age as me. I remembered the day Rosie the Ripper and I glimpsed the Queen, on camera behind the clueless Jester, frazzled as a hit-and-run driver. Did she know that day? Must've been the source of her unseemly display. I get her. For once, I do.

Now what, you ask? I'm left to puzzle these pieces together alone, that's what. For sure the Heiress will post updates as she sifts through the collateral damage.

If you're still conscious—stay with me.

During the routine course of my sifting I rediscovered the hidden path behind the Royal's behemoth plantation, the place where I was raised. This road less traveled used to aid my many escapes from the Queen's prying eyes and her annoying insistence I attend school. As if paved by the gods of sneaky behavior this few-miles-long trail dumps out at the highway.

Convenient. No?

I happened to pass the old stomping ground on my way to. . .okay, not exactly on my way, but I did pass it. Well, I would've passed it if I hadn't turned onto it. Before I knew what overtook me I found myself at the empty but pristine stables far enough from the main house to hide my presence but close enough to trek on foot without much ado. Slim to no chance of discovery by any groundskeeper since the sport of kings had long since lost its allure for the Royals. I parked, hoofed the rest of the way right to the back door. Good sense prevailed. After almost waltzing in, I scampered like a scared rabbit back toward my SUV.

I felt the Queen's eyes on my back as I made tracks. I stopped, turned toward the house through no fault of my own. Royal She controlled me. I saw Mother standing at her bedroom window like a woman carved from stone. Dusk fell, so I felt fairly confident she couldn't actually see me, like I could see her, backlit. I stared at the Queen's still form, willing her to acknowledge me, scared bug-eyed she might. Her hand glided to her neck, where that hideous scar resides.

Words formed around my throat but stuck. I stepped forward.

Then I saw her.

The Irishman's, and now the Jester's, Chica. She came up from behind the Queen, a beautiful, dark-haired apparition, stood still a few seconds, then led Mother away by the arm. I felt my lids bat open, close, open, close, as if I could blink out some Morse code of understanding. Could I trust my jaded eyes? Could the Jester's balls, once missing, now have inflated on such a scale that he'd move his girlfriend into the house he shares with the Queen? Is such growth even possible?

What do you make of these devilish developments, my faithful?

The Invisible Heiress
Rain your wisdom down on me.

Comments

Jack

My head spins. I've no advice other than make sure New Dick is on speed dial. BTW, maybe the Queen did see you. Would that be the worst thing?

Reply: Too bad you can't ask her yourself. She'd part your hair with the Royal wrath. You should know by now New Dick might be the same old, same old. I've made baby steps toward trusting him.

Maggie May

OMFG. Poor Irishman. Hard to believe these things happen in real life. I'm so sorry for you. But an upside is the Queen's innocent! Now you can patch things up, can't you?

Reply: Why would we do that when things have worked out so swimmingly for her?

Well Hung Jung

I never thought the Irishman was man enough for you. Too much blarney, not enough stones, you know what I'm sayin'? Didn't you say Chica's mamacita has a connection to the Royal She? Maybe Chica's an innocent bystander helping out after the Queen let her lay low at your house.

Reply: The Chica's connected to the Jester's codpiece. You know what I'm sayin?

Well Hung Jung

Or maybe the Royal She is keeping her enemies close.

Reply: Finally something not idiotic.

Norma B.

I'm very sorry and sad to hear of the Irishman's terrible death. I think the new detective sounds above board. Let him help, particularly if your FIL chief of police delegated you to him. Maybe the old regime is out. I told you that nonsense about the Queen doing harm to her son situation would work itself out. Too bad I was right about the Jester and his Chica.

Reply: Yes, you are my supersmart Siri, Norma.

Norma B.

Well, where there's smoke there's fuego.

Chapter Forty-Five

Isabel

I'm no sitting duck.

Wary of Sherman's doings or motives I decided to take the reins, again. Some say if you're not sure what to do, do nothing. Some would, but not me. I'd do something even a wrong thing.

First, I cruised Sherman's new swank townhouse to see if I might catch the weasel in the act. No such luck. I didn't see any red flags, but I couldn't very well knock on the front door. No way I'd give him the satisfaction. From what little I could see, slowed to a crawl, neck craned toward the front windows, the place looked peaceful as a monastery. Of course none of that meant anything. He could be orchestrating a Caligula-style orgy in the garage for all I knew.

I drove on.

Guess it's never dawned on Preston that I know her address or how easy she is to follow. Almost ran into her head on but I don't think she saw me. Probably too stoned, as I doubt she'd stay clean. No reason not to go back to her old ways.

Because my bribery plan flopped, I'm vigorously looking down new avenues for conspiracies. What better avenue than Preston? I've tailed her for days. She didn't even notice I almost rear-ended her when she turned off the highway onto a dirt road. I didn't dare track her down what looked like an almost hidden path.

So I waited.

A convenient mess of roadside shrubs let me camouflage my

car until I saw Preston drive out. Soon as she sped out of sight I retraced her drive. The road meandered for a few miles surrounded by dense forest. Before I knew it the trees cleared. I found myself parked behind some barns or some such. I'll admit I broke a good sweat not knowing where or what the hell. I got out to inspect.

Sometimes my nerve surprises even me.

A giant, swank, white house with black trim and striped awnings filled my field of vision. I knew right away I stood on Harrison Blair's sacred grounds. Everyone knew the Blair Fitzgeralds lived a genteel, frozen-in-time existence on one of the few, still-standing (albeit extensively renovated) privately owned plantations in the state—Beverley. I Inspector Gadgeted my way from behind one Greek-type lawn ornament to the next, mincing closer to the magnificent estate, grateful for the near darkness. Mid-tiptoe a light went on in the grand old house. I froze.

Harrison Blair, plain as the crazy on Preston, looked right at me from an upstairs window. I ducked down, peered around the side of the faux Venus de Milo. The lamplight illuminated the space all around Harrison, lit the old bitch up like an angelic apparition. Wished I could remember how that all worked. Could she see me if I saw her? Not if it's dark out? I took a gamble, inched my way up to an almost standing position.

That's when I saw him.

A man.

A *young* man appeared alongside the matriarch. I rubbed my eyes, certain I hallucinated. Nope. A super-sized, young, blond man sidled up beside Harrison, draped a log-like arm around her shoulders. So shocked I couldn't move, even though it looked like he stared at me too. My chest expanded, felt tight, from the breath I drew in but didn't exhale. Then, just like that, mystery guy leaned down, kissed old lady Blair smack on the lips.

Fuck me six ways from Sunday. Harrison Blair's gone cougar.

Chapter Forty-Six

Preston

"Pull over."

"Why?" Smiley turned the radio up louder.

I turned it off. "You can't drive my car. Range Rover's twice the size of your heap."

"Hey, that heap's new. Old one got totaled. Too close to Brendan's car when it—"

"You drive like an old lady with a dog in her lap."

"We're not even off your property for chrissake."

"I could've driven myself to my own husband's funeral."

"I'm sure. Safer this way though, so humor me."

"Better slow down. Gate guard thinks he works at the Pentagon since the last press stampede. He'll want to probe our cavities before he lets us out."

"He knows the drill now. Gate'll open in time for us to make a clean getaway from the media frenzy."

Smiley slammed the gas pedal. We sped through the yawning gates and the howling wolf pack of press like Bonnie and Clyde.

"They think I killed Brendan."

"Buck up, Preston. You don't seem like you give a fuck about what anyone thinks."

"Who says 'buck up' anymore? Golly gee whiz Howdy Doo—"

"What's the deal with your staircase?" In the clear, Smiley slowed to a reasonable pace.

"Where'd that come from?" I said. "What are you talking

about?"

"I noticed you don't walk near it. You cut a wide berth to go around the damn thing."

"Aren't you observant?"

"I *am* a detective."

"Then detect," I said.

"Okay. I'd guess upstairs is where it all went down with your mom."

"Good job."

"You haven't gone up there since—"

"That night. Right."

"Do you plan to move or just live on the first floor for the rest of your life?"

"What's it to you, nosy?" I watched the hills and trees through the window as we drove past, didn't watch Smiley.

"Might help to face it," he said. "It's just a room, after all. I'd go with you."

"What happened to your daughter?" I looked right at him this time.

Smiley's skin blanched pale, his hands turned white, clutched the steering wheel. "You do go right for the throat, don't you?"

He jerked the car back over the yellow line.

"Oh, I see. You know all about me, but I can't know about you."

"How do you know anything about my daughter?" Smiley said.

"You're as bad as my dad. Ever heard of Google? It's the wave of the future. I knew I'd seen your mug before. In the papers a few years back."

"Corey's on Google?"

Hearing him say his daughter's name hit me like a slap. After that smack down, I didn't feel so superior. Even if I didn't already know, I could've guessed she'd come to a bad end just by the way he said "Corey"—his tone low, dreadful. I wondered if my mother sounded the same way when she said my name or Cooper's. My own voice softened.

"Yes," I said. "Online newspaper articles. After I read them, I remembered. My father talked about the case ad nauseam."

"Then you know what happened to her."

"Yes. She was—"

This topic definitely didn't feel like a good idea anymore. I couldn't repeat the awful details of her brutal rape and murder.

"I'm so sorry. What a terrible—" I couldn't think of a word horrible enough to finish my sentence. "Did you catch her killer?"

"Yes. Didn't Google finish the story for you?"

"No."

I hadn't looked too deep. I'd seen the headline trumpeting her murder and the ongoing investigation then got distracted by who could remember what.

"Well, Google it again."

I'd hit a raw nerve. No way he'd chat about his daughter as if she were cocktail party conversation with someone he barely knew—someone who showed an embarrassing disdain for his feelings. I checked my watch. As was often the case, the more I thought about my insensitive and cruel behavior, the more I felt compelled to take it across the finish line unimpeded.

"We're late. Can you speed this up so we at least get to the cemetery *today*? Bad enough they think I killed my own husband. Best not to mosey in like we'd rather be at the mall."

Chapter Forty-Seven

Preston

While a dour Smiley piloted us toward the cemetery, I worked to settle my nerves. Pushed Smiley and his murdered teenage daughter out of my thoughts. Felt horrible I'd brought Corey up. I'd think about that later. Maybe even apologize. Profusely.

I arranged my hair to hide my Frankenstein forehead. Brendan married me in part for my looks, thought I should make an effort. Checked my face in the visor mirror. Seeing the bandaged wound felt like a bitch slap.

Brendan died. No joke. Murdered.

Last time I'd laid eyes on my husband, I'd tried to string him up by his sober chip chain. Self-loathing made me withered and ugly, like the picture of Dorian Gray. I mushed my lids shut with the heels of my hands ruining my puttied-on eye makeup.

"Your money's not stolen is it?"

Smiley concentrated on the road ahead, tense. I knew it cost him not to throw my rude ass out of the moving Rover.

"Why would you think it was?"

"Your father talked to me about it," Smiley said. "Wanted me to trace it."

Goddamn Dad. His laser focus on my money was really starting to piss me off. Especially since I'd come home. Paid all my own bills. Even though the topic annoyed me no end, I felt grateful for something else to talk about, dabbed a tissue around my stuck-together lashes, black smudges under my eyes, cleaned up the best I could.

"My father is aware he has no right, under the law, to know anything about my money. Both my parents are lawyers. So I know too."

"Which is what I told him," Smiley said. "So it's all good?"

"Absolutely."

"That's what I detected," Smiley said. "Every time I've dropped by the same maid answers the door. There're a bunch of gardeners, damage from the explosion's cleaned up, new fountain installed in record time. You've got money somewhere."

"A little-known fact: the rich've always got money sitting around. Mother's got more riches under her divan cushions than most people make in their lifetimes."

"You got the same couch as Harrison?"

"Kind of. I moved every last hard-earned-by-someone-other-than-me dime."

"Ah, yes. All things are possible for the Blairs."

"Anyone with a laptop, the right security code and access to a phone can wire money away from prying eyes and sticky fingers. We live in the twenty-first century for chrissake."

****

"We're getting close to the graveyard. Start looking for Hill Avenue."

"I know where it is," Smiley said. "Think your parents'll show?"

"What? Of course."

Why I felt entitled to their support after what could only be described as my indescribable behavior said a lot about me that I didn't want to dwell on.

"Appearances mean everything to my mom and dad," I said half convinced.

"The keeping-up-appearances ship sailed when you Zorro'd Harrison's—"

"Stop your gabbing," I said.

Smiley didn't usually speak snark. I deserved it, which as usual, irritated me. "Keep an eye out for the turnoff," I said.

"I'm familiar with the cemetery, thank you." Smiley slowed.

I almost wondered aloud if Marcella would show up. Tempted to blab that I saw the hot nurse at Mother's side when I spied on her at Beverley, I refrained. Still on the fence about Smiley, not sure he wouldn't run right to my parents, or someone with influence, with any information he reconnoitered from me, especially about a person of interest. But if she meant my mother harm, I mean she *was* diddling my father. I pressed my eyes shut again. I couldn't think anymore. My throat tightened, panic seized me.

Smiley said, "You haven't talked to your mother since you've been home?"

I took a few deep breaths, got a grip.

"No." I flipped the visor down again to check my now-beyond-repair mascara and to calm my breathing. "You really are nosy today."

"Hello Pot? Kettle calling."

"Okay, whatever."

"Kind of surprising, isn't it? She showed up at the hospital. Thought a reconciliation might be in the works."

Smiley said out loud what I'd thought, but I didn't feel like getting into a whole yadda yadda yadda at the moment. Why would Mom care about me after what I'd done? Care she did. I could feel the love while she sat on my hospital bed. I could even feel it while she railed against me at Haven House. I knew Mom'd show up here to help bury my husband. Why? None of the potential answers squared with my impression of the woman I'd spent most my life detesting—one who snuffed her son, accident or not, but wouldn't own up. I'd concede. The two faces of Harrison Blair didn't gel—a dignified, recently gentle and tactile mother, and a crazed baby killer. At the very least, one who's smothering carelessness resulted in her child's death.

I wouldn't be the first daughter to get her mother wrong.

Thinking through my theories surrounding Cooper's death didn't make sense anymore. My mother might've been cold and aloof, but murderous or neglectful, especially where her adored son was concerned, didn't feel right anymore. It never really did no matter how I tried to talk myself into it. So what was that written confession about? Why did we fight to the near death about it? Or did we? My wound pounded my head like a ball-peen hammer. I filed my mother predicament away for another day.

"Whoever murdered Brendan's gonna be at the funeral, right?"

"It's a private burial. Remember?" Smiley said.

"They don't lock the gates. Anyone can drive in."

"Think someone's gonna show wearing an "I'm the Killer" sandwich board?"

"Don't you watch cop shows? The killer always goes to the funeral."

"You know TV's not real life, right?"

"Thanks for the enlightenment."

"If you think the guilty party's on the invite list you must have an idea who killed Brendan."

"My parents might know."

"You really think so?"

I'd admit to myself that idea felt tenuous too. Every sinister deed I'd dumped on my parents now seemed ridiculous. My parents owned this town, owned its justice system, got their way as a matter of course, but murdering Brendan? It didn't sit.

"Drug deal gone bad is the only scenario that makes sense," I said, meaning it.

"I'm open to changing my mind if you know something. Anything?"

"Shit. I knew it. You missed the street."

****

Another herd of smut-rag reporters pawed and snorted outside St. Gertrude's cemetery. The fact they didn't intrude on the congregated meant the Blair Fitzgeralds still brandished *some* clout. I steeled myself for another assault. Smiley gunned the SUV through the iron gates. Some of the waiting reporters scattered, some didn't. He weaved toward the persistent ones, pressing harder on the gas, then slammed on the brakes right as one jumped just in time to avoid the Rover's front end then threw himself to the ground. The screaming almost drowned out our cackling.

"That was fun," he said.

"It so was."

We raced down the winding road past the neat, gray headstones lined up like tiny infantry. Drove 'til we got to the tail end of a long line of parked cars.

Smiley whistled. "Whose Bentley?"

"My dad's."

He'd pleaded to escort me, but I couldn't handle his overbearing futzing.

"Of course." Smiley slowed. "I'll let you out ahead, then park."

He chauffeured me to the gravesite dotted with more attendees than I'd anticipated. Guess they came to rubberneck. All dressed appropriately in black, their milling around and discreet waves to one another looked like birds gently flapping their wings—a murder of crows. How appropriate.

Brendan's sleek black casket up on its stand, wreathed in flowers I'd chosen, rocked me. I stared from behind the tinted windows of my Rover. The hole in the dirt, hidden by the best box money could buy, waited to embrace my Irishman for eternity. Soon he'd belong to the earth, to the god I'd never believed in. Whatever life I'd lived with Brendan had run its course. No more chances. I wouldn't wake up from this.

"Preston, you've got to get out," Smiley said.

"I can't."

"You can."

I hardly recognized anyone. Brendan's usual crowd didn't do funerals, particularly those surrounded by the police. I hadn't heard one peep from the Finneys, which I still found difficult to fathom. Brendan's parents disapproved of his life and his death. Stubborn Irish don't like to bend, but I knew they loved their son.

No one who mattered to my husband showed—except me. No one came for me either. My friends, the few I'd had, voted themselves off the island when I got carted off to the psych ward. Parasites attached themselves to me like swine flu for drugs, money, entre into the hottest clubs, or the occasional blurb in the society page. When access to living la vida loca dispersed so did my peeps.

"See your parents?" Smiley said.

"No. They wouldn't come together."

"The rich are different, I guess."

"That's generous. I don't remember a time they didn't live separate lives. My mother will come with her driver. You saw my father's here under his own steam."

I opened the passenger side door a crack, which opened the floodgates. Brendan deserved my crying. Smiley double-parked to see me safely to my seat. The assembled parted like the Red Sea to let me through. Staring daggers.

"What exactly is going on with the Finneys?" I said. "Do you have any idea? I get they blame Brendan for his own downfall but—"

"You didn't hear?"

"Hear what?"

"They've left town. Finney up and retired then split to an unknown destination."

That got my hackles up big time. No way. Smiley wasn't an idiot. He wasn't looking at me when he dropped that load, his tone sounded oh so casual. He suspected something. I felt it.

Before I could ask what, he said, "Didn't you say that was your Dad's Bentley?"

"Yes."

He pointed to the empty seat reserved for my father, craned his neck to take stock of the gathered.

"He's not here."

Chapter Forty-Eight

Isabel

"I don't care if you're on the fucking moon, you lying, two-headed snake," I yelled into my cell. "You've always got some excuse. If you think for one second I'm—hello? Hello? Are you there?"

Goddamn you, Sherman.

I rammed my phone off, tip of my new fake nail sailed to the carpet in my apartment living room. Immediately I regretted my outburst. Pissed as I felt I couldn't afford to shoot my gift horse. I'd need Sherman's money more than ever if Jonathan's wife was indeed our bugger and cut off his funds.

Now what?

I needed to put a lid on. Think. Grabbed my decanter off the table, marched across the cheap linoleum to get a glass. After a glug my heart slowed—inhaled, deep, mind-clearing breaths. Don't go off half-cocked. Sherman could still be telling the truth. But why had he only invited me over once now that he'd rid himself of the albatross? I'd make good on my promise to drop over, this time I'd storm the place. No more mamby pamby drive-bys. Sherman could bet his spiked dog collar on that.

One thing did settle my nerves a little. He kept coming back, didn't he? Sure, he'd exclaim, hand wring, protest, but couldn't stay away more than a few days. We were *in the family way*.

Maybe he wanted to surprise me. That was probably it. Why hadn't I thought of that before? Sherman said he wanted us to start clean. I'm sure that meant he planned to propose. I could tell. Probably on one knee at some expensive, exclusive, destination resort. We'd fly first class.

Of course. *That was it.*

My fury dissipated like e-cigarette vapor. I pitched backward on my couch. Imagined how I'd try to act surprised when we returned home from the Four Seasons Resort Bali, where a new mansion, bigger than Preston's, grander than Beverley, waited just for me. Sherman would cover my eyes with both hands, then yodel, "Surprise!" I'd say something like, "For me? Oh you shouldn't have," while he pressed the keys to the kingdom swinging from an Hermès keychain into my palm.

I punched out numbers on my phone. Wait 'til my mother hears all this. She'd die, stingy hen. Well, I knew I probably shouldn't say anything yet. Better to underpromise then overdeliver. It might not go the way I imagined. Truthfully, I suspected it wouldn't go that way at all. In fact, the heave-ho was probably coming my way, and I'd get the I-told-you-so from Mom.

Then again maybe not.

What the hell—I'd risk it. Didn't I always?

I finished dialing. No answer. Again. Tried to remember how long since I'd talked to her. Husband didn't pick up either. Couldn't remember the creep's name. Rich as a Trump but the tight ass never traveled farther than the Indian casino for bingo or the Piggly Wiggly for smokes.

I patted my stomach. The old penny-pincher would be excited about the baby, wouldn't she? My mother, never in a million years, would think she'd become a grandmother. I laughed to myself. She'd have a better shot at winning the lottery. Mom would finally be happy about something I did. She—

Why didn't anyone pick up?

Chapter Forty-Nine

Preston

After a cursory search for my father, Smiley came up empty, then ever so gently pushed me into the chair meant for me. He peered over my head still looking for any relative of mine. Didn't see one, so he regretfully left me alone then headed for the rear. "They'll turn up," I'd said. "I'm all right."

Father O'What's-his-name chatted up a woman I'd seen at my mother's Tuesday luncheons back in the day. No one had taken their seats or addressed me. Most of the hush-voiced, tastefully dressed funeral goers were members of my parents' prehistoric sphere whose nonnegotiable rules kept the planets aligned. Anyone who was *anyone* registered Republican, worshiped Episcopalian, inherited fortunes, attended Ivy League schools as a legacy, merged rather than married and said things like *toddy* and *the Vineyard*.

Never mind the Irish existed solely to burrow up the WASP ass. When one finagled his way into their circle, then exploded in their historically significant neighborhood, attendance at his funeral took precedence, even if the service collided with a Seven Sisters' alumni luncheon.

So busy scoffing at my parents' peers I didn't notice my mother until she took the seat to my right, escorted by the only faithful man in her life—the driver—who, despite knowing him forever, I couldn't pick him out of a lineup and didn't know his name. The communal intake of breath drew my attention. I wouldn't say she smiled at me but something similar warmed her features, maybe sedative induced. After all the Catholic cemetery was the closest Mother had ever been to the ghetto.

She looked beautiful in black.

Father O'What's-his-name sidled up to ask if he could start. Other than dealing with the funeral home, *um, whatever you think* and *how much should I donate* had been the extent of my contribution to the actual service and my relationship with the padre. So we both deferred to Harrison Blair who said, "Please do" in a gritty, slurred but measured, tone. Like a drunk who thinks no one knows they're shit-faced.

My dad's late entrance to my left hedged my bawling. I divided my parents in every circumstance. Where'd he been? Something about Dad seemed wrong. Couldn't put my finger on what. His skin flushed too pink like he'd just come in from the cold or a tryst with a lusty Latina. Only after he checked the cell phone he gripped, straightened his tie, and pulled down his cuffs did he acknowledge me, oddly preoccupied. While the priest intoned scripture Dad stopped adjusting to pat my arm. The long, pink scar that zagged across the back of his hand startled me, like it did every time I saw the thing.

"Many of those who sleep in the dust of the earth shall awake." The priest's voice sounded far. *Why'd you cut your mother's throat?*

I jerked my head like a punch pummeled it up. Who said that? The priest, right? I looked to both sides. My parents hadn't flinched. Both studied their funeral programs.

"And those who lead the many to justice shall be like the stars forever," the priest carried on. *How'd you get away with it, Preston?*

A steady thud battered my temples. I looked behind me. Countless heads bowed in reverent silence. Didn't anyone hear what he just said?

"Fear not, for I have redeemed you," the good father chanted. *Why did you kill him?*

I jumped to my feet. Thought I might stroke out. Why didn't anyone stop him? Kill Brendan? Me? What kind of monster did they think I was?

"Preston." Mother pulled the back of my skirt. "It's almost

over. Sit down."

"But he—" The words jammed. Every eye that wouldn't meet mine before accused me. "Make him—" I wanted more than anything to take flight, but my heels sunk into the grass, clipped my wings. "Why is he saying—"

"Saying what? He's praying. Sit, Preston. Please." My father's pink face burned red. Crowd shifted, murmured. Someone said sotto voce, "She really is batty." The priest stepped out from behind the small podium.

"It's fine, Father. Please continue," Dad said. "Hard day, that's all." He waved away Smiley and one of the cops on standby that responded to the ruckus.

I sat, crinkly program wadded in my hands. If the priest resumed the service I couldn't hear him above my rib-splitting heart. Leave it to me to pick the worst time to get a conscience. One that wouldn't keep its big crazy mouth shut. Mother put an iron hand over mine. I couldn't decide if she tried to calm me or keep me from bolting.

"Ashes to ashes, dust to dust."

Hearing those solemn words reminded me of the permanence of death. *I'd never see Brendan again.* I didn't think things could get worse. Wrong. I breathed through my nose, swallowed a bunch of times, tried to self-soothe, but my dress squeezed tight. I might be the next to explode. How could I humiliate myself with psychotic theatrics over imaginary voices in front of *them?*

Didn't dare turn around to face the seats behind me again. Seats filled with those I'd grown up around, but belittled, and never bothered to remember. They remembered me all right. I'd made sure. Now Oreo'd between my parents, who despite the unspeakable acts I committed and their own personal troubles, united to get me through. I crumbled. I felt exposed, skinned. My self-pity and grief gave way to a painful realization.

Who was I to look down on anyone when I'd lived most of my life from the floor?

Chapter Fifty

Isabel

Rang my mother one more time. Still nothing. I'd love to tell her about Harrison Blair's unseemly liaison with the pool boy. Of course, I didn't know if the fella cleaned the pool or not, but isn't it always the pool boy? My mother loved it when the upper crust stooped low.

I could call her neighbor to see if they'd check in at her place. But what neighbor? I didn't know Mom's neighbors. Why couldn't I remember new stepdaddy's name? Knew less than zero about that dud. Mom moved across town with her winnings, an hour's drive tops with traffic. But I steered clear. Oh, I'd been once or twice uninvited, but seeing me in person didn't move her.

Maybe now things with her could change. Once she knew about the baby.

Except she wasn't answering my calls. Discouraged but not defeated, I'd decided to try again later when my phone rang, still in my hand.

"Got the tapes back," Jonathan said. "Or the video or whatever the hell."

"What?"

"From the security cameras. Parking lot? Remember?"

"Oh right. Those," I said.

"Am I interrupting? You sound ruffled or something."

"I'm, I'm, you know, dusting. Not everyone's got a housekeeper."

"Anyway, not much to report," Jonathan said.

"How's that possible?"

"Cameras cover a limited space. I didn't spring for any sophisticated security system when we expanded and added the extra lot, you know. My money goes elsewhere as if you didn't—"

"So you got nothing?"

"Glimpse of a car at the curb but no way to know if the thing belonged to whoever broke in."

"What *do* you know?"

"A lone person in dark clothes running across the lot. Head down, so can't make out much of the face."

"So still pretty much nothing," I said, wondering why he'd bothered to call.

"Investigator not real jazzed to spend a lot of time on this because nothing bad happened."

"Yet."

"You'll have to take a look," Jonathan said. "See what you think."

"You there now?"

"Yep."

"Grabbing my purse as I speak. I'll—"

"One really weird thing. Unusual anyway. Culprit's a woman."

"How do you know?"

His wife. I'm sure.

"Hair's in a bun."

Chapter Fifty-One

Preston

"Doing okay?" Smiley said. "At least it's over. That's about the best that can be said about funerals."

Smiley must've been remembering his own young daughter's burial. Guilt gave me a hardy jab. Why'd I go there? Me and my gigantic flapping mouth. Before I could break down for the umpteenth time my father sidled up beside me. Put an arm around my shoulders. He seemed less frazzled than when he'd arrived, late. I opened my mouth to ask what he'd been doing, to see if he'd blush, but felt I'd doled out enough damage today and kept it shut, plenty of time for inquisitions later.

"Come on, Preston. I'll take you home," Dad said.

"Listen Dad, Smiley's gonna drive me home. Aren't you?" I'd have been disappointed if he said no.

"Of course," Smiley said.

My father didn't argue but said to Smiley, "Thank you for bringing her and for all you've done to help. I hope you can figure out what the hell happened to Brendan Finney."

"Working on it," Smiley said. "Any word on Chief Finney?"

"Sadly, no. Other than he put in his papers and left town. Sometimes a change of scenery is the best thing." His arm squeezed my shoulder tighter. "Hard to lose a child, as you know. You lost a daughter, didn't you? If I recall that was a real tragedy. Hard to fathom such things go on in the world."

I couldn't tell by Smiley's face how he took Dad's remarks.

"You also lost a child. A son?" Smiley said.

An outside observer might think they were two dads, commiserating. Like a dog that knows an earthquake's coming I sensed a low volt current moving through the air.

"Yes, our son, Cooper. That was a long time ago." Dad let go of me, took a couple of backward steps. "What say we go to dinner, Preston? Six o'clock? We'll go to that Italian place you love."

"I don't know," I said. "Maybe another night."

My father creeped me out now. What with his goofy-looking face, sleazy dalliances and preoccupation with my trust fund. I'd need to think before I'd agree to sit alone across a table from him.

Smiley stepped toward my father.

"Don't you think it's odd the Finneys missed their son's funeral?"

"Not necessarily," Dad said. "People deal with grief differently. No rule book."

"He didn't say a word to any of us," Smiley said. "Finney was tight with his cops. Why didn't he tell anyone goodbye?"

"Probably didn't want any fuss."

"Probably?" Smiley said. "You don't know? Thought you two were best buds."

"Marv Finney doesn't owe me any explanations," Dad said.

"Surely you can think of one, right? Something? Anything?" Smiley waited but got nothing from my now zip-lipped dad, so he went on. "Since Brendan was murdered have you considered the Finneys disappearance might involve foul play?"

Smiley moved even closer. Space invading at its finest. The undercurrent wasn't so under anymore. My father and Smiley faced each other like gunslingers.

"Maybe I've been an attorney too long, but this feels like an interrogation," Dad said.

"Not at all. I just get curious when things don't add up."

"You know what they say about curiosity," Dad said, his eyes hard.

"Let's go, Smiley." I broke it up. "I'm tired. This has been a long day."

Smiley took my arm. I felt obligated to wave my father on his way, but he'd beat tracks already. No sense in yelling goodbye to his retreating back.

Smiley said, "I think your father just threatened me."

****

My dad looked weird, acted weird, and his young girlfriend was weird enough to run free in my parent's house right alongside my mother—the trifecta of weirdness. I tried to make sense of it while Smiley and I meandered through the cemetery toward my car. He didn't say anything so I assumed he mused on the same subject.

"Well, everyone cleared out pretty fast," Smiley said at last.

Whatever I thought he'd say, that wasn't it. I was all for tackling a different topic, however inane.

"Not like anyone knew Brendan, or me, really."

They'd all avoided me like patient zero after I'd shown my ass graveside. Remembering my embarrassing performance made me uncomfortable so I walked faster as if I could outrun my behavior. Smiley had to have seen the whole bizarre incident.

"I never saw your mother leave. Did you?"

"Driver whisked her off."

I left out the part where she'd brushed her gentle hand across my wet face on her way by or how the evocative scent of jasmine and roses stayed with me long after she'd gone.

"She came. That means something, doesn't it?"

"Maybe. Maybe not," I said.

I noticed right then that Smiley had held on to my arm the whole way, our elbows looped. I felt safe with him.

"So," I said. "What was that with my father?"

"That was Todd Fitzgerald on defense."

I stopped short. "So you do think my parents are involved with Brendan's death."

"I'm a long way from that, but no one's off limits in a murder investigation."

We walked again.

"What do you think happened to the Finneys?"

This time Smiley stopped. "Don't look now, but someone's hiding behind a tree across the road."

"Where?"

"I said don't look——"

Too late. A feminine form, a flare of a skirt, tweaked my attention. In the split second I caught her face as she turned away from the old oak she'd hidden behind, I recognized her. Head down, scarf covering her hair and part of her face, hurrying away in the opposite direction—didn't matter a whit. I'd know Brendan's mother anywhere.

Chapter Fifty-Two

Isabel

Jonathan leaned away from the conference room table where he'd set up the video on his laptop. "Well? Any brilliant ideas?"

"Nope," I said. "None."

Jonathan stopped studying the parking lot film to study me. "Well, barring any unfortunate related event I guess we'll never know, will we?"

"How would I know? Whoever bugged us probably got bored to death. God knows you're tedious as Al Gore."

"Why do I think these bugs are your doing?"

"Why would I bug my own office you nitwit?"

"Oh, I don't think you did the bugging, you're obviously not that engineering, but I wouldn't be surprised if this whole fiasco is connected to you."

"Leave the thinking for those better equipped."

"If you aren't involved in this I'll be shocked." Jonathan refocused his attention to his computer screen, dismissed me with the back of his head.

I didn't need more time to tell that our mystery spy was Brendan Finney and not Jonathan's wife. After Preston tried to kill Brendan with his own hippie bling at Haven House, Nurse Judy held him for observation and questioning until we could evaluate whether or not he'd been seriously injured or seemed even moderately litigious. I'd watched Preston's artsy-fartsy husband wind up his bun with nervous abandon then secure the stupid thing with a thin paintbrush (of all the preposterous props).

Brendan Finney didn't scare me. He died. Whatever he knew, which I doubt amounted to anything important, blew to bits along with him. Probably wanted to know if I knew anything interesting about Preston. Like if she planned to try to kill him again. If not, the meddling detective that dropped in on Preston at Haven House would've come poking around, wouldn't he?

Yes, he would, for a few reasons. All bad. Better to plan my wedding instead. I flirted with the notion of telling Jonathan about Harrison's new young stud but decided against loosening my lips just yet.

"What on earth are you smiling about?" Jonathan said. "These bugs are serious."

"Thinking about my new life, the wedding, if you must know."

"Ah, yes. Do let me know when you decide on a date. Wouldn't miss that circus." Jonathan turned his frown upside down at the thought I might actually get out of his thinning hair.

"Of course. Shall I add you and what's-her-name to the guest list?"

"An announcement after the fact will do me fine."

Let the jackass enjoy feeling superior. He didn't know, but I'd saved a treat just for him. A reverse wedding present, if you will. I'd decided to never let Jonathan off my hook. Why would I? He wanted to hide our tryst from the little woman in perpetuity, didn't he? Not to mention the ensuing pregnancy and abortion. It'd serve the two-timing, rutting pig right.

"Brendan Finney's burial hit the news today."

Speak of the rocket-launched devil.

"Really?" I said. "Haven't been paying attention."

"Do you ever? So you missed the big announcement?"

"What are you talking about?"

"Weird day for such things but nothing the Blair Fitzgeralds do surprises me anymore."

"Spit it out," I said.

"Todd Fitzgerald announced his retirement from the DA's office today. At the cemetery gates."

Chapter Fifty-Three

Preston

"Looks like the Finneys aren't missing after all," Smiley said. "At least Colleen isn't."

Of course, he could identify my mother-in-law. She'd been the boss's wife for umpteen years. As close as Marv was to his cops, I'm sure the boys in blue and Colleen crossed paths more than once.

"Yeah, wow," I said. "Guess not. Thought my eyes were playing tricks."

We'd waited until the drive home before we started talking about seeing Colleen Finney traipse through the trees at the cemetery. Baffling.

"Why on earth would she hide at her own son's burial?" I said. "She doesn't like any of the Blair Fitzgeralds, but still. We wouldn't have had to mingle, for God's sake." I thought about my mother-in-law and her scarf. "Why incognito? Undercover's not her style, hardly a wallflower. And if she's here, where the hell is Marv?"

"Good questions." Smiley drove at a steady clip.

We both shut up for the rest of the way. Smiley knew more than he let on. He sped past the press through the gates to my house, waved to the guard on our way by, stopped in front of my new fountain.

"Parents shouldn't bury their children," he said out of the blue. "I'm sure the Finneys are in a lot of pain."

I fiddled with the passenger door handle. The space inside

my car felt squirmy. The stink from what I'd said to Smiley about his daughter before lingered. "Listen," I said. "I'm so sorry I brought your daughter up. That was low. Even for me. I feel terrible about it."

"Don't worry about that, I'm fine. Grieving is an ugly process."

I could see this day had taken a toll on Smiley too. The skin around Smiley's mouth hung loose, the half-moons under his eyes looked swollen and dark. He'd aged years between the cemetery and my house. I didn't press him on the Finneys. That could wait.

"Wonder why the press seemed so interested in your father," Smiley said. "Better him than you. But it was kind of surprising to see him holding court at the cemetery gates of all places."

"He probably called them." I remembered my father's just-in-time harried arrival graveside—phone in hand. "Haven't you noticed my dad loves the camera? I'm just grateful he didn't give phone interviews during the eulogy."

"Why now though? Tacky, if you ask me."

"That's my father," I said, "the titan of tacky."

"Luckily, you're the flavor of the moment for about two days, then the newshounds move on to some other salacious event."

"Fingers crossed."

I didn't want to get out of the Rover, so I made no move to do it. Several peaceful seconds passed. I felt comfortable in the quiet with Smiley. Didn't feel the need to fill the silence with zingers, quips, or anything at all—a first for me.

"Sure you're okay?" Smiley covered my hand with his but this time didn't snatch it back.

"You know," I said. "I read once that one usually loves more than the other in a marriage. Brendan loved me more. He left but couldn't stay gone. I didn't miss him. He knew helping me wouldn't end well, but he helped anyway. Brendan was full of kindness. I was cruel."

"Try not to think like that. You'll drive yourself—" He stopped before *crazy* came out. I almost laughed. "You can't do anything about any of that now." His neck turned a delicate pink. "Go forward."

"I should go in," I said with no enthusiasm. "I've kept you

too long."

"No worries. I'll park the Rover by the garage."

I swung the door open, dropped one leg out. "You'll let me know if you find out anything about anyone?"

"I'll tell you what I can. I promise."

I wondered if he really would. Close-mouthed, this one. I'd need to do some more digging myself.

"Thank you for escorting me," I said. "I'm sure you've got better things to do."

I still felt the imprint of his hand on mine.

"My wife probably thinks so. She'll let me know when I get home to her ever-growing list of honey-dos."

Chapter Fifty-Four

Preston's Blog

Musings from the Dented Throne

Four Secrets and a Funeral

I survived my husband's funeral, but I'm not the same carefree Heiress. Since the topic depresses me, I won't dwell. Best that can be said is, as the New Detective told me, it's over.

How's the New Detective, you ask?

Oh, my faithful, the copper's got secrets.

Secret number one: New Detective's fourteen-year-old daughter, his only child, got kidnapped and murdered by a serial psychopath. This is public information (how do you think the Heiress got it?), but he didn't breathe a word to me. Yes, I'm one of those stalker Google-ites. Almost anything worth knowing is simply a finger stroke away.

His daughter's horrible end caused him to take a hiatus from the police force and from life itself, as far as I can tell. When I think of what he's gone through, how his rage at the random cruelty of the world must eat his insides like a parasite, I can barely keep from weeping. Somehow, I feel simpatico. I'm sure it's just me making everything about me. This knowledge pains me though. I promise you.

Secret number two: He gunned down daughter's killer for attempting to escape police custody. That was his story anyway. If the *real* story got covered up and he shot the guy for revenge (why wouldn't he?), the crafty detective got away with it. Google didn't say exactly that but you know the Heiress, she loves to extrapolate.

Secret Number Three: Detective told me a wife waits in the wings. I'll own up, only to you, I felt a mix of alarm and disappointment. Not that I harbored any delusions of romance, what with the Irishman only recently deceased. But if I'm confessing, the Heiress is a sucker for a strong jaw. Something about the guy gets me where I live. Couldn't believe I missed such an important stat during my online research so I surfed once more.

Guess the fuck what?

Secret Number Four: Missus New Detective committed suicide six months after their daughter's horrible demise. That's a pile of shit news if I ever saw one. Means my new detective's the only survivor (although I'm not sure he'd call it that). How much can any man take?

I'm a woman divided between admiration—cut with a heavy dose of empathy for the saddest, handsomest detective—and irritation he felt compelled to make up a living spouse. I wasn't groping him or doing anything that would induce lies to keep me at bay. I'm hopeful you, my followers, can advise me.

A final perplexity: Who popped out from behind a tree at the cemetery after the Irishman's burial but his mother? Yes, you remember mom-in-law? Her halfhearted attempt to go undercover couldn't conceal her real identity.

At first, mom-in-law's appearance surprised me, but after some serious thought, it makes sense. She brought her son into the world—she'd see him out—peevish husband be damned. I thought they might've up and moved. But no, Colleen would never leave. She'd stay where the memories of a child gone too soon still seemed fresh—home. It's what mothers do.

Even mine.

The Queen kept up regular visits to the psych ward, even if she wanted to hate me, showed up at the hospital when the explosion that killed my husband injured me, made her alliance clear for all to see at his funeral. I could still feel the champagne tickle of her touch on my skin.

Some bonds won't break no matter how fierce the beat down.

I've given you a lot to kvetch over, my faithful.

The Invisible Heiress

In the immortal words of Chaka Kahn—tell me something good.

Comments

Jack

So you're saying New Detective says his wife is alive but she's not?

Reply: Yes. It's a real *Sixth Sense* situation.

Jack

Isn't it possible he remarried?

Reply: Hmmm. You got me there. I'll do more snooping.

Amy W.

That poor New Detective. You should make nice with him no matter what about the dead wife. I mean, really. What a cruel twist of fate to lose a wife and a daughter in such violent ways.

Reply: I've taken that suggestion under advisement.

Maggie May

Makes perfect sense the Irishman's mother would show. You're right about mothers. I hope you and yours can kiss and make up. Now what? Are you going to try to contact mom-in-law?

Reply: Can't imagine it, but I'm considering any and all possibilities.

Masked Man

New Dick's lying to get laid. There's nothing more appealing to women than a man who's wanted by another woman. I lie all the time about a Missus Masked Man.

Reply: If you weren't such an asshat I might take this possibility seriously. New Dick will keep little New Dick packed, I assure you.

Norma B.

New Detective's personal tragedies make him the perfect candidate to help figure everything out. He wants to protect you. Show your Mom-in-law kindness. You two might bond in ways that could surprise you.

Chapter Fifty-Five

Isabel

I planned to take a cursory look at Jonathan's video then hit the slots. Instead I slogged to my office, pushed paper around, gave my current state of limbo some thought.

"I've filed for divorce. These things don't unravel overnight." Sherman assured me over and over, but a nagging doubt thumped the back of my brain. The lout forced me to call twenty odd times before he answered.

"I'm locking up. You staying?" Jonathan poked his head in my office, a whack-a-mole begging for a mallet. "You'd think I'd learn my lesson by now but dare I ask what you're so deep in thought about?"

"Someone tried to break in last night." Didn't mean to spew that out. I'd intended to tell Sherman earlier but didn't get the chance.

"Here?" Jonathan looked around my office, crossed immediately to the window, rattled the latch.

"No. My apartment."

"Really? Well, I'm not surprised. Like I said, those listening devices have everything to do with you. Someone's out to get you. I better not get caught in the crossfire."

"Or you'll what?"

"I don't know. You won't want to find out."

"Ooh, snap. Jonathan found his balls. Wife'll want them back by end of day. No worries anyway. I'm sure I imagined the whole thing. Don't know why I even mentioned it to you, of all people."

My teeny-tiny, inner sane person smacked herself on the forehead. I didn't connect the bugs to my prowler until Jonathan threw the idea in my face.

"Did you call the cops?"

"Yes. That's exactly what I did. Called them last night. Right away."

"What'd they say?"

"Couldn't find anything. They took note though, yep. Took note."

"Okay, well. You'd better be right." Jonathan tucked his phone back in his pocket. "Look Isabel, I'm probably wrong. Just blowing off steam. Can't expect me to feign happiness over this situation considering our history. I'm sure your imagination's working overtime. You know how you can get."

****

I really didn't have a care in the world, did I? I shouldn't worry so much.

Sherman would make an honest woman out of me (honest probably isn't the right word) sooner rather than later. No one tried to break into my place. I'm sure Jonathan was right. I imagined the whole thing. My head played tricks on me. Jonathan knew me well. I could get a little—no other way to describe it—undone. Good things came to those who wait. I waited, if not with much patience, at least not psychotically. Well, not the strict definition anyway.

I flirted again with the idea of going to the club, but the thought didn't lift my sagging spirits. I steered my beautiful sedan home. I drove like a ninety year-old, followed the back roads, thinking, churning.

Sherman wouldn't try to pull one over on me. Would he?

Spent a wad on my wedding dress. Soon the glorious confection won't fit. Goddammit. I'd need to double up on the Spanx to get my expanding belly in a size six dress, but I'd give it a go. Jonathan keeps commenting on my weight gain, but if he hasn't guessed I'm pregnant by now maybe I can fit into that gown.

What if Sherman really did dump me? Then what? I wondered what alleyway I'd have to go down to get a late-term abortion. I absentmindedly yanked a wad of hair out at my neckline. *Stop, Isabel. Don't go there.* I needed to calm myself before I made another terrible mistake. Sherman gave his word. I believed him. That was that. I felt a drip down my neck, wiped it away with an impatient hand, came back red. Shit. The gob of hair in my hand stuck to the gooey mix of sweat and blood. My neck started to hurt where I'd pulled, kept bleeding. So engrossed in stemming the flow, I about missed my street. Jerked the wheel, scraped the curb.

Now what? Police parked in front of my apartment building?

Chapter Fifty-Six

Preston

Not sure where to begin my investigation, I'd driven to the Finneys' place. Didn't even need to slow down to see the place looked locked down tighter than a librarian's thighs. Only sign of life was the old cop sedan parked in the driveway, stripped of its insignias, bought at the annual auction probably.

I turned too sharp and my purse fell off the seat onto the floor, spilling girlie crap plus Brendan's apartment keys. I'd forgotten about them until that second. Changed my mind about making peace with my in-laws. My husband's apartment seemed like as good a place as any to start my look-see.

I parked in the first open space, not caring if it was reserved for a resident. I was technically a resident, since I kept paying the rent. Couldn't let the place go. Not yet. Good thing. I trudged around the complex looking for the number that matched the one scribbled on the paper tag clipped to the keys. Didn't need to search long. Neon yellow tape crisscrossed the front door.

"Crime-scene tape? Still? Jesus, how lazy is the landlord?" I said out loud to no one, ripped the yellow announcement of Brendan's dirty dealings off the front door of his apartment. "Overkill."

I stepped in, touched a light finger to the hair-shirt gash on my forehead, a forever testimony to the part I played in my husband's ghastly death. The seeping cut refereed the outrageous games I played with my thoughts. Every time I gave myself a free pass, my wound cried bullshit, stung and wept like I'd used kerosene as antiseptic.

"Christ. What a fucking mess."

I kicked piles out of my way to clear a path. Mining Brendan's apartment seemed like the thing to do a few minutes ago. Now I didn't feel so sure.

I picked up a dual metal food and water dish, a smudge of dried food stuck to one side. Poor Jesse Pinkman, the furry, four-legged, innocent bystander. Why did the thought of an animal I never knew about make me want to throw myself to the ground in an operatic fit? I held Jesse Pinkman's dish under an armpit instead. Didn't own an animal, but I'd keep the dish.

I weaved through toward the galley kitchen. The small apartment felt like Brendan. His smell, a mix of paint thinner, peppermint soap and musky sweat hung in the air. One of the few personal things about my husband I knew for sure.

I couldn't remember much of my life with Brendan. Maybe I chose not to. Flashes of tenderness sometimes popped up in my head. Did I really cuddle up to his backbone in bed, one leg thrown over his? Did he kiss my neck, brush my hair or rub my feet? Did we ever share the small intimacies that separated the fly-by-nights from the built-to-last? Or did his death already polish his rock-of-a-life into a gem?

I felt suspended on the ragged edge of despair. Blairs didn't cry. A rule I'd broken with impunity lately. Needed to steady myself on the fridge, opened the freezer for the hell of it. I reached in past the ice cube trays, one tube of hamburger meat, empty box of Hot Pockets and a brown butcher paper package. Tore open the plain wrappings to discover a wad of cash. I remembered Brendan used to hide drugs and/or drug money in the freezer but assumed the cops would've found them. Hiding shit in a freezer didn't exactly ring original. How lazy had the cops gotten? My guess was they'd found the stash but didn't want to log it into evidence to protect Marv's son. At least they didn't steal it.

Smiley called it right. My Irishman tangled himself back up with his druggies. What I'd told Brendan was true. Can't blame my parents for everything, or anything at all—my brother's death, Brendan's. But what would my world look like without archenemies?

Wasn't there always someone other than me to blame?

I dropped the cash bundle at the kitchen sink, used a filthy sponge to scrub the dried food clinging to Jesse Pinkman's dish under running water for something else to do. Grabbed the first thing that resembled a towel and dried with vigor.

"What's this?"

I held the towel out, studied the familiar navy embroidery—CFB—in a classic font. *Jesus, Mary and Joseph.* My brother Cooper's monogrammed blanket.

Chapter Fifty-Seven

Isabel

"Ma'am, are you all right?" One of the two uniformed cops planted in front of my apartment pointed out the blood smeared on my neck.

"Oh, yes. Fine." I rubbed my hand on my skirt to get rid of the sticky hair. "Cut myself, um, shaving." I'd parked my new car in the covered lot, tried to keep my blood pressure at a reasonable level. Keep calm and carry on. "You're not here to see me, are you?" I put my key in the door.

"Are you Isabel Warner?"

I wondered if it'd help to lie.

"Yes."

No use.

"Can we step inside?"

"Sure."

My voice sounded breezy, didn't it? Why shouldn't it? I'd broken no laws. Not real laws. Well, not any these cops would be clever enough to know about. We all strode in easy peasy. On autopilot, both cops removed their caps at the same time. I dropped my purse on the coffee table, offered my unwelcome visitors a seat that they declined. Worked like a mother to keep my face neutral. One opened his mouth to speak, but I cut him off.

"I'm sure whatever it is can be cleared up in—"

"It's about your mother, Ms. Warner," he said. "Jeanine Turner?"

"Yes, that's my mother."

I knew what he was getting at. The reason she hadn't answered the phone. I steeled myself for the blow by trying to keep the cop from saying what I already knew out loud.

"I told the klepto cheapskate last time I'd let her stew in the pokey if she—"

"She's dead."

Chapter Fifty-Eight

Preston's Blog

Musings from the Dented Throne

Good Golly, Miss Molly

Call me crazy (I know you already do), but something funny's going on. Funny as waking up in the middle of the night to find a clown perched on the end of your bed.

I found my brother's monogrammed blanket in the Irishman's apartment.

Let that sink in.

The last time I laid eyes on a similar cashmere square I held it clenched in both fists before my excursion to the cuckoo's nest. One of the few details I remember distinctly. Could it be the same one? I brought the evidence home from the Irishman's. Smells fresh, clean, unlike everything else in my late husband's apartment. Despite the small size, I can't overstate how significant it is. Like a letter bomb.

Jester's decided, suddenly and shockingly, that life on the public dime doesn't suit anymore. Financial planning's his new gig. He plans to spend, I mean invest, other people's money. The only kind he knows. Saw the doofus's press conference on the news. I suspect the Royal She's somehow cut his funds off at the knees on this one. The Queen considers herself a politico's wife. She'd never agree to finance a private side hustle so he'd need to start scheming like his ass was on fire via Ponzi.

Then there's his wonky appearance plus attitude. I've given

you the 911 on his face and hair but since he talked smack to the Queen that day in therapy he's turned goon. No more doormat dad. The only explanation for all these oddities indicates something bigger is afoot. What? Got me.

On my way home from the Irishman's apartment you'll never guess who I pulled right alongside at a stop sign. Shrinky. Driving what looked like a new luxury car, well, luxury for someone like her. Get this. Had a weird near miss with an unknown car near my gate a while back. Looked a lot like this same one. I noticed the crazy skank this time because she had the driver's side window rolled down. Shrinky didn't see me because she was too busy talking to an invisible friend and pulling out handfuls of her own hair.

Welcome to my world.

Random reminiscences come my way. The window in my old bedroom at the Royal's doesn't lock. Latch broke moons ago. Queen is old school. No alarm systems. A gun in the bedside drawer is her version of high-tech security. She conceded front-gate cameras, but they hadn't been upgraded in eons to my knowledge. If the Heiress felt like a quick B&E she could get 'er done easy. A clandestine stroll down the hidden path, and some catlike maneuvers up to the second floor, is all it'd take. I'd done similar throughout my formative years, sneaking out to the closest rave or whatnot.

The Invisible Heiress

P.S. Such is my state that I brought home Jesse Pinkman's dish. The Irishman could pick a great dog name. I don't own a dog. It's a reminder that only a man who loves dogs, and is loved by dogs, could put up with me.

Put down that joint. Tell me how you feel.

Comments

Hubba-Hubba

Who buys babies cashmere? You fuck nuts deserve whatever happens to you.

Reply: We absolutely, positively, never, fuck nuts.

Dr. Frank

You should turn Shrinky into the AMA. She's definitely bonzo. Why not look me up? I'd treat you for free. We could chat over dinner and drinks? Wear something slutty.

Reply: To think I'd used a shrink playing with half a deck when I could've gone to you. My bad.

Maria N.

I can't for the life of me think why the Irishman would keep the Littlest Heir's blanket. Did he get it from you? I think your poor dad needed a break. Maybe financial management's easier?

Reply: It is easier because he's always had someone manage his. Nope, makes no sense. I'm with you, Maria. I can't, for the life of me, think why the Irishman owned baby bro's blanket either. I'm blank but certain it's not a good sign.

Maria N.

BTW, you're a tender heart, Heiress. Sweet you'd keep Jesse Pinkman's dish.

Norma B.

Maybe the Irishman spent more time in your house than you think while you were gone. Or searched the crime scene? I can't believe Shrinky doesn't get under your skin enough to prick your interest. God knows she gets under mine, just from reading about her here.

Chapter Fifty-Nine

Isabel

"Bun-wearing bugger's a guy," Jonathan said in my ear. "*Was* a guy, I should say. Preston Blair's husband, Brendan Finney, if you can believe that."

I thought finally answering his call would be less annoying than hearing it ring. Not so. I didn't have the wherewithal to feign surprise.

"Okay, whatever," I said. "Listen I've gotta—"

"*Whatever?* Are you kidding? Expect a visit from a Detective Smiley. He's already talked to me. He did say there's no proof Brendan actually did any bugging or even broke in. Not from the photos anyway. Common sense dictates—"

"Got other things going, if you must know. Some big, scary creeper tried to break in a few minutes ago."

"Again? You sure this time?

"Definitely. I fell sleep. Heard a noise. Then a shadowy figure. Saw his outline, tried to pry open the window right here in my bedroom." I'd tucked myself in early, phone by my pillow in case Sherman called.

"You okay? Is he gone?"

"Um, yes. Think so."

I'd opened my mouth to scream but fear froze me. The second I thought *this is it,* a chorus of voices then the slam of a door surprised both the creeper and me. Creeper booked, followed by the giggling couple from next door probably on a last-ditch booze run.

"Isabel, you still there?"

"What? Yes."

"Cops. Did you call?"

"Not yet."

"Call right now. Mention the bugs again. They've got to be connected. Maybe Brendan didn't do anything. If he didn't the bugger's still on the loose."

"Well, I—"

"Dial nine-one-one, Isabel. It's not complicated. A monkey can do it. I'll hang up." And he did.

I'm on it.

Pulled the covers up around my neck, ears out, listening hard for any squeak or sign the bogeyman returned. Didn't give a hoot for the late hour. Dialed Sherman. Straight to voicemail. Goddammit. Fine time for his phone to completely break, left another message.

After the cops conveyed the news about my recently departed mother, naturally I called Sherman to tell him the news. No answer. I left a message. Okay, a couple of messages, maybe ten or fifteen. I left so many because Sherman told me he's had trouble with his phone lately, can't hear the ring or retrieve messages. Oh so busy. Oh such a liar.

A blocked number called over and over, which I ignored. I'd fallen for that creditor ruse before. Then Jonathan called, like a million times. Ignored the obsessive-compulsive dialer until the millionth time. Thought I'd feel comforted, telling Jonathan about my brush with disaster. His broken record, call-the-cops chorus wore thin in a hurry. Sherman could calm my nerves, couldn't he?

Of course, Sherman didn't know a thing about my harridan of a mother. Neither did Jonathan. Humiliating that the biggest, single lottery winner in the United States wouldn't help her own daughter. Besides, if they thought I might get money out of dear mummy, they'd feel disinclined to pony up. Well, Sherman would. Jonathan's pony will stay saddled forever.

Police told me no sign of stepdaddy whose name is apparently Dwayne (what else?). No immediate evidence of foul play. The scroogess dropped dead with no fanfare. Surely stepdaddy Dwayne recognized a winning hand when he saw one (probably dumb as Camille Cosby most days), absconded with everything worth taking.

No sleep for me, so for giggles I thought I'd see if I could still squeeze into my wedding dress. Didn't look too bad. Seams puckered a bit what with the weight I'd piled on playing the waiting game, but I put on two girdles, which helped.

I lay back on my bed, all dressed up, nowhere to go, one eye on the window the other on my phone.

Someone's moving in for the kill.

Chapter Sixty

Preston

"We need to talk." Detective Smiley wriggled out of his coat. "We pulled security tapes from around Brendan's neighborhood. Anywhere we thought he'd go."

"Oh good, great."

Smiley beat me to the library, tossed his trench on the ottoman, pushed piles to the side on top of my antique heirloom desk. I snatched the monogrammed blanket I'd tossed near the stack of unpaid bills, shoved it into the top drawer before Smiley got a gander.

"That desk's an antique," I said to distract. "Belonged to my Aunt James."

That stopped Smiley's rearranging. "Oh, I'll be careful. You didn't know her, did you?"

"No. She died well before I arrived. My mother furnished this house."

"Look at these. Stills from the security footage." Smiley spread photos. "Anything jump out?"

I rotated pics. Smiley plucked one out. A beautifully restored Victorian smack in the center of two parking lots.

"What about this?" He said.

"A house turned office?"

"Your therapist's office."

"Shrinky? You sure?"

"Yes, if Shrinky is Isabel Warner. That's the converted offices she shares with a partner, Jonathan Meyers."

"What about it?"

"Brendan might've bugged the place. Jonathan Meyer found the bugs. Uniforms dumped their security cameras. Brendan's on film in their parking lot, as is his Tesla."

He handed me another pic of what looked a lot like Brendan's head and bun.

"Brendan never found anything that would throw suspicion on Isabel. If so, he never mentioned it," I said. "Then, well, he couldn't tell me."

"She's on the radar now."

"I think she's following me." I pointed out the red car in the parking lot.

"Why?" He stopped tossing photos around.

I confessed I'd almost run into the same car the day I'd made Brendan's funeral arrangements, plus I'd seen her right next to me at a stop sign. What an idiot I was for not telling Smiley earlier. I could never take Shrinky seriously. Right about now underestimating her felt like a big mistake.

"Any idea why she'd follow you?"

"Other than she's mad as a hatter? No. But I could be wrong. It's not like I own the roads. She could've been going anywhere, right?"

He'd taken out a pad. Wrote fast, made a few more notations, then said, "It's possible, but I'll reserve judgment for now. All we know is Brendan was in the parking lot a couple of weeks before they found the bugs. But his prints weren't at the scene. If they were they would've come up. He's in the system."

Brendan knew how to break the law. Of course he'd never leave fingerprints.

"If Brendan thought nosing around Isabel would turn up anything useful, can't believe he didn't tell me."

"Maybe he would've the day he died, if he'd found something."

"So nothing but more questions," I said.

Leaning against the desk with Cooper's blanket stuffed in, I decided to come clean. I opened the drawer, pulled the thing out. Smiley was trying to help me. My natural inclination to hoard info would only hurt me.

"I found this in Brendan's apartment."

"A hand towel?" Smiley said.

"My brother Cooper's receiving blanket."

I showed him the monogram.

"That's odd. Why would Brendan have that?"

"No idea."

He took the blanket to get a closer look.

"Cooper died, what? Decades ago?"

"Yes."

"Don't you think this blanket looks new?"

I grabbed it back. "I don't know. It's not like it got used much."

"Can I take it?"

"No." I shoved the blanket back in the drawer.

I felt Smiley thinking. Wondering, like I did, about the blanket's significance and how the thing could be new. I'd never noticed anything but the small embroidered initials. New or old its randomness made it feel important. He wrote on his pad but didn't press me to give up the blanket.

"Probably doesn't mean anything," he said. "It's not a crime to own a baby blanket."

Smiley thought it *did* mean something. I could tell by the way his brows scrunched together and he kept adding to whatever he was writing.

"Back to the bugs," he said. "I need motive. Why would Brendan have bugged Isabel's office? For all we know he went to talk about you. Or make an appointment. Nothing solid connects Brendan to the bugs. Love to get a look at Isabel and her partner's computers but can't get a warrant."

"Why not?"

"HIPAA laws for one. They're psychiatrists. For another, far as we know, *they're* the victims in this. Keep looking through the photos." Smiley shifted his weight from one foot to the other. We'd stayed standing behind Aunt James's desk.

I flipped through a few more. One showed Brendan's Tesla blurred by its motion caught in still frame, passing by an almost imperceptible building with no clear identity. I pointed.

"This?"

"Private fetish club."

That staggered me.

"What? Drugs and freaky shit sex too?"

How could a man I've known since nursery school end up a complete stranger?

"Just because he drove by it doesn't mean he indulged." Smiley held the photo up toward the light.

"True."

Still. I didn't think he'd have a Chica either.

"Security footage from inside gave no clues. Everyone's masked."

"Freaks."

"Casino in the front. Nothing obvious there either," Smiley said. "Anything else?"

I shuffled through more pics, aware of Smiley's nearness, his earthy scent. No matter how seductive his packaging, or how much I trusted him, there *was* some info I still needed to hoard. Like, my peeping at Beverley. I wanted to keep anything that might make me look peculiar, *more* peculiar, to myself.

Thinking of hoarded info and Beverley reminded me. I'd never shown Smiley that last photo of me and Cooper.

Even though it seemed less and less likely that my parents had done anything criminal, whenever I ran across the photo I'd tossed on Aunt James' desk, I felt uneasy about their innocence. Smiley worked his ass off on my behalf, I needed to help, not hinder. I dug the photo out from under the accumulation.

"What about this?" I held out the pic.

He looked taken aback for a sec.

"Well, let me see. This is you?"

"And Cooper."

"You were beautiful even then," he said. "Cooper too. Definitely genetically blessed."

"Beautiful? Cooper's dead in that picture." I heard myself talking too loudly.

"What?" Smiley jerked the pic out of my hand. Looked at me, then the pic, then back again. "Preston, I've seen more dead people than I care to remember in person and in photos."

Somehow, I knew what he'd say next.

"Cooper is very much alive in this picture."

****

"Sorry to disturb, ma'am."

The biggest dog on earth stood at attention next to the guard.

"Couldn't leave my post," he said. "And since you let the cop posted at your front door go I wasn't sure what to do with him, exactly."

The beautiful beast stood still, bearing proud, military like. A bright orange vest yelled "Do Not Pet" on both sides. A lone reporter snapped shots from across the road. I'd fallen far on the ladder of interest.

"Holy Mother. Is that a Dalmatian or what?"

I jumped out to get a good look at the most gorgeous animal.

Guard shuffled through the file in his hands. "Oh no, ma'am. Great Dane. A harlequin."

"It's a he?"

Guard peered around the Dane's south forty. "Yes, but neutered." He read through more of the paperwork. "Says he's trained. There's a list of commands. If you take off the vest he relaxes. Vest on he's at work."

"Work? What's his job?"

"I'd say protecting you."

"Where'd he come from? Or who?"

"No idea. A real nice lady dropped him off. She said to give you this."

I tore open the envelope he handed me. A plain piece of typed paper read, "He can use the dog dish."

"A nice lady from where?" I said.

"Training place, I thought. But now that you mention it she didn't say exactly."

"What'd she look like?"

Guard scratched his chin. "Well, normal, I guess. Nothing special. I can pull up the surveillance." He pointed to one of the two cameras looming at the gate.

I followed him into the guardhouse where he pressed keys and scrolled up, down, and around on the monitor.

"Here she is," he said.

I looked over his shoulder. "You're right. Nothing special. Never seen her. White van, unmarked."

"I've got the license plate. I can run it."

"Please do."

"If you don't mind my saying, you're gonna need a dog run."

"Huh? What's that?"

"A place in your backyard fenced off just for him. These types of dogs make a hell of a mess. If you know what I mean."

"Oh right. Great Dane-sized shit."

"Dinosaur sized more like it."

"How does he know he's supposed to protect me? I didn't train him. He's never seen me before."

"He'll know. They just do."

"You a security *and* dog expert?"

"Danes are just about the best dogs ever. My daughter's got two. He'll die for you if need be."

I reached to pet my new friend, who stepped back.

"Don't." Guard pointed at the neon vest. "Take it off him when you get back up to the house. Then you can get to know each other."

"He got a name?" I said.

Guard referred once more to the folder. "Let's see. Oh, yep. Here it is—name's Walter, of all things. Walter White."

That froze me. Whoever sent the dog knew about Jesse Pinkman.

He opened my car door, said, "Up."

The magnificent creature hopped into the back, reclined like royalty on the leather seat, neck craned, ears alert.

Chapter Sixty-One

Isabel

"Christ. What do you want now, Jonathan? Sun's barely up. You're phone-stalking me."

"You never mentioned your mother. Not that I ever wondered. But—"

"My mother? What are you—"

"Across town this whole time?"

"Yeah. So. What about her?"

"She died."

"Yeah, I know," I said. "How do you know anything about my mother?"

"Morning paper, second page. 'Biggest Lottery Winner's Luck Ran Out.'"

****

I sprinted to the corner 7-Eleven for the day's paper, still wearing my nuptial dress, now ripped at the seams. In a tizzy, I'd stuffed my swollen feet into the footwear closest to my bed, Uggs.

"Love the walk-of-shame outfit," said the mouthy cashier, with at least three missing teeth, to my back, as I dashed out with a fresh copy of the *Tribune*.

Just like a convenience store brainiac to get all judgmental while she counts fingers to give back change for a fucking Slurpee.

Rooted in the parking lot, I tore open the newspaper. Jonathan said the second page. Why didn't I anticipate media interest? She'd made the papers when she won. I sped-read through the crap I already knew. Focused on the important blips: *Survived by her husband, Dwayne Cooney, and her only child, daughter Isabel Warner, a local therapist. As of press time, calls to Mister Cooney and Doctor Warner have not been returned. It's unknown if either or both inherit Ms. Turner's record-holding lottery winnings.*

My name didn't come up when she raked in millions but leave a decaying corpse and suddenly *family matters*.

****

"That her?" the coroner's office minion said.

"Yes." Mom looked mostly the same dead or alive, same casino pallor, gray hair long, stringy, dirty. To my shock, a tear bubbled to the edge of my fake lashes. I touched her cold, hard-as-concrete face but resisted the urge to bid my lifelong archenemy adieu with a kiss. I studied her for several minutes, taking her in. I wondered if my baby would resemble her at all.

The baby I'd grown to love, more or less, despite not wanting to at all.

"Listen, it's late," the minion said. "I shouldn't have let you in."

"You did though. Can we move on?"

Minion yanked the sheet over Mom's head. How surprised was I when he pushed the refrigerated drawer shut and it felt like a fist to my windpipe? Fighting the urge to keel over, I leaned against the cold steel, reached for my belly as was my habit these days. Reality slapped me hard. All these years, I'd waited for my mother to love me. Now she never would.

"Autopsy won't get done for at least forty-eight hours. Plenty of time to get your ducks in a row." The oblivious minion hustled me out then locked the door behind me.

I took Lamaze breaths, consigned my unexpected grief to the back burner of my mind, then tooled over toward Sherman's part of town. Planned to have a come-to-Jesus with my duck *tout de suite*. With that in mind, lo and behold, my route took me right to the winding dirt road off the highway on Beverley's backside.

Did I dare? Again?

I'd need to exercise caution in broad daylight so I parked farther away from the stables than last time. Wished I'd have worn sturdier footwear than Uggs but managed a quick lope across the yard that brought me flush against the back wall of the Blair Fitzgerald plantation. I ducked down near a window, then peeked around the frame, and saw Harrison plus young buck clear as a summer sky.

What in jumping Jesus were they doing?

Harrison sat prim, proper, coiffed, on what I'd call a settee of some sort, across from her boy who operated a video camera. Rapt, I watched for who knows how long. Harrison's fuchsia lips moved, then the boy fidgeted with a whatchacallit on the camera. Boy's lips moved, then Harrison's, then boy adjusted some doohickey on the tripod. If I had to guess, I'd say he asked questions, she answered, he filmed. No network logo on the camera that I could see. Did that mean he wasn't a reporter conducting an interview? No, the boy asking questions was the same one I saw kissing Harrison last time.

Was a Harrison Blair pool boy movie in the works?

Chapter Sixty-Two

Preston

"I believe you or someone who works here dropped off a dog at my house earlier," I said to the tie-dyed onesie, puka-shell wearing woman behind the counter. Looked like the one caught on my security camera. Gate guard IDed the van's plates, owned by It's a Dog's Life kennel and training.

"Walter White," I said, in case she'd need me to identify him.

"Oh, yes, he's a great dog. Don't you just love him?" she said.

"Um, yes. But I'd like to know who bought him for me. You know, so I can thank them."

"Hmmm." She sounded concerned, like she thought my request would prove problematic. "Actually, the nice young man who made all the arrangements asked that the gift giver remain anonymous."

"What nice young man? What'd he look like?"

"Big, strapping——." She pointed a short stub of a finger at me. "Oh, you almost tricked me. I'm sorry. We promised to honor the request."

I felt like jumping over the counter to shake the shit out of this annoying hippie of a clerk.

"No such thing as dog trainer/client confidentiality, you know," I said.

"Oh, silly. I know that." She didn't seem ruffled in the least at my obvious irritation. "Is it against the law to give a gift? Would you like to return him? We could do that if you insisted."

"No. Never mind."

I stomped out. What the fuck? Whoever gave me Walter knew about Jesse Pinkman so they had to have read my blog and watched *Breaking Bad*. A lot of people probably did the latter, not so many did the former. Sure, I had a hundred thousand or so blog subscribers, ditto Twitter followers, but I'm hardly a Kardashian. They also assumed I'd come looking for them. What had she said about the guy who picked him up? Maybe Smiley. Had to be, didn't it?

Whoa.

If the gift horse were Smiley, he'd read my blog. He couldn't know about it, could he? Shit. I flung open my car door. What about my father? I'd made excuse after excuse to avoid him. Maybe Walter was his attempt to break the ice. Dad's frozen face and too-cool-for-school hair flashed through my mind. No. He wasn't the giver. But who just decides, out of the blue, to get someone else a dog? Still. It all came back to my blog. Whoever sent him read *Musings from the Dented Throne,* kept up with cool TV shows, *and* knew my address.

A snippet of something jabbed me. I sat behind the wheel, closed my eyes. My brain searched its files for I didn't know what. I smacked the steering wheel with my fist. Nothing made sense. My delightful Walter White. Cooper's blanket, new? Cooper alive in that photo? The top of my head might come off if I thought harder.

Time to move on to something else.

I'd already planned to drop in at Beverley. The trainer visit had been a last-minute add-on. Curious about Smiley's situation, I could sneak over to his house too. First, I'd need to find his address (Google, don't fail me now), check in on Walter, who I'd let roam free in my yard. I'd need to stop at some pet place to buy supplies. The big galoot had probably already dug a hole to China.

****

Didn't expect to find Smiley's address so easily, but when I did I took that as a message from my higher power—my creepy, stalking, inappropriate higher power—to go ahead.

He lived in a so-so area of town, not far from the Finneys, in a cop's neighborhood. I planned to do a quick drive-by, no harm, no foul. Perhaps get a glimpse of the life of Smiley, see if he'd acquired a new wife then sleuth the shit outta my parents' house. I intended to find out why Marcella set up shop at Beverley. Plus, I needed to see my mother. Even from the yard like a pervy peeping tom, I wanted to see her.

So focused on the dreamy detective's situation and Walter White's unknown buyer, I forgot where I left my car keys. Scoped out the library where I thought I'd last seen them. Jerked the top drawer of Aunt James's desk open too hard, the rickety thing fell to the floor, spilling all the doodads, pens, papers, my car keys, out across the Persian rug. I grabbed the keys then noticed the monogrammed blanket I'd stuffed in so Smiley couldn't take it. Dropped to my knees to scoop up the spillage but changed my mind. I needed to get going. The mess could wait. I crammed Cooper's blanket into my purse—a macabre, good luck charm.

Chapter Sixty-Three

Preston

I parked across the street. Hoped hiding in plain sight worked. I could tell at first glance by the frazzled yard and peeling paint of the façade that no woman lived in that house. Maybe a slovenly, muumuu-wearing, sponge-roller sporting frump but no woman I could imagine catching Smiley's eye.

Nothing covered the picture window at the front of the house. In the near darkness with lights blaring from inside, I could see whatever went on in what was probably the living room. Not content to snoop from afar I got out of the Rover, then slinked closer. From a convenient spot alongside Smiley's car, parked on the weed-infested driveway, I could observe from a safe place, get my bearings.

Smiley, shirtsleeves rolled to the elbows, lingered behind a TV tray with frozen dinner rubble and a half-full bottle of tequila. The sight of the handsomest detective unguarded, and alone, filled me with longing. I wondered what he'd do if he saw me. Probably wouldn't care much about me kicking around his yard, but he sure as hell wouldn't want me anywhere near his soul. Nevertheless, I fought the urge to race in, to do . . . what?

Could I put my mouth to his, ease his burdens? Could I lay my head against his heartbeat to ease mine? Smiley's loneliness reached out to me across the dead, dried grass. I felt it, a palpable living thing, as heavy as my own. He turned toward the window, as if he could sense me there, wondering what his naked skin felt like. If I closed my eyes, I could smell him—a clean, crisp, starched linen freshness—undercut with a musky desperation. Before I could make up my mind to go to the door Smiley dropped his head into both hands. I could see his shoulders rise and fall. Even though we didn't occupy the same space, his grief enveloped me like an executioner's hood.

I've heard the real measure of a man is what he does when he thinks no one is looking. How could I help but fall for one who cried for his lost wife and daughter?

****

Driving away from Smiley's House of Heartbreak, not paying attention to the road, I made a wrong turn. Drove several minutes lost in thought before noticing I'd accidentally made my way onto the Finneys' street. Why not drop in?

When in Rome.

Street stood empty. Caution to the wind I parked curbside. Even in the dark I could see the house looked abandoned. Like before, no curtains opened, newspapers piled up on the porch. No car in the driveway this time. Halfway up the pathway the front door opened. Colleen Finney stood two yards away from me. We stared, both stunned to see the other. I realized the only reason I'd attempted a visit was because I felt sure no one would be home.

"Go home, Preston." Colleen planted herself on the porch.

"Colleen . . ." I didn't know what to say, hadn't planned any speech, heartfelt or otherwise. "I saw you. At Brendan's funeral," I said for lack of something better.

I adjusted to the twilight enough to see Colleen's face. The ashen pallor of her skin, deep lines around her mouth, eyes lifeless—she looked like a woman who'd seen her son buried. We'd never been what I'd call friends, but I felt pained my husband's mother saw me now as an enemy. The air between us popped with accusation.

"Colleen, I'm so sorry—"

"I knew Brendan wouldn't live through marrying you."

I couldn't respond. Guilt and shame sat on my tongue like rocks.

"What do you want, Preston? You took my son. I've nothing

left to give you."

"I don't want anything, Colleen. Not sure why I showed up here. Maybe because I felt sure you'd be gone. Guess I wanted to feel a connection to Brendan."

"You don't expect me to believe that."

"No, I don't, but I believe it. That's enough for me right now."

A taxi pulled into the empty driveway. Driver tapped the horn.

"Where are you going?" I said, not expecting an answer.

"Far from this place."

"What about Marv?" The house definitely looked unoccupied. "Is he going with you?"

"I've got to go." She stepped around me, then stopped. "Marriages often don't survive the death of a child. Or one with murderous intentions toward their own mother."

It took a few seconds for me to catch on she was referring to my parents' marriage as well as her own. "What are you talking about? You're leaving Marv? My parents are together and—" I started to say *fine* but I knew that was a lie. *Fine* hadn't described them in a long time.

Colleen opened the taxi door with me right behind her.

I don't know why I thought to do it right then but I pulled Cooper's monogrammed blanket out. "I found this in Brendan's apartment."

Colleen stopped, back straight, stiff.

"Do you know anything about this?"

Even in the dim glow from the taxi's headlights I saw Colleen's face go gray. "Yes."

She talked. I listened.

Chapter Sixty-Four

Isabel

"You're there. Thank God," Sherman said.

"It's you? Why are you calling me from a blocked number? I don't normally answer those." The hairs I had left on the back of my neck stood at attention. "Where'd you think I'd go? What do you mean, *thank God?*"

"Take it easy. I couldn't reach you, so I worried," Sherman said.

"Why a blocked number all of a sudden? Better give the number to me too."

"Why don't I give it to you in person?"

Sherman's tone turned flirtatious yet was salted with something else. Desperation?

"Someone tried to break into my apartment last night. I don't think it was the first time either. I got really scared. I needed you last night."

"Who'd want to hurt my tootsie-wootsie?" he said.

Normally, Sherman's baby talk made me want to kick him in the nuts, which he enjoyed, but not today.

"Time to get married."

I couldn't believe my ears. Finally.

"When?"

"Right away," he said. "Then we'll get a place in the safest neighborhood. Best money can buy. We can go today. Shop around for one big enough for a family."

I guess I assumed we'd move into his new townhouse, place

was huge and luxurious, but I'd go with getting something grander. Emboldened by Sherman's kindness, I said, "My mother died."

"You're kidding?" he said. "Your *mother*? Wait. Did I know you had a mother? Well, of course you did. Everyone does, or did, obviously. You know what I mean. Was she ill?"

"Not that I know of. No cause of death yet."

I wasn't sure which way this conversation might go. Of course, Sherman would feel annoyed I'd been less than forthcoming about my mother's existence—particularly the lottery-winning part. Why bother after she'd gone to great lengths to rub my face in my disinheritance. As we spoke, Mom's hillbilly husband, Dwayne, probably ran wild, snapping up satellite dishes, Corvettes, and KFC franchises as fast as he could yell, "Bingo." I'd bet on that.

"Her death made this morning's paper. Second page. The *Tribune*." I put a toe in.

"Must've missed that," he said.

"Mom and I weren't close."

Damn it. Should I have said that? Did not being close to my mother say something unsavory about me?

"I'll handle everything," he said.

Whew. Guess I said the right thing or the okay thing. I couldn't believe Sherman's capacity for sympathy. Sounded like he might cry.

"Investor calling. Sit tight. I'll pick you up in the morning. Rest up. You'll need it. If you know what I mean." Sherman's girlie giggle accompanied his hang up.

I talked to my unborn baby, "See? Daddy loves us. We're going to get married, just like I said."

Who'd want to hurt my tootsie-wootsie?

Weird Sherman would think someone wanted to hurt me. But maybe someone did. Jonathan? Much as he'd love to get rid of me, hard to see no-guts-no-glory Jonathan as the perp. But no one else would want me gone, would they?

I put that thought, along with my mother's death, somewhere in the far reaches of my mind. Busy assuring myself of Sherman's unbridled devotion, no telling how many times the phone rang before I noticed. Blocked number. Sherman.

"You're not canceling, are you?" I said.

"Hello? Is this Isabel Warner?" said someone who wasn't Sherman.

"Who is this?"

"Is this Ms. Warner?"

"If I say yes?"

"This is Ernest Shaw from Shaw, Smithson, and Price. I left my card in your door a couple of days ago. Thought that's why you called."

"Called? Not me."

"Someone called, a woman. Said she was you. Not even an hour ago."

"Never got a card. Never called. What the hell's going on?"

"I need to tell you—"

"Listen, you're not getting any more money out of me. I don't have it. Just write off whichever debt this is about. Trust me, it'll be much less trouble for you."

"Ma'am you misunderstand, I—"

"No, you misunderstand."

"Understand this." I hung up. I'd need to change my number again. After Sherman married me I could pay everything I owed. Could. But won't.

Chapter Sixty-Five

Preston

Head hammering with Colleen's reveal about the blanket, I'd raced through the front doors, catapulted up the stairs I'd successfully avoided, determined to see for myself what secrets the scene of the crime held in check. What Colleen told me couldn't possibly be true. Could it? How could she relay something so shocking while standing in the middle of a driveway next to an idling taxi? I felt electrified, nerve endings at the top of my skin, sharp as glass shards. Fear's force surrounded me. Fate pulled me onward.

I prodded the door open.

The cold, near-empty room embraced its prodigal daughter. I resisted. My race to its threshold caused a sweat. I stopped, clawed my wet neck. An invisible force impelled me. I put one foot in front of the other like a death-row inmate led to the gas chamber.

The floor underneath my shoes, in this room, felt different than anywhere else—soft, pliable, too much so, like it might give way and suck me under. Quicker than the flip of a switch, I saw the whole night. Details marched across my brain like a disciplined, determined army. Every accusation I'd slung at my mother dissolved. My perceptions of the past fizzled.

Colleen's words crackled inside my brain.

"That's not your brother's blanket. It's your baby's blanket, Preston. Yours and Brendan's Baby."

I kept going even though I felt like running out. The enormity of what I'd done, what happened, hit me hard, over and over like bullets. *This* kept me at Haven House. I'd been scared shitless of this place, this moment. I covered my ears to dull the crackling rumble.

When your world collapses it sounds like thunder.

****

I grabbed the crib to keep from reeling. I leaned over, smoothed the sheet still clinging to the small mattress with gentle fingers so as not to mar the invisible imprint of my son's tiny body, gone forever.

"What happened to your baby, Preston?" Smiley said from behind me. I didn't startle, ask how he got there, or why. I didn't care or feel surprised. I knew I needed to say my son's name out loud, tell his story. I'd been his mother, the only one who could. I slid to the floor, lied curled up on my side. Smiley followed me down and lay prone next to me. We stayed quiet for I don't know how long.

Every memory I'd kept at bay roared back to me.

"When Brendan left, he didn't know I was pregnant. I didn't want to have a baby alone. Or, at all," I finally said.

"But you *did* have a baby?"

"I *didn't* get an abortion—totally different thing. I only worried about how to keep the drugs coming, since my supplier husband bailed. I stayed pregnant because I didn't get off my ass to do anything about it. Didn't leave this house. When I thought about food instead of drugs, I had it delivered. Maid got groceries for a while, but I think I fired her. Don't know. All I know is she was gone."

"You didn't leave this house the whole time you were pregnant? No doctor?"

"Nope. A doctor would've turned me in, or at least bitched about my drug taking. Didn't want to deal with either."

I'd kept these demons contained so long, cemented inside. Now they'd gotten free. I could stay trampled down on the floor until the end of time.

"No one knew?"

"My mother showed up, let herself in. I didn't know she kept a key. We'd stopped talking by then. Mom knew, asked me how far along I was. I had no idea. Thought I looked same as always. She kept turning up. Finally, it occurred to me to get the locks changed."

"Then what?"

"I felt so sick that day. I'd ordered monogrammed blankets, of all the dumbass stoner things. CFB—embroidered in beautiful script—Cooper Finney Blair. Exactly what my mother had done for my brother—Cooper *Fitzgerald* Blair. Don't know why I assumed a boy or why I'd name him after my brother, who I barely remember, except the jealousy I felt. I remember I opened the door for the FedEx guy because I wanted those damn blankets."

"Did you give birth here, alone?"

"Eventually, yes. I couldn't get the fucking blanket box open after FedEx delivered. Too high, drunk. Between that and feeling like shit, couldn't tackle cardboard. Labor never occurred to me. Like a good junkie I concentrated on the box. I cut at it and cut at it, bit by little bit."

"You must've been terrified."

"Are you kidding? If only I'd had sense enough to feel even a little nervous. I might not, maybe I wouldn't have, oh, I don't know, I might've done everything differently. Maybe my son would've lived."

"How'd he die?"

I couldn't control my fact telling. After I'd squashed reality so long, the truth wouldn't be denied. Would it set me free? No, it'd run me over like a freight train, leave me for dead.

"Miraculous I stayed pregnant long as I did. Drugs killed him. Born dead. I used the cutter to cut the umbilical cord. Picked him up off the floor, the tiniest boy, still and silent." I sat up, barfed on my lap.

"Hang on, Preston." Smiley jumped up, brought toilet paper out of the adjoining bath, wiped my face and mouth. "Let me get towels from—"

Nothing felt more right than sitting in a pool of my own vomit, the sour vile stench radiated from my core. Smiley parked near my head, leaned against the crib. "What'd you do after he was born?"

"Born? Cooper wasn't *born*. He dropped out of my body."

"Okay, what then?"

"Funny, I can see the whole scene so well, like a YouTube video. I pulled my bloody pants back on, stuffed the box cutter in my front pocket. Because people with their load on think things like that are important."

"Go on."

"Tried to give him mouth to mouth, as if I knew how. I wrapped Cooper in one of the monogrammed blankets, finally out of the box. Laid him in the crib. Made a lame effort to clean up the birthing mess, smeared muck all over. I couldn't stand seeing him so small in this big crib, alone, so I held him, already cold, stiff." I looked around the nursery. "Rocked him in that rocker, held him close, rocked and rocked, so he wouldn't feel scared."

"How long?"

"All day, a couple days, who knows? My memory seems covered in gauze. I think I tried to bathe him. He stunk. Couldn't get rid of the stench. Finally, my mother railroaded me, then my father. She broke a window to get in. I heard the crash. The alarm shrieked. I thought Armageddon landed, probably what brought my father-in-law rushing over."

I stopped to get a breath to let my mouth catch up with my brain.

"The good chief handled our family personally," I said. "Never sent uniforms. Mom tried to get Cooper out of my arms. I didn't want her to take him away, so I pulled the box cutter out of my pocket. Standoff went on for what seemed like hours. Out of nowhere, my dad showed up, tried to intervene. Everybody knows what happened next."

"You must've sobered up. All those days shut in."

"Wrong. Stayed loaded the whole time. Every time I felt pain, I'd knock it back with a substance. Kept my drugs close always."

"The written confession?"

"Mine. Not intended as one. A page ripped from my journal. I grabbed it and Cooper's blanket when I got carted off. Only the journal made it to Haven House where it sat like a powder keg on my desk. I could've looked in it whenever I wanted but didn't. No idea who ripped the page out and sent the thing to my mother."

"What happened to Cooper's body?"

"I don't know. Knowing my parents, I'm sure they hoped I'd never remember. If I remembered I might want to talk about it. God forbid any fucking thing gets talked about in our family." All of a sudden Brendan's voice told stories in my head. "Brendan told me once he'd heard someone died that night."

"Certainly, his parents would've told him."

"No. Colleen told me Marv didn't tell her until after Brendan's death."

"She didn't know where Cooper's buried?"

"I didn't ask. I raced home."

"You could ask your father or your mother, couldn't you? Surely they're not that heartless."

Hearing Smiley refer to my father brought my nausea up again. Given his strange behavior, he was the last person I wanted to ask about anything.

"My mother might not remember it either."

"Want me to dig around? I'm sure I could find out."

"I don't know. Probably won't do any good. You won't find what my parents don't want you to find."

"Maybe. Maybe not."

Smiley let me cry unimpeded for a long while.

"This is as hard as it's gonna be, Preston. Now you can start again," he said when I took a breather.

"As you already know, some pain is always new. To be honest, when I entered this room tonight, I came back to where I've always been. I'll never get away from what happened here."

"Feels that way now, Preston. But later—"

"If I close my eyes, I swear I can hear him cry, even though he never did."

****

I don't know how it happened. One minute Smiley helped me into the tub to wash off. Next minute he carried me to a guest room. His smooth cool skin calmed mine. His mouth burned hot across my collarbone. The reasons why I should've stopped him dissolved when his hand on my back guided my hips toward his.

He entered me fast, hard, sure enough for the both of us. Of all the terrible mistakes I've made in my life, maybe this was yet another. My judgment only ever failed me. Didn't matter, I couldn't stop, *wouldn't* stop. We licked each other's wounds, filled our empty places. On a never-before-used mattress as a battlefield, Smiley's torment met mine on equal footing. Every sigh called out a ghost. Every shudder exorcised a demon.

The man lit me up from the inside out.

Chapter Sixty-Six

Preston

I thought Smiley would split before morning, but here he stood in my kitchen. I couldn't read him. His silver-specked hair adorably rumpled, his face creased from sleep, but still brutally handsome.

"You ok? How you doing this morning?" Smiley said.

"Good as I look."

My hair couldn't look worse if I'd limbo'd underneath a barbed-wire fence. My face felt chapped, swollen, sore from tissue rubbing. Exhausted by my crying and confessions, nevertheless I'd slept fitfully. Smiley kept his thoughts to himself, stood as close to me as possible without touching me. I could feel his uncertainty. It matched my own. Smiley poured the coffee I'd made, then we both settled in at the table, drank without talking for a few blessed minutes.

"Well, now what?" I sipped the hot dark roast. Wished for a stiff Jameson kicker and a Valium.

"I'll try to find out what happened to Cooper's body."

His simple sentence felt like a slap. "You'll arrest me then?"

"Christ, no. For what?" He covered my smaller hand with his bigger one. "Stillbirth isn't a crime, even with the drugs. Not in this state."

"I deserve punishment, don't I?"

"You're doing a bang-up job of that on your own."

"How'd you get past the guard last night?"

"I hired him. I get special privileges."

"Why'd you come?"

"My neighbor saw a crazy-looking blonde skulking around my yard."

Under other circumstances this discovery would've flattened me with embarrassment but today not so much. Smiley'd heard the worst.

"So, you don't know any other blonde, crazy ladies?"

"Not one who drives a Range Rover," Smiley said. "It's a neighborhood full of cops. They don't miss a trick. I got worried, so after some arguing with myself and losing, I drove over."

He reached over to ruffle my wreck of a hairdo.

"I'm pretty sure Colleen left Marv, or Marv left her," I said. "I went there right after skulking duty. She was on the way out the door when I stopped her. Their place looks like a mausoleum."

"Not surprising. Marv's view of Brendan was harsh. Colleen's more forgiving. Now that Brendan's gone I'd guess she couldn't bear his point of view."

"Maybe. But something's off."

"Like?"

"I don't know exactly. Why would she spirit away in the dead of night? You don't think that's odd? Plus, she knew about Cooper."

"Mothers usually know more than they let on."

"Exactly. I think she, no *they*, know more than they're telling."

"Cooper's death is a pretty bad thing to know, isn't it? Their grandson died under terrible circumstances. I mean, that's quite a painful secret for them to keep," he said.

I felt my face cave in on itself. I'd only thought about myself. Not my parents, or my husband's parents, who'd suffered in so many unbearable ways, or my husband who died in service to me.

"I'm sorry, Preston."

"Me too. There aren't even words to describe how much." I rubbed my sore eyes to keep from crying again. "So now what?" I said. "We're still nowhere."

"The investigation's like running a gauntlet. Before Marv cut out he made it clear he thinks Brendan's death was a drug deal gone bad. Which, as you know, was code for 'Leave it the hell alone' to the guys."

"He could be right about the drug deal. I hate to say but he could."

"Gang shootout at a club downtown. One of the dead is someone Marv said Brendan did business with—someone known for threats. Likely the guy killed him."

"How likely?"

"It's the most obvious choice."

"What's your choice?" I drained my cup.

"To keep looking."

I got up to pour more coffee.

"Jesus Christ," Smiley said. "There's a horse in your yard."

****

Smiley intended to leave. I intended to usher him out the door. We ended up in my bed instead. I woke up in darkness, alone. I'd spent countless days and nights alone in this room, this house, but recent events wore me down. Feeling frightened and abandoned, I pulled on my clothes and made a beeline for the kitchen.

"Hey sleepyhead," Smiley wore his trench coat, obviously ready to walk out the door. I interrupted him gathering his stuff off the messy, kitchen table. "I didn't want to wake you. God knows you need some sleep."

"You're leaving?" I hoped I didn't sound as desperate as I felt.

"There's still an investigation underway." His face turned the palest shade of rose. He shoved his cell into his inside coat pocket. "I got sidetracked. Now back to work."

"Why'd you tell me you had a wife?"

Smiley fumbled with the buttons on his coat. "Habit, more than anything. That and I couldn't stand to say I don't."

"I'm sorry. About what happened to her. I—"

"That all feels like a lifetime ago right about now."

Smiley put his arms around me. We stayed pressed together for several minutes.

"That picture of you and Cooper," he said. "Makes more sense now, what you thought."

"I was so fucked up. Obviously, my memory of that day got mixed up with what happened upstairs. It's why I felt so sure about

Mom and my brother. That I knew the *real story* about his death. I thought she'd written that confession, that we'd fought over it."

"You ever look through that journal? Might be something useful in there."

"No, but I've got it here somewhere."

Now I felt embarrassed he knew about my journal. How new agey could I be? Never mind *Musings from the Dented Throne.* I'd never told another living soul about my blog. I trusted Smiley. Hell, I was falling in love with him, but I wasn't ready to talk about "The Invisible Heiress." I fished around the pile of crap strewn across the table. Found it at the bottom, fanned out the pages.

"Someone stole this when I was at Haven House but returned it a few days later. Must've torn out pages. I never looked."

"Who would do that?"

"Someone with more nerve than brains."

"Doesn't narrow it down much."

"Think it's connected to what happened to Brendan?"

So many pieces didn't seem to fit.

"I don't know," Smiley said. "At first glance, it doesn't seem to be, but you never know." He started toward the entryway, stopped to kiss my forehead.

"Do you have a first name?" I said, thrilled he didn't ask to take my journal.

His laugh sounded a lot like a love song.

"Yes, It's Sean."

"I'll stick with Smiley."

"What's wrong with Sean?"

"Nothing. It's good. But Smiley's great. The happiest name in the world."

"If you put it that way."

He pulled me to him, one big hand cradling the back of my head in a way that felt protective with a tinge of sexy. I might've finally met the man who could declaw me.

"Thank you," I said.

"For what?"

"A memory that's not broken."

Chapter Sixty-Seven

Preston's Blog

Musings from the Dented Throne

To Be Honest, I'm a Liar

I don't think I've ever let so much time pass between posts. I needed time. Yes, I know a couple of months away from the blogosphere is a lifetime. Although I found that time does *not* heal all wounds but stretches and reshapes them into a well-fitted, permanent second skin. I remembered things about myself I can't possibly tell you because some things feel worse for the telling.

So what do I want to talk about? Other people, that's what. I've spun some unbelievable tales but none more than the following.

I'd mentioned to New Detective that an unknown, pilfering sod stole my journal during my confinement. He got the why-didn't-I-think-of-it idea to check the cameras sure to be in the entrance of the psych ward. Turns out there were cameras, but they tape over all footage every thirty days.

Welcome to my big, fat, dead end. But it gets more promising.

Remember I told you about Shrinky's appearances in my hood? Well, I told New Detective, who took a leisurely stroll through her financials. Large cash deposits appear in Shrinky's account, source unconfirmed. Could be she got it from her lottery winning but now deceased mother. But from what she'd told me about the woman (yes, Shrinky unloaded on me about her stingy mama) that didn't seem likely. Until proven otherwise the deposits are above board. New Dick's interviews with deranged harpy also turned up zero. Shrinky's a smooth operator.

I leveled with New Detective about the Chica's liaisons with both the Jester and the Irishman and her appearance with the Queen at the plantation. If he disapproved of my jaunts down the hidden path, he never let on, and for now, I've stopped.

My handsome detective finally ran down the Chica, who coincidentally got hauled in for questioning that mostly went nowhere. The sultry siren admitted my husband had reentered the drug trade with no help from her. So far, no one's proved otherwise. The Chica says she looked in on the Queen from time to time at the request of her mother, the Queen's former right-hand woman.

The Queen, the Jester, and Chica's mother confirm.

All parties deny any funny business between Chica and the Jester, or for that matter, Chica and the Irishman.

What the devil is going on?

I'm sure the Jester and the Chica still cavort undetected by the Queen. Sadly, bad taste in women is not a crime. Nor is cheating on your wife.

One final stunner: The Irishman might've bugged (quite the Renaissance man, my husband) Shrinky's downtown office. No one, including the Heiress, can figure why, but I'm certain his reasons would withstand any scrutiny. No one knows for sure who killed my poor husband or why. The likelihood that drug selling took his life looks more and more convincing, which would explain the wad of cash I found in his freezer. Did I mention that? Well, no matter.

But the beat goes on.

The Jester's become more of a pest. He's called, left rambling weepy messages, emailed, texted. Begs to see me. I finally stopped paying attention to them. I refuse to acknowledge his efforts. My feelings for my father are complicated. While I don't necessarily blame him for stepping out on the Queen, I'm still pissed. When I think of his bizarre, hostile exchange with New Detective at the graveside and his smarmy run at my money, my hackles rise. Before I forget—New Dick is *not* currently wed. He lied to disguise his heartbreak, which I get. The handsome, sad detective crushes on the Heiress, which I don't get. How could a man of such caliber see good in a girl like me?

I recognize New Detective as a man, fully formed. Not a boy, like the Irishman, who taught me a lot about love but not the Sunday kind. In my handsome detective's arms, the world feels like an extraordinary place. Like the acrobat who danced between the Twin Towers on a tightrope, he illuminates an otherwise ordinary space—then leaves an emptiness that won't quite recover from his absence.

The Invisible Heiress

P.S. I love my new dog. Thank you to whoever you are. The giver is yet one more mystery in my ever-mysterious life.

Not sure I want to know what you think, but let 'er rip.

Comments
Maggie May

So much has happened. Like you, I don't know what to think. Shrinky's in the mix now? The Irishman went on some covert operation with listening devices? Makes no sense at all. However, I'm thrilled for you and New Dick. A man like him couldn't love you if you're so bad. So you must be good inside. I know you love the Queen.

Reply: No motive for killing meaner than love.

4 Christ R Lord

Your sins will find you out. Your husband barely dead, and you're defiling the marital bed already?

Reply: My sins saw me coming a long time ago. Defiling is the least of my problems.

Well Hung Jung

Just so you know, I like dogs. I think you need a spanking for letting New Dick in where I called dibs. Maybe Dick sent you the dog. Could be a whole kinky kind of dog-spank-the-monkey situation.

Reply: Why didn't I think of that? You're too smart for me, WHJ. If I'm ever in the market for a good paddling, you'll be the first to know, although I gave the dog your collar. You and I are *simpatico*.

Well Hung Jung

Didn't you once say Dick's old enough to be your father?

Reply: And you thought I only had mommy issues.

Amy W.

Maybe the Irishman's ways did catch up with him. It could be as simple as that. Is it possible Shrinky was involved in drugs? Sometimes the most obvious choice is the right one. Weird, he'd have anything to do with her office. Odd their paths would cross.

Reply: Odd is right. Hmmm. Now you've got me thinking. And remembering.

Norma B.

I've got a crazy idea. Why don't you ask the Queen about the Chica? Or Jester? He acts like he's dying to talk. Let him. See for yourself what's what. You're avoiding the inevitable.

Reply: As always you are wise, Norma. I believe I'll take another stroll down Beverley Lane.

Part III

Beverley

Chapter Sixty-Eight

Preston

Just like old times I scrambled up the wall of Beverley using an ancient trellis for a foothold. Up, over my old balcony, I got in. No one fixed, or knew about, the broken latch on my bedroom window, as I suspected.

I maneuvered around my old bedroom, which offered a vignette of time stood still. Dark wood floors covered with hip yet classic hand-woven rugs, which complemented the top-of-the-line furnishings, fixtures, and deceptively casual artwork worth more than a lot of people's houses. My mother had exasperated me with luxury at every turn. No wonder I couldn't stand her.

I tiptoed through the children's wing of Beverley to the grand stairway landing. The bottom floor, as far as I could tell, stood empty. I crawled toward the top stair. The centuries-old house moaned like a bored hooker. Voices stopped me.

I recognized my mother's but not the man she was talking to. Man? What man?

I listened, for what seemed like hours, to Mother go on and on about the history of Beverley. Maybe *Architectural Digest* was finally getting its story about the plantation. The editor had asked before. Mother always said no.

Her roughed-up voice sounded like it always should've— lush, hidden, loaded with secrets. Hearing her here, in my childhood home, made me wish I were brave enough to really see her.

I think I'd started to nod off a little when I heard this gem.

"I knew what sort Todd was when we married. Yet his betrayal slapped me straight on," my mother said.

That sat me straight.

"Betrayal? You mean the power of attorney?" the man said.

I almost fell over. Luckily, I caught myself before that could happen, which would've ruined my whole mission.

Who was this guy?

"No, that power of attorney has existed for years," Mother said. "Money's mine, but if I were ever incapacitated, bills would need to be paid. At the time, like everyone, I never thought Todd would need it. At any rate, the power of attorney was *limited*, not unlimited. Only to take care of both our living expenses, the house upkeep and any medical bills. But he went beyond that."

I inched, still on all fours, close as I could to the stairs without tumbling down them. I realized they both spoke louder than normal. I shouldn't have been able to hear them as well as I did from my vantage point.

Mother went on, "For the first time in our married life, Todd felt like a man. Got to call the shots. While I lay comatose, he got brave. First, the inch, then the mile. Preston almost killing me was the best thing that ever happened to Todd. Carte blanche with the checkbook."

Preston almost killing me—hearing that from her felt like a gut shot. Why in hellfire was my mother suddenly a spewing fountain of information? She'd undergone a personality transplant of some sort. Mystery Man mumbled something, which refocused my attention.

"My setback really gave him courage. All the drugs I'd started taking for everything from pain to anxiety to depression zonked me, plus he convinced Alicia's daughter, Marcella, the ethically challenged nurse, to up the dosages and thought I didn't know. Too bad for Todd that even drugged my wits are more intact than his. Plus, I quit taking them, unbeknownst to him." Her laugh sounded like midnight and cigarettes. "He carried on like I was still comatose. You'd be surprised what people will do in front of you when they think you're blind."

I knew she'd faked it.

"Like?" Mystery Man prodded.

"Like paying for a new wing at Haven House and selling my sister James's estate," Mom continued. "When I found out he'd sold my sister's house I figured he was trying to get up the nerve to leave me, use the proceeds as startup funds for his new life."

"Ah. Tricky," Mystery Man said.

"No. Purposely dumb. Todd's an experienced attorney. He knows the difference between limited and unlimited. But no one questioned him. Not to mention, he might've forged the document he needed. A lot of people in this town would do his bidding without a blink."

She stopped talking. I thought for a second she'd quit all together until she said, "So he did as he pleased. I'm sure he thought I'd die and he'd never need to pay the piper. He opened a separate account with proceeds from the sale, plus some cash he pilfered from our joint account, which always has a lot of money in it. He didn't need any power of attorney to move money from there."

"You'd said the bulk of the Blair fortune goes to the boys and skips the girls. There're no boys. So, if you'd died, wouldn't Preston get everything?"

"Right. But Preston wasn't sober or responsible in any way. Todd could manipulate and take advantage of her no end. Or so he figured. She'd have been a lot easier to bamboozle than me. I'm sure he figured she'd go right back to her old ways."

I latched on to the top stair's edge to stop myself from falling over. Brendan had been right. Dad sold James's house for pocket money.

"So I divorced him," Mother said.

Nearly convulsed with shock by that humdinger, I decided to go for broke. Took off my shoes, crept down the stairs. I felt a dire need to see what I couldn't believe I heard. The drawing room beckoned me forward. I hugged the baseboard like a seasoned burglar. A giant, antique mirror still hung over the hearth, which allowed for all-points access from my vantage point. I used to sneak downstairs in my jammies to spy on my parents' parties using the mirror's reflection.

Like everything else under Beverley's roof, Mother's beauty remained reliable. She held court like always, from a damask-covered chaise, faced in the direction of a camera.

A *camera*?

What dimension did I enter? Did my mother consent to do an interview on film? She really wasn't the same since—hell's bells. That's why they sounded so clear, for the microphone. As if all that TMI wasn't enough to make Jesus weep, she said, "Todd never could keep his pecker stowed."

First divorce. Now pecker. Death by a thousand cuts.

I reminded myself to breathe.

Mom droned on about the many grievances visited on her by Dad's pecker, freed from stowing, while I tried to block her out and wondered who, in the name of Martin Scorsese, was the young, broad-shouldered guy behind the camera? Information, like fire ants, crawled hot all over my brain. Harrison Blair and Todd Fitzgerald divorced? When? How did that dish not hit the news?

As if the camera guy and I were on the same wavelength he said, "Preston doesn't know about the divorce?"

"I don't think so, she hasn't mentioned it. It's recently finalized but private," Mom said. "We do that in the South. We're discreet when it comes to those things, if at all possible."

Wait. What? *She hasn't mentioned it?* When would she have heard me mention it or *anything at all*?

"There's a lot Preston doesn't know," Mom said.

"Like?" Camera guy said again.

My ears felt like they actually flapped. The silence expanded, heavy as a grudge. Camera guy fidgeted in his silk-covered, club chair.

"I don't think she knows about Todd's girlfriend," Mom said. "Or that they used Preston's house as some kind of lair."

I almost yelled "What?" out loud. Wasn't Dad the sly fox and a smooth half-truth teller? Marcella, the slutty Spaniard, *did* use my house, with my father, of all the—.

"I found out about her and James's house sale all in the same week. I'd planned to confront Todd, throw him out. Stormed to the DA's office. By dumb luck, I didn't get the chance."

Rosie and I'd seen her on TV that day. The disheveled Lilly Pulitzer, the horrible look on her face. I could tell something *else* bad happened. No way could Dad flip Aunt James's manse, or cavort with a sizzling senorita in my house and Beverley, with Mom none the wiser.

"So, I came home," Mom said. "Thought over my options."

"If you've already divorced him, what options are left?"

Mom draped a Givenchy'd arm across the back of the settee.

"Oh, there're lots. For one, I'm suing him for fraud or threatened to. I don't think I'll have to go that far. He'll see the error of his ways pretty quick. His power of attorney was limited, not an ATM machine. The snake enriched himself. A real legal faux pas, if you will. Todd forgets I know my way around the law too. But even so, that's easy, run of the mill."

"So what else?" younger-than-me camera guy said.

"Nothing."

"Huh? Nothing?"

Her expression ignited the mirror, ferocious enough to crack a crab. "Todd wants a new life with his young girlfriend. Let him have it. He can have that and everything else that's going to come with it."

Chapter Sixty-Nine

Isabel

"Guess your new husband and *that*," Jonathan pointed at my burgeoning belly, "takes all your time. You haven't put in an appearance here at the office in weeks and weeks. Not that I've missed you. Although I have to say I'm surprised you never brought the poor bastard by. Show off your new toy."

"Well, it's been a whirlwind. Aren't you delighted to be on a need-to-know basis?"

"*Delighted* doesn't come close." Jonathan doodled on his ever-present pad for several moments. I'd about decided to walk out of his office when he said, "By the way, I've replaced you."

"With who?" I hadn't worked since who knew when. Didn't plan to work again. But I didn't like the sound of *replaced*.

"Not that you should care but with an ethical, experienced gentleman from Atlanta, who isn't a felon."

"'Sounds like a dullard."

"He starts next week. Can you get your stuff out?"

"Jesus. You jump in my grave that fast?"

"No point dragging things out. Let's both start fresh," Jonathan said from the catbird seat.

"Depends how you define fresh."

"Haven't read a thing about your pals, the Blair Fitzgeralds, or their dead son-in-law in ages. Guess that's settled?"

"Far as I know. Last I heard one of Brendan Finney's stoner pals did the deed. They found some nurse chick that backs up the story. Something about her gangland cousin. I put the whole clan behind me, right along with that wiseacre detective who got all up in my face about following Preston. Twit saw me, I guess. I denied it, of course. No law against tailgating is what I told him. That seemed forever ago.

"Guess that's it then," Jonathan said.

"Far as I'm concerned the whole incident never happened."

I sashayed (or so I imagined) toward Jonathan's office door. "Gotta fly. I'll send someone to get my things." I had *someones* now.

"Yes, well, you look good, considering you're obviously about to pop. Get a makeover?" Jonathan's confidence that I'd matrimonied myself right out of his life made him magnanimous.

"Backhanded compliments get you nowhere."

Jonathan leaned back in his chair. "For a minute there I forgot you and that kid aren't my problem." Asshat stood, held a hand out to shake on it. "Good luck to you. Your new husband can finance you now."

"Yeah, well, about that."

****

"If you think you can blackmail me forever, you've got another thing coming, you leeching bitch."

Jonathan's parting words, like the wind beneath my wings, ushered me out the door to my waiting sedan. I hoped he heard me snickering at his empty threats. As scared as the nutless wonder was of me—the wife got him shaking in his Tevas like nobody's business. Sure, I didn't need the money anymore, but not everything's about need, is it? It's about winning. I'd celebrate my continued winner's streak with a quick run at the roulette wheel.

Sherman isn't a fan of my visits to the club. Not like I'm angling for a man since I bagged the elusive *perfect catch*. What else could I want? I'll tell you what—a quick now-I-can-afford-to-lose-here-and-there friendly game of poker.

I've given up drinking for the baby.

The thudding beats of "Another One Bites the Dust" boomed out of my purse. My new ringtone. Took one hand off the wheel to grope for my cell. Unknown number. Shit. When I got married, I got a new number, new phone. The calls stopped until this second. Creditors can find you. I'd changed my number plenty over the years, and still they find me. Bloodhounds.

I'd hoped to temporarily flummox Visa, American Express, and every other place with my name change after I married Sherman. But still they homed in. Or maybe whoever called wasn't a creditor. Maybe someone wanted to sell me something because I'd just married rich. Couldn't get *that* lucky. At any rate, no way I'd waste money paying creditors, but I didn't want my new husband to know all my secrets. I let whatever scumbag collector it was go to voicemail. Speak to the hand, jackwad.

Chapter Seventy

Preston

I'd slept late, past noon, a fitful mercifully dreamless sleep, troubled and unmoored, by what I'd heard and witnessed at Beverley. I could conjure no reasonable explanation for the boyish cameraman who appeared to commit Mother's every utterance to film. I got stuck on her *she hasn't mentioned it* comment. As if we spoke on a regular basis.

I wandered my house with no direction, Walter White at my heels, whining, nosing my legs. When I passed the staircase to my baby's room I felt a burn spread through my lungs like a bird on fire unfurled its wings inside my chest. I wondered if I'd ever get used to knowing about my son.

I could call Smiley, but I didn't feel like telling him yet that I'd broken into Beverley again or what I'd overheard. I'd take a breather first. The library seemed as good a place as any to look for something to do. Maybe read, or look through my mail, consider next steps. Like a shark, I'd need to keep moving to live.

The maid, vexed I'm sure, finally moved the contents of the drawer I'd dumped from Aunt James's desk on the floor, back to its top, where it's sat for eons. In my susceptible, depressed state, my eyes welled, knowing her desk was all the Blairs had left of James. I didn't need to know my aunt to feel melancholy about her fate or how her last act of desperation changed the direction of my mother's life. I nuzzled Walter, wallowed a few minutes, then dove back into my intended chore.

I'd been so proud of how I'd organized my bills, paid them

on time, created a spreadsheet of expenses, like a real grown-up. James's desktop looked a fright. Now it was a mess—a sticky note, piles of paper, disaster. Time to shake off the darkness that plagued me and get it together.

Brendan's case was closed but not to anyone's satisfaction. Both Smiley and I felt we'd missed a crucial clue. I picked through the pile determined to reorganize, throw out some crap, get back on track, curtail my confusion with busy work.

Walter stood watch next to the desk chair as I scavenged through endless notes, postage stamps, pizza delivery menus and old invoices until I landed on a heavy ecru envelope, the sort used for wedding invitations or birth announcements. Before I could turn it over to read the front, something else caught my eye.

Video stills.

The same ones Smiley'd brought for me to examine months before. "Give these a good once over. Call me if anything jumps out at you," he'd said. I'd gotten sidetracked with the whose-its and the whatnots or fuck knows. I shuffled through the ones I'd already seen—Shrinky's office, then the one with Brendan's car blitzing past the pink neon sign on the freak club. Same ole.

Then one I didn't recall seeing before. An interior shot of what I surmised was the casino portion of the fetish club. Slot machines, gaming tables, gamblers, then something jumped out at me.

I shoved what was left of the pile back into the drawer to make room for the spread of shots. I feasted my eyes on the lone woman wedged between several men, seated, with a few stacks of chips in front of her. I'd recognize that self-inflicted haircut anywhere.

"What do you know, Walter White?" I said. "Shrinky got her game on."

****

"Brought a few straggler stills caught on various security cameras from the surrounding area." Smiley held out a manila envelope. "Soon as you called I scoured the evidence room, every drawer and cabinet in the precinct. Found this in a random desk, loose, not bagged, no tag, zippo. Looked like trash, a miracle it didn't get thrown out."

"What's the deal with that?"

We trudged through the entry to the library and our now homey spot at James's desk. Walter White circled Smiley's legs, stubbed tail wagging as much as a stub could. Smiley ruffled his ears, pulled another chair up to the desk with Walter at his feet.

"I guess whatever lazy cop stored these photos figured no one would care about their existence because Marv pretty much cut the investigation off then left town."

"Wait'll you see the doozy I found." I fetched the pic of Shrinky at the poker table.

He studied a few seconds. "Well, still weak. If Brendan was sitting next to her, or even standing out front, we'd have a little something to go on. Just driving by the place is too thin."

"Still. Doesn't make any sense—Shrinky at the same place as Brendan? They're not exactly from the same circle." I remembered a comment made by one of the Heiress's followers. "Maybe she bought drugs from him."

"Do you know if she uses drugs?

"No. But she acts like she could."

"That's a thought," Smiley said. "But it's not evidence."

"What about Marcella's eeny, meeny, miny, moeing between my husband and father? That can't be a coincidence either. What if my father found out about Brendan and Marcella then decided to off the younger competition?"

"That's the first thing I looked at," Smiley said. "I do know how to work a case."

"And?"

"Your father denies any liaison between him and Marcella. We've got no solid proof otherwise."

Right then I blabbed what I'd heard at Beverley.

"I'll talk to Harrison," he said. "I'll just say I'd heard a rumor about Marcella and Todd. I won't mention anything else you heard. Sounds like she's got all that covered anyway. That'll keep you out of it for now. I can't promise I can do that forever, depending on what I find out."

"Deal."

"It's probably as simple as it looks," I said. "Brendan drove by a club in the same neighborhood he dealt drugs, Shrinky's a lowlife who hung out in the same neighborhood. Camera caught Brendan driving around. End of story."

"I'm not convinced of that," Smiley said for both of us. "Possible? Yes. All we've got now are threads. But enough threads make a blanket. So, I'll keep looking."

"Even though I act like an ungrateful brat, I appreciate what you're trying to do for me. Working a closed case must involve all kinds of rule breaking."

I could still feel the kiss on my mouth from his greeting.

He smiled, a small simple thing. But I saw a more complicated story in his eyes.

"I'm breaking all sorts of rules with you, Preston."

"I know," I said in a small voice.

"But I stopped caring about the rules after Corey."

Smiley rearranged his features, smile gone, handed me the photos he'd carried in that I'd already forgotten about. He let me peruse in peace a few moments. I didn't comment on his daughter. I'd done that once and still felt horrible about it.

"What's this?" I said looking through the pics.

"What?" Smiley leaned in to see.

My pulse hammered in my neck. Shrinky malingered at the curb, pink neon sign on the club exterior bright behind her. A closeup of a man stepping out of what looked like a car with one arm extended, as if she might grasp his outstretched hand to hoist him the rest of the way out. Before I could form a thought, Smiley held out a second photo of the two locked in an embrace still at the curb.

Chapter Seventy-One

Isabel

"How's the unpacking going?" Sherman's voice blared through my car speakers. Fancy ride came with Bluetooth.

"It's not. I'm not at the house yet. The movers got the last of everything. What there was of it. Our stuff is in."

"Good, good," Sherman said.

"Just called to see how things are going on your end," I said, suspicious as always that he was doing something I wouldn't like. "Am I interrupting something? You sound weird. I don't know—preoccupied? You're cutting in and out."

Our marriage hadn't improved Sherman's phone etiquette. It still took umpteen messages to get a call back.

"Actually, I'm in the middle of something," he said. "Why don't you go to the house, get settled. I'll meet you there later."

"Pulling into the drive as we speak."

He'd hung up already.

I'd been worried our new house wouldn't be finished before the baby was born. But we made it with a few weeks to spare. I couldn't gripe about the new place, all things considered, but it's grandeur disappointed. A newish, planned community, filled with McMansions. Not the historical neighborhood I wanted. I'd hoped for a well-established community with Tudor or Neoclassical homes, a high-priced old money kind of place. Not this nouveau riche, cookie-cutter place. I planned to upgrade sooner rather than later. I'd already saved a few available estates, more to my liking, on realtor.com.

I let myself in with my new shiny key. "Hello?"

I knew no one was home but wanted to hear my voice echo through ten thousand square feet of emptiness. I padded room to room, puffy feet and cankles swelled over my new Chanel ballet flats. Much to my fiancé's dismay, I got rid of all our old crap stuff to get new. Sherman had never really furnished his place so not much to chuck.

I brought the couture clothing I'd recently purchased (in my prepregnancy size) plus the maternity wardrobe I'd ordered from one of those exclusive boutiques for celebrity A-list mommies to be. New, glossy hair extensions attached by *the* hot in-demand stylist, facial, discreet Botox, and Juvéderm injections, complete with mani/pedi, compliments of the aesthetician du jour.

I aimed for the only room in the house with a chair. Even though I'd vetoed any existing furniture, Sherman brought in his fey, precious desk with its Tiffany lamp. I sank down into his plush, desk chair—the buttery leather hugged my now substantial ass. I hadn't even put down my new YSL bag, since there wasn't anything to set it down on until I sat behind the desk. File folders, newspapers, cartons halfway unpacked, contents spilled over, balled-up trash scattered around the high-shine hardwood floor.

I looked over my elite surroundings, felt a twinge that my mother didn't live to see me finally living the life I felt owed. I missed the old bag. One of these days, I'd try to track down her white-trash husband, Dwayne, who'd taken the money and run, just to fuck with him. Make him think I'd fight him for the winnings. Nostalgic, I swung my bloated legs up to prop my swollen feet up on the desk, knocked my purse to the ground.

With a grunt, I plucked my wallet, makeup bag, and pen out of the rubble, kicked Sherman's crap that already littered the floor, out of the way, before I dumped my purse contents on it. Underneath my travel-size pack of Kleenex I picked up a business card. I held the small rectangle aloft to better see it.

Shaw, Smithson, and Price stared back at me from the center of the card in black, bold, masculine print. The name Ernest Shaw decorated the bottom left.

Why did Ernest Shaw sound familiar? My unborn baby kicked me square in the ribs as if to jog my memory. I racked my hormone-soaked brain. Shaw . . . Shaw . . . Ernest Shaw. I'd heard that name recently. I knew I had. Wait. Was he the guy who called sniffing around for money? Yes, that's what he'd said his name was. I felt confident.

What else did he say? I couldn't remember, but he'd said something else. I looked closer at the card—attorneys at law. I'd assumed Shaw called on behalf of a department store or bank—a creditor of some kind. Did attorneys make collection calls? Maybe. I'd expended a lot of energy avoiding creditors most of my adult life but knew little about them or their process.

Where'd the business card come from? If I remembered right, he'd said something about leaving his card in the front door of my apartment. Had I put it in my purse? No, I didn't think so. I must've. How else could it have fallen out of my bag?

Unless Shaw's calling card didn't fall out of anything that belonged to me. If the card hadn't been lying dormant on the bottom of my purse, where'd it been? Already here, that's where, on the floor with the rest of Sherman's stuff.

Chapter Seventy-Two

Preston

"I'm going to take these photos to our photo analyst. He'll clean them up, enlarge them," Smiley said. "Maybe we can salvage a little something."

"Wish we could see from the front, at least more of the car. It's almost blacked out completely. Hard to identify someone from their back, especially in the shadows." I squinted to focus. It didn't help. "How convenient that whoever this guy is, he almost disappears in the darkness." I pointed to the murky man in Shrinky's arms.

Smiley sorted through more photos. "Here's another one."

"Well, it's closer but still from behind and dark."

"Never know what we'll see after my guy does his mumbo jumbo."

Both of us jumped at the sound of Smiley's ringing cell. He made listening sounds while I further examined the pictures. Soon he held his phone between his ear and shoulder to write on his pad.

"That was interesting, unbelievable actually." He jabbed the phone off.

"What?"

"When I talked to Isabel's partner at his office, I noticed they had a reception desk but no receptionist. The partner, Jonathan, said he'd fired her. As far as he knew she left town but gave me her name and number."

"Why would you want to talk to her?"

"Routine. Gotta talk to everybody. I couldn't reach her. Thought she really had left town—which she had—but only for a few weeks."

"And?"

"That was the missing receptionist, Rhonda Hopkins. Jonathan fired her for stealing from petty cash, only she says she didn't do it."

"They always say they didn't do it."

"She said she thought Isabel stole it."

"Why would Isabel need to steal petty cash?"

"Rhonda says because Isabel is a . . ." he referred to his notes, "a certifiable psychotic."

"I could've told you that."

"She spent time in a psych hospital out of state."

"Of course, she did. My father can really pick a therapist."

"Your father picked her? She wasn't assigned to you?"

"Nope. The chick they assigned to me couldn't handle me. So they brought in Shrinky. Takes one to know one, I guess."

"Well, Rhonda had quite a bit to say about her."

"The receptionist always knows everything."

"She says Isabel and Jonathan were lovers." Smiley kept reading. "Last year he broke it off, so she put a bomb in an office trash can. Set the place on fire."

Chapter Seventy-Three

Isabel

I spent the next half hour nosing through the sea of cartons that Sherman had left dispersed over his office floor. Found nothing of great interest—spreadsheets, graphs, calendars, files of junk, normal office paraphernalia. Who kept a paper calendar anymore? A copy of his divorce papers gave me pause but no surprises there. I'd even uncrumpled all the wads of paper he'd rained down everywhere, spread them out one by one for close scrutiny. I wasn't sure exactly what I thought I'd find. So far, Sherman was the definition of tedious, as I'd expect.

What about that business card from Ernest Shaw though?

Maybe I did, indeed, cram that little thing in my purse during some kind of hallucinogenic seizure. Other than me barking orders, I didn't remember Ernest Shaw's conversation. I think, yes, I think he said I'd called him back once. Is that what he'd said?

Nothing stopped me from calling Ernest Shaw now to find out. I searched for my cell on my knees, belly hanging, to find where it'd landed. A thought interrupted my rescue. What if my mom left a shit heap of debts? Maybe he called to see if he could squeeze me for payment. I knew I probably couldn't be held responsible, but who needed the aggravation? How would I know until I called?

Wait.

Even my loopy mother couldn't blow through more than three hundred million dollars. But knowing her she could've gotten into some pissing match with an old crone at bingo.

Territorial about her troll dolls, bingo cards, and taped-to-the-table trash bag, maybe she assaulted some granny on Social Security who saw her as a meal ticket.

Maybe they couldn't find Dwayne.

Only one way to find out what Shaw wanted. Call.

I pulled my phone from under the desk, my jiggly arm barely long enough to reach, pitched myself back into the chair. Poked out the first couple of numbers I read on the card, then stopped. Why worry about mundane bullshit now anyway, especially someone else's bullshit? I tore the business card into little pieces, sprinkled them like confetti into my purse.

So immersed on the floor of meaningless treasures, I'd forgotten about the desk drawers. What a moron. I yanked them open on both sides—one empty, one with a small, leather-bound notepad. Like the ones the police carried who came to my house to tell me my mother had died. I set it aside, gave the last center drawer a healthy tug. Didn't budge. Tried again, this time put all my weight behind the effort. Almost jerked the hardware off, the stubborn thing still didn't open.

Then I noticed the tiny keyhole. Shit. Locked.

I opened the notepad instead.

Chapter Seventy-Four

Preston

"Well, Isabel's in the wind," Smiley said.

I held my cell between my chin and collarbone to feed Walter White from his two-ton bag of dog food. "Already?"

"She vacated her apartment, no forwarding address, according to the landlord who's primo pissed because she owes him back rent and left the place a mess."

"Did you ask what's-his-name? The partner?"

"Um, yes," Smiley said, a teensy bit impatient with my assumption he'd need a reminder. "He says she left to get married, of all the crazy things. No idea where she'd gone or if she'd come back."

"Why didn't he report her when she tried to blow him to smithereens?"

"He denies any of that happened. No affair, no bomb. Just a freak accident."

"What? Really?" Walter's chomping got on my nerves, so I left him to his dinner, sat at Aunt James's desk.

"Fire chief said the fire definitely started because of a homemade explosive device. Not a very-well-made one either. Amateur. Said Jonathan stayed tightlipped about the whole thing then too."

I had no idea where Smiley was calling from, but I imagined him at home in his sad, empty, living room. He didn't seem like an office kind of guy. I couldn't envision him traipsing through a precinct full of cops. He seemed above all that, above everyone, a man who worked alone.

"My mumbo-jumbo guy wasn't able to do as much with those blurred photos as I'd hoped either," Smiley said. "But I'll drop them by anyway. Maybe something will stand out to you."

"Crap. Okay."

"Showed Isabel and Brendan's photos around at the casino. A couple of dealers and a waitress recognized Isabel but other than that nothing. They all said she came alone, gambled and drank alone. Brendan's face didn't ring a bell with anyone and he never showed up on any security camera inside."

"I don't know why that makes me feel better. None of my business what Brendan did at that point. We can't still be nowhere, can we?"

"I'd say we're somewhere," Smiley said. "The Asphyxia manager got a lot more cooperative. He—"

"Asphyxia?"

"The fetish club."

"Naturally," I said.

"Anyway, the manager gave me the member list."

"Look at you, on the downlow. You're super detective."

Smiley laughed. "There're no fetish club client confidentiality laws. The owner handed it right over, didn't want us to get a search warrant or subpoena, which would shut him down for days."

"Any names look familiar? Like Isabel's?"

"Most don't use their real names. The club owner couldn't care less who they are as long as they pay in advance. The list is pretty much a tally of run-of-the-mill, freaky, sex names."

That cracked me up. "Are there run-of-the-mill, freaky, sex names?"

"Yes, actually," he said. "Marquis de Sade, yeah that's original. Here's Heidi Fleiss, Monica Lewinsky. Of course, Bill Clinton, Eliot Spitzer."

"Brother. I guess originality got spanked out of them."

"Here's a standout."

"What?"

"I don't think General William T. Sherman was known for his kinky side."

I laughed. Might as well.

"No telling then if Brendan ever actually went inside the club," I said.

"I doubt if he did. But someone else interesting did, on the security camera in the casino, plain as day."

"Who?

"Judge Seward. Right next to Isabel."

I almost toppled over onto the desk. "No way. My parents' Judge Seward?"

"That's the one."

Chapter Seventy-Five

Preston's Blog

Musings from the Dented Throne

I'll Have the Bonkers with a Side of Get the Fuck Out

As you can see, my followers, I titled this post with my usual joie de vivre but find I can't continue in that vein. Fact is, I'm mighty low on joie and pretty much out of de vivre.

My chief of police father-in-law killed himself.

Yes. You read that right.

How can it be that both my Irishman and his father are gone quick as a whisper in the dark? My late husband once said to me, in a pique of frustration, "My father would hate me if he could."

I think my Irishman got his dad so wrong. I believe the man couldn't continue to live in a son-less and wife-less world. While he and I weren't close (that's an understatement), I feel a deep pang at the thought of his despair. I'm no stranger to anguish.

What of my own father?

I've gone back and forth between love and hate in light of Dad's obvious grief over my predicament and failed relationship with Mother, his inability to keep the little Jester sheathed, his embezzlement, and their subsequent secret divorce (yes, it's true. I know. I can scarcely believe it myself). Then there's his fixation on my trust fund. But I know now that it's possible to love someone and cut them from your life. Even if I could forgive my father his many sins, and I don't think I've even scratched the surface of what those sins are, I can't forget.

I should talk, right? I've committed plenty of unforgivable sins.

You see my dilemma.

I want to throw stones but can't take the high ground.

I guess melancholy made me listen again to all the voicemails my father left the past weeks while I, in a passive-aggressive offensive, punished him with my silence. He never mentioned the divorce in any message, but I assume he'd want to tell me that in person.

One alerted me he'd changed his phone number. Made sense because he'd retired from the DA position. I called the new number several times over several days to ask if he'd left the Queen for Chica but went straight to voicemail every time. In light of his best friend's death, you'd think he'd keep his head aboveground.

What's up with him do you suppose?

By now, you're used to me saving the best, most shocking, for last. Try these bits.

Evidence points to Shrinky killing the Irishman.

Read that again.

Shrinky's a bomber, done it before. Pictorial evidence puts Shrinky, my late husband, and a third shockingly familiar face, at the same place. But in the Irishman's case, not the same time, at the kink club where Shrinky cavorts alongside someone completely out of her league. Who? Here come da judge is all I'll say.

Maybe those pictures are one smoking gun away from incriminating Shrinky and her unlikely judicial mate. While my husband's reasons for bugging the psycho's office remain unknown, maybe she found out he'd listened in, didn't like what she thought he'd heard, then kaboom. Bye-bye, Irishman. Maybe that's too many maybes.

The Queen found out about Chica (hence the divorce). She's got a do-nothing-but-get-everything Ivana Trump post-divorce plan. Not sure of details. Maybe the Jester's off the grid or faked his own death to avoid the Queen's formidable rage. Who could blame him? When it comes to dishing out, my money's on the Queen.

Before I forget the Royal She's giving interviews. I've watched for said interview to show up somewhere on TV or online but nothing so far.

Shitstorm's coming, I can feel it about to rain down on all our heads.

The Invisible Heiress

Speak.

Comments

Hubba-Hubba

Of course the Queen's got a get everything plan. It's bought and paid for by her rich daddy. She didn't earn any of it.

Reply: You obviously never met her daddy.

Norma B.

I'm not surprised in the slightest that Shrinky's a bomber. I can't believe you are either.

You should get the story from the Queen directly. Maybe she knows what's up with the Jester? Why don't you go through the front door this time? Are you going to stay away forever?

Reply: I hate to say I'm long on scared shitless and short on nerve.

Norma B.

By the way, I am sorry to hear about your father-in-law. Seems suspicious, doesn't it? Considering the timing. And one more thing—I think the Queen would see you in a heartbeat. Don't count that out.

Reply: As if I didn't have enough to figure or count out.

4 Christ R Lord

I know you don't like me, but you are in my prayers. A suicide is the saddest thing ever.

Reply: You do annoy me, but I'll take any prayers I can get.

4 Christ R Lord

If you ask me, your father-in-law knew something he shouldn't have, or did something he shouldn't have and was afraid he'd get caught. Don't you ever watch *Law and Order?*

Reply: I'd say you just received your first real message from God.

Chapter Seventy-Six

Isabel

Sherman's mood has taken a decided downturn since our big day. Even pinching his balls with the needle-nose pliers didn't raise his spirits. He's been jumpy, terse. If we hadn't already gotten hitched I might've felt alarmed. Soon as this baby arrives I plan to do what every sane married woman does—live a separate life from my husband. I'd also thought of divorcing him after a decent interval. No prenup (shocking, no?), so I'd get half plus upkeep for the kid. But half's not all. I want it all.

Too greedy for my own good is why I found myself in this mess to begin with. A mess I might not get out of.

Armed with the shocking pages from the notepad I'd found, and directions to what looked like the stables at Beverley, I needed to make a trek to the mighty mansion. Strange thing about the notepad—the author's unknown. I'd searched every page, no clue about the writer. Well familiar with Sherman's handwriting (he'd left me plenty of stern notes), whoever scribbled in this thing was definitely not Sherman.

Mysterious notes in hand, I parked farther from the stables, walked slower. I'd no more than reached the stable doors when I heard one of the gardeners (I assumed) yell something in Spanish. I dashed inside.

Big enough to house a mid-size family in comfort the swanky barn and stalls stood empty. The whole building shone immaculate, concrete floors polished to a high sheen, the sweet smell of wood shavings, fresh, clean. No horses though. The conversation in Spanish sounded closer so to be safe I darted into the stall nearest the back wall, pulled the gate behind me.

It took several seconds to adjust to the semi-darkness, several more to figure out what heap of crap I'd nearly tripped over. I crouched down (no easy feat in my condition) to see better. Saw some boxes. I opened one. I opened another and another—looked like a security camera graveyard.

Just like it said in the notes.

I think I might've found my ace in the hole.

Since my swollen feet and legs forced me to walk in geologic time it took the better part of an hour to get them all in my car.

****

Tired from my stint at Beverley I was in no mood for Jonathan and his mansplanations. I'd started to unload my treasure trove from the stables into my house when he called. Old habits die hard is the only explanation for my answering.

"I knew I'd regret giving you my new number," I said. "What do you want?" I waddled into the house, backed into one of our just-delivered custom chairs, for a cat-and-mouse chat.

"What are you up to, Isabel?"

"Don't you sound menacing?" I said. "If you must know I'm in the middle of decorating my new mansion. You?"

"Get off it. Your lawyer called."

"What dribble are you squawking now?" I didn't have a lawyer but didn't want to admit that until Jonathan sated my curiosity. "Why would I need a lawyer?"

"You tell me. I hate to ask."

"What would pique your pea brain to wonder if I'd hired an attorney for Lord only knows what."

"He called here looking for you."

"He who?"

"Elmer—" Jonathan paused. I imagined him peering through his professorial bifocals at a scribbled note. "No, *Ernest*. That's right, Ernest Shaw."

That gnat buzzed around again? "What'd he want?"

"So he *is* your lawyer?"

"What if he is?"

"Why is he calling me?" Jonathan's voice turned adolescent squeaky.

"What'd he say?"

"Only that he was following up on some paperwork he sent you."

"What the—"

"Are you suing me?" Jonathan yelled now. "This is it, Isabel. I'm going to—"

I jammed my phone off. What the fuck's up with this Shaw guy? Paperwork? What paperwork? What about his business card I'd liberated from the floor? Couldn't say for sure where the stupid thing came from.

The hairs that'd started growing back in at my neckline tingled. Bad juju wriggled over my stretch-marked skin like worms. I waddled quick as I could to Sherman's office to try the drawer again. With no proof whatsoever, I knew the contents would change my life forever. I'd bet the McMansion on it. Gave the bronze pull a jerk. Still locked. I'd need to pick the damn thing now. Where'd we put the steak knives?

Chapter Seventy-Seven

Preston

Not much from Smiley since Marv ate his gun.

I'd never been a Marv fan, but his suicide still caused a twinge of sadness. Brendan's heart would've broken over his father's self-inflicted demise. Losing a parent is usually a defining moment in an adult child's life. One made more difficult when the two are estranged. Brendan and Marv had both gone to their graves without any understanding of each other at all.

I'd planned another snoop session at Beverley but could never get myself to go. Brooding and self-pity took up most of my waking hours. If it weren't for Walter White and Smiley I'd cave.

And what on earth had Marv done? My blog follower might've been on to something. What did he know that drove him to such an extreme? Or worse, did someone do it for him? Hard to get away with a murder trumped up to look like suicide these days. Modern forensics took that kind of misdirection off the table. But no one ever said killers were smart. Maybe an idiot killed my father-in-law. Who's to say? Never knowing the whys of his suicide seemed likely.

Some secrets do go to the grave. Maybe a lot of them.

The paper reported Chief of Police Marv Finney's accidental death, not the truth. Of course, the department would do what it could to sneak in that designation, instead of suicide, to preserve his benefits for his family. Did Marv have a family anymore? Who would bury the poor man? Could they find Colleen? Would she care? Should I offer on Brendan's behalf?

Mother would know what to do, she always did. Her pitch-perfect decorum buoyed many a calamitous situation. She'd known Marv Finney for more than thirty years. I don't think she cared much for him or any of the Finneys for that matter. But now two out of three were dead, she'd put the past where it rightly belonged, behind her, at least long enough to do the right thing. Wouldn't she? The Finneys were family of a kind.

I almost called her, still knew her number by heart. But stopped. The blood on my hands killed my courage.

I corralled Walter to take him to the dog park where I blended with the rest of those annoying weirdos who considered themselves puppy parents and paraded among them with a plastic glove on my hand, held aloft like I'd just given a prostate exam.

With Walter shimmying and chattering beside me I went on my usual hunt for car keys and phone. In my fog I couldn't keep track of a damn thing. Aunt James's desk was where I usually got lucky. Sure enough, my phone lay next to my checkbook where I last paid bills. With Marv's death throwing the precinct into a bit of a flux, Smiley hadn't the time to check in on my father, as he'd promised as a favor to me. He was trying to find Colleen, which was job enough. A quick search on the small desktop didn't turn up my keys.

I pulled the top drawer open. Right on top sat the cream-colored, unopened envelope I'd run across the other day. I flipped it over to see *Harrison* handwritten on the front in a calligraphy-type penmanship—only her first name, no address. I grabbed my silver letter opener, intended to slice it, then didn't. Opening the letter felt wrong. My mother still lived. The correspondence had been addressed to her. Besides, if I opened it, no way could I make the thing look like new again. I should forward it.

Or I could use the letter as an excuse to ring the bell, go through the front door like Norma B. suggested. I swallowed hard. Could I summon the boldness? Before I could make a determination, my phone rang, scared the bejesus out of me. Guard gate. Why could I never remember their names? I answered anyway.

"Detective Smiley dropped off an envelope for you. Said to tell you he'd come up later. After he gets Chief Finney's—well, takes care of that sad business." Guard paused, cleared his throat. "I can bring the envelope to the house when the shift changes."

"No, I'm on my way out. I'll pick it up."

Chapter Seventy-Eight

Isabel

I barreled home with my finds from Beverley's stables focused on Sherman's locked drawer. I needed to get in that thing. I'd started to bring the cameras in but decided to worry about them after I found whatever lay hidden in that desk. I lumbered through the house to Sherman's office, reminiscing.

One of my previous fiancés, the wacko from Waco (as my mom loved to call him) taught me to assemble a fertilizer bomb, kite checks and pick locks. None were as easy as I remembered. When I'd busted in to Preston's prissy husband's crap apartment to muss it up it took so long I think three neighbors saw me. Didn't help his little dog yipped and pissed all over the place. I hadn't meant to squeeze it so hard, but the thing wouldn't shut up. Why would a man own such a fem dog anyway?

Neither bomb I concocted solo got me the expected results. One fizzled, started a lame fire in the office. The other blew a car to the sky along with that pesky Brendan. So far, my attempt at opening Sherman's desk drawer didn't work so great either. The steak knife tip proved too big for the hole. I scoured Sherman's office boxes until I found a box of paperclips.

That did the trick. You'd be surprised how many of life's conundrums can be solved with a paperclip. It's when you try to get fancy that fucks things up. I no more than heard the "click" of success when my cell rang. Sherman. Shit. Well, I'd need to know where he was, how close to home, so I answered.

"Jesus, did you sprint to your phone?" I said. "You're huffing and puffing like a rutting pig." If the pig fit.

"No, I'm—" he stopped to catch his breath but wasn't too successful. "I'm—never mind. I'll explain when I get home. I'm going to be late. Not sure how long." His voice trailed away.

"Hello? You there?"

"I wanted to make sure you're going to be home later."

"Where would I go?"

"I don't know where you go half the time."

Walked right into that one. "Yeah, well, I'm home. Planned to stay. Where are you? Outside somewhere?"

"Movers gone?"

"Yes, why?"

Sherman composed himself somewhat, his breathing slowed. "We haven't spent a night uninterrupted since we got married."

"Great, now I need to find the lube and—"

"Don't worry about that stuff." He trailed off again. "I've gotta go."

"Wait—"

He'd gone. Oh well, all I cared about was time. Now I had plenty of it with Sherman out of my hair. Didn't need to ruffle through the drawer at all. On top, an ominous, yellow envelope lurked, addressed to me. The neat, black-bordered address label matched the business card I'd found from Shaw, Smithson, and Price, Attorneys at Law.

Chapter Seventy-Nine

Preston

I hadn't planned to bring Walter White with me but couldn't stand to see his sad face when I told him the dog park would need to wait. He hung his big lunk head, stared at the floor. His disappointment palpable Walter couldn't bear to look me in the eye. I fell for it.

Equipped with Walter, the still sealed correspondence addressed to Mom as an excuse, and the envelope from Smiley, I sped to Beverley. With every intention of marching up to the front door, I didn't. What kind of crazed, homicidal maniac didn't possess backbone enough to rap on a door? The pep talk I'd given myself on the drive over hadn't helped. Even Walter, whose unconditional love made me feel worthy, couldn't close the deal.

I'd seen my mother up close and personal at Haven House but that was my turf, not hers. Plus, I'd been so angry then. Without rage to buck me up, the thought of facing my mother, her scar blazing, in the house I grew up in, made me woozy. The thought of breaking in unseen again didn't seem too gonzo anymore.

What about Walter? Even I knew I couldn't leave him inside the Rover where he might bake to death.

I parked near the stables, my usual spot. Since they couldn't be seen from the house I latched Walter's long leash to the gate of the first stall. He could sit in the shade just inside or get some sun outside. My visit wouldn't take long. I didn't know why I felt compelled to at least catch a glimpse of my mother. I only knew I needed to see her.

****

As if I'd never left I took my usual place under the stairs. Mom sat in the exact same spot, camera guy across from her. Mother touched the corners of her mouth, a lipstick check. I'd seen her perform this unconscious act countless times growing up. I felt comforted, like that small gesture signaled divinity. I was meant to be in this spot at this moment. Didn't even have to wait through a lot of their boring chitchat. A few minutes in and I was rewarded.

"How'd you find Preston's blog by the way?" camera guy said.

Oh, Lordy.

As soon as mystery guy said "blog," I knew his identity. Jack. Jack the documentarian who dogged me to let him film my life story, *our* life story. He'd halfway succeeded. How? Why?

"I took her journal from Haven House," Mother said. "I snooped in her room, found it on the desk. Swiped it. She'd written about the blog in the journal. I'd wanted her to stay at Haven House forever, until I read that blog. Sure, a lot of what she wrote hurt. Her rage scared me. But I read other things that gave me pause. Well, I realized my daughter wasn't beyond help. After that, I wanted to reach out to her to know whether or not she was okay. My online ruse was born."

"Norma B." Jack said.

I felt like I'd just lifted one foot off the high wire.

"Yes, as you know." Mom smiled in that way that made you feel like the only person in the universe.

"What's the B stand for?" Jack said.

"Bates. Norman's mother."

The room went silent then Jack laughed too loudly. Like his boss told a mediocre joke at the company party. They both laughed. Mom sucked him in. I wasn't too stunned to notice his crush. Norma Bates *was* a clever pen name though.

"How did her journal page get back to you? Isn't that what some nut used to try to blackmail you?"

"I'd forgotten I tore that page out of Preston's journal, kept it in my purse. I'd made an appointment with Jonathan something or other, Isabel's partner. Somehow it got away from me while I was there," Mother said, shocking the living daylights out of me. "That pompous Jonathan probably sent it. Looked desperate to me."

"Why'd you alert the authorities?"

"I never would've had I known they'd show Preston the journal page. I could tell she didn't remember much of anything that happened that night or the months preceding. I'd have known it when I finally saw her at Haven House. No idea why that detective would involve her. But I don't tolerate threats. Best to nip those in the bud. We've received our share over the years."

"Why'd you tear that page out of the journal?"

"I didn't want Preston to see it."

"How did you know she hadn't already?"

"She definitely would've mentioned that in her blog or hinted at it in that way she has. She didn't. I read all the posts back to the first one."

"You didn't want her to know about her own baby?"

"Not until she was well. I felt she'd remember when she got strong enough. If she didn't, well, some things are best forgotten."

So Mother did remember something. My baby.

"What else do you remember about that night?"

My thoughts exactly.

"I remember her poor, stillborn baby, Preston holding him. Maybe that wiped out everything else." Her voice broke. "I couldn't bear it, seeing her pain. She looked so frightened. Even the drugs she'd taken couldn't numb her enough to withstand it. I knew I was to blame, in large part, for where Preston ended up. She didn't get the love and attention she needed from her mother." She stopped. I don't think I'd ever seen her cry. I could barely breathe. Mother continued, "I reached for her and that tiny dead baby, then it's all a blur, a black hole. Next thing I knew, I was in the hospital."

Jack let the silence sit unchallenged. Then, "You said you'd dropped the journal page at Isabel Warner's partners' office. Why'd you want to see him?"

"Isabel's a disaster. Jonathan wouldn't say much about her

when I went to see him. He tried to assure me. My experience with her, and my intuition, told me to be wary of Isabel Warner."

"You could've replaced her with someone else."

"Todd thought she helped, said we'd never find a therapist who wasn't crazy or one who'd put up with Preston. Which I believed. I knew from the blog that Preston dismissed anything Isabel said, so I didn't worry she'd have influence either way. Then when I found out the truth, I told Preston, or Norma B. told Preston, to get out."

What truth?

"Do you think Brendan planted listening devices in their offices? Did you ask him to?" Jack leaned forward, elbows on his knees.

Wait. Wasn't he going to ask her about whatever *truth* she found out? Come on, Jack. Get with it. Mesmerized, I'd crawled farther toward the living room. Scooted back in a hurry.

"No, I did not. I've got no idea why, or if, Brendan did anything."

"Did his murder make you fear for Preston's life?"

"Of course. That and everything else."

"Is that why you bought her the dog?" He fiddled with a knob on the camera.

She bought Walter White? Wait. Again. Wasn't he going to ask about *everything else* either? Shit. They'd had several conversations that I'd missed. No telling how many. Damnit.

"Yes. And I knew that detective had taken a shine to her. I noticed that right away at Brendan's funeral. I knew he'd protect her. As a silly aside, Preston always wanted a dog, but I didn't allow dogs in this house or on the furniture. I knew she'd love him."

That made me cry. Quietly.

Jack closed the space between Mother and the camera with a couple of long strides. I hadn't realized before how big he was, like a tree. He sat beside her on the chaise meant for one.

"What do you hope happens next?" he said.

She looked away from him. He cupped her chin to turn her toward him again, a gentle intimate act. They were lovers—that was a fact not in dispute. I could tell immediately.

"Do you want to see Preston?" he said.

"Of course."

"Even after all she's done, you'd give her another chance?"

"You never run out of chances with your mother."

Chapter Eighty

Isabel

Good Lord, fuck a duck.

Though not versed on the lingo I figured out quickly what I'd found. The heading screamed: Certificate of Revocable Trust. I jumped on the second paragraph, which read: Trustor: Jeanine Elizabeth Turner. Then, Successor Trustee: Isabel Grace Warner.

No mention of her husband. I flipped a page.

I'm a married woman. It is my intention that my husband, Dwayne Ray Cooney, receive the monies and items stated and agreed upon in the legally binding, attached prenuptial agreement, signed and witnessed May eleventh, two thousand fourteen.

I thumbed through until I found the prenup, read the short, to-the-point document several times. Dwayne got what he came with—his personal effects, guns, Ford F-450 truck, Vista Alpine camper shell and ten thousand dollars thrown in as a thanks-for-playing-asshole parting gift.

So engrossed, I almost forgot to wonder how and why a copy of my mother's trust was in Sherman's drawer under lock and key. As a grifter myself I knew funny business when I saw it, and *this* was funny business. Tingling with anticipation, I continued through the jargon. Eyes feeling close to crossed, I skipped to the last page, which turned out to be a cover letter from Ernest Shaw that cut to the chase.

I'd inherited every dime of my mother's more than three hundred million dollar estate.

Chapter Eighty-One

Preston

My snoop session at Beverley got cut short. By Smiley of all people. Fortunately, the stars were aligned. He called over first. My mother's phone sat within arm's reach, giving me time and opportunity to skedaddle. Only after I felt sure I'd skipped away unnoticed did I get the chance to let what I'd heard at Beverley marinate. The lengthy walk back to the stables gave me time to fret over it.

My mother. Norma B?

A picture of Mom, in frozen repose, rode herd in my brain, while I tried to recall her incognito comments. Hard to believe beneath that icy reserve Norma B. lived. My memory of Norma's observations might've already taken on a nostalgic sheen but from what I could remember, some were a rebuke, most sensible but calm, a few hopeful, even kindhearted. I looked forward to her asides after every post.

Then Jack?

The one who nagged me constantly about some kind of film? He and my mother had thrown their lot in to make a documentary? What else could it be? Plus, they clearly knew each other in the biblical sense. My head felt thick with scenarios, possibilities. Before I could stop them the tears started. I slapped them away like gnats.

Mom had gifted me with Walter. The best present ever—for protection. From what? Apparently, she'd already covered that topic out of my hearing. She must've known, or thought she knew, that whoever killed Brendan might come after me. Yet she thought I should leave Haven House.

What had she said about Shrinky and *the truth*?

Something like, "Preston dismissed anything Isabel said, so I didn't worry she'd have any influence when I found out the truth." That's when she (Norma B.) told me to get out. The truth and Shrinky were linked, at least in my mother's mind. Mother had been shut in for months. I could count on less than four fingers how many run-ins she'd had with the wackiest therapist on earth. Maybe the unexplained *everything else* she mentioned was the proof.

And what had she said about Smiley? She could tell he *took a shine* to me? Geez. Mothers really did know everything. I never noticed a shine or even a glimmer, not then. Did I? I didn't think Mother noticed anyone, or anything, at Brendan's funeral—except all the dead Catholics surrounding her.

I threw my head back to look at the dusky sky, as if the clouds and the sinking sun could guide me. Nope. No messages written overhead so I walked on, wondered. Heard Mom's shot-of-tequila voice on repeat: "You never run out of chances with your mother."

Now my mother seemed like someone from my dreams, lesser than her myth. If I looked hard enough, I'd find the real woman inside that exquisite shell, one who could give me the love I yearned for.

****

I meandered toward the stables, thought about my father problem. Tried to remember what I'd overheard my mother say about my father and his girlfriend. Had my mother said Marcella's name or did she refer to her only as Dad's girlfriend? Dammit. I couldn't recall. It'd been too long ago and now my head was full of every word my mother uttered *this* time.

Did my mother know why my father disappeared or where he'd gone? Doubtful. Dejected, I opened the driver's side door to get in, saw my plastic glove stash, then trudged over to get Walter from the stables. He wasn't where I'd left him. I know I'd tied his leash in a tight knot. The stall slat I'd hooked him to hung splintered and torn off in jagged pieces. He'd jerked so hard to get free he'd broken the stall board. What the hell?

"Walter White," I said loud as I dared. Probably could yodel the stable walls down and no one could hear. "Walter White, come," I said louder.

Rabbits. Goddammit. I'd forgotten about the wildlife that roamed around here, irresistible prey for a dog. I'd also forgotten his strength, size, and speed. Shit. He could've run miles away by now. I called his name a few more times, stomped around the immediate area with no luck.

I turned in time to see brake lights ahead, far ahead. If I'd have been a second slower I'd have missed them. I looked around, noticed tire marks and footprints all around. So many, more than one person might've left them. Someone, or more than one someone, had obviously been here and just left. I always parked far away from the stables, far enough to not be seen unless you looked really, really, hard. If they'd have been here before I would've run into whoever it was when I walked Walter over to tie him up.

Had they noticed my Rover, despite my attempt at subterfuge? Had Walter already bolted by the time they'd arrived or had he chased them?

Knowing I could search all day for Walter and never find him, I jumped into my SUV and gunned it. Maybe I could catch up with whoever owned those brake lights and find Walter at the same time.

****

Of course, I'd dallied too long. When I hit the highway, cars whizzed by like normal. I'd missed my chance. Shit. I'd turned my cell off, shoved it deep into my front jeans pocket, to avoid dropping it or letting its ring rat me out at Beverley. The phone dug into my thigh. I fished it out, saw I missed five calls. I listened to messages while I drove aimlessly.

"Preston, it's me," Smiley's voice fit my ear perfectly. "Listen, I talked to Harrison. Nothing concrete there about Todd and Marcella, but she definitely suspected an affair. She did do me one giant solid though. I'm getting in to see Judge Seward. Your mother really does run this town. See you tonight at the house, probably late."

The last four calls came from the same, unfamiliar number, seconds apart. Two hang-ups followed and one butt dial. All I heard was muffled, airy noises. Last call.

"Preston, it's Dad."

I turned my already low playing stereo off. "Preston, where the hell are you? Preston, come on." His exasperated hiss came across clearly. I pressed the phone harder to my ear, the better to hear his anger. "Preston, I mean it. Where are you? Jesus Christ, what the—" A weird, throaty rumble came next, then nothing.

I replayed. Listened close over and over. He sounded breathless, outdoors. I could tell he talked and walked at the same time, walking faster and faster, talking angrier and angrier. I could count on two fingers the times I'd heard my father angry. These days, when he talked to me he was crying. I figured he'd be hurt, annoyed even that I'd distanced myself, but furious? Besides, he's the one who went off-grid with his Latina lover. I'm the one who had the right to be mad.

What was that rumbling at the end? I listened one more time, couldn't put my finger on that sound. Whatever was going on with my dad didn't sound good, that was plain. I hit redial. Went straight to voicemail like the phone had been shut off.

I couldn't think straight 'til I found my dog. Walter White meant everything to me. How could I have lost him?

Chapter Eighty-Two

Isabel

I couldn't contain all the ifs, ands, or buts swirling through my mind. I thumbed through the complicated legalese but came to the same conclusion.

I was rich. Really rich. Richer than fuck rich.

My skin felt iced, my throat raw. I'd attended one Lamaze class then grew bored and quit but tried to take deep breaths as the teacher had instructed to self-soothe. In, then out. In, then out. In, then—I spied a final thin sheath of papers clipped together at the top, lying all by itself toward the back of the drawer.

On the first page, copies of my Social Security card and a driver's license.

What the fuck?

The driver's license bore my name but most definitely not my face. The room turned darker with the sunset. I clicked on the desk lamp, illuminating the fraud. I peered closely at my impersonator, a beautiful girl, Mexican or Spanish probably, who definitely did not look anything like me. But since no one in my mother's life, including her banker, knew what I looked like, it didn't matter. I gnawed my already bleeding thumbnail. Who was she? I didn't recognize her. A stranger who stole my name and probably my money.

I moved on to the second page. Copies of Sherman's Social Security card and driver's license, his real name, of course. No forgery there. I felt choked with apprehension. Even if I'd wanted to throw everything I held in my hands in the trash, I couldn't. Curiosity and horror gripped me.

Last page. After a few minutes of study, turning the page over and around, I surmised it was a copy of a money transfer from one account to another. I flipped through the trust documents, matched the number. Still making a meal of my fingernail, I re-examined the lid on my coffin.

If I read correctly, and I'm sure I did, Sherman and fake me had recently transferred more than three hundred million dollars from my newly discovered, personal trust account to a different, jointly owned, bank account.

Thought I'd pulled off the ruse of a lifetime. But I'd always been underwater when it came to Sherman. I knew my way around his psyche. He knew his way around the law. I thought I'd prevail. I was mistaken.

The con got conned.

Chapter Eighty-Three

Preston

I'd driven through several unfamiliar neighborhoods looking for my dog. Hunting for Walter in any of these areas was nonsensical, I knew. Somewhere deep in that forest he was eating whatever small animal he'd happily chased down. I could withstand losing my dad but not my dog. I stumbled around a while more, yelling my dog's name 'til I'd gone hoarse. Disheartened, I climbed back into my SUV.

Knee deep in frustration I looked over at the envelopes I'd brought along when I'd planned to actually meet Mom face-to-face with a personal delivery. Shoved the one Smiley dropped off in my purse for later, ripped open the envelope addressed to simply: Harrison. I pried out the single piece of heavy stationary to read the letter written in an elegant script.

My dearest Harrison,

I forgive you. A sister's never been loved as much as I love you. I don't begrudge your happiness but am certain it's short lived. As for me, I fear for my life. If you're reading this letter, it's because I'm dead. Todd Fitzgerald could think of no better way to get out of our engagement. I shouldn't have been so forthcoming with him regarding our inheritance. Since I'm first born Todd naturally assumed I'd inherit. He suffers from intentional blindness where Daddy, and his obsession with you, is concerned. He fears, rightfully so, that if he unwinds our impending nuptials, Daddy will extinguish his ambitions, which I'm afraid far outweigh his abilities. I overheard him in a compromising telephone conversation that leads me to believe I'm not long for this world. What's worse is Todd knows I heard. Could I do anything about it? Who would believe me? Not you, because you love him, always have. If you won't see the truth, no one will.

You know how I've struggled to defeat the darkness that overcomes me. Followed doctor's orders, taken every pill. Power over my own life eludes me. I'm not sure I care how, or where, I end up. Please know, Harrison, no blame lies hidden in my heart. Take care of yourself. If you feel the slightest disturbance where Todd is concerned, do what I couldn't—leave.

By my own hand or another's, my demise is imminent.

Your ardent fan and best-intentioned sister,

James.

****

My father's transformation from mild mannered wimp to lying, conniving, cheating ass had happened before my eyes. Even though it'd taken a while, I'd adjusted to his new reality. But murder? That one was tough. Could I picture it? Just because James thought he might didn't mean he did. But he did. I knew it. I shut my eyes as if being sightless would change the obvious. My mother had never seen this letter.

Was killing in our DNA like eye or hair color? Were we a family of murdering sociopaths who croaked those who inconvenienced or annoyed us? I turned the ignition on to roll my window down for air. I thought I might suffocate. Stuck my head out in time to see a Bentley speed by me.

My father? As if Bentleys were common. It had to be him. Who else?

I stepped on the gas to follow, almost honked to get his attention but thought better of it. I really didn't know him at all. He slowed in front of a huge, new house. I eased up on the gas. I sucked at these PI type activities. If Dad was paying a cat hair's worth of attention, he'd have seen me. He slammed to a stop, idled for a few seconds, then took off like a bullet train.

I sped up too but changed my mind. Instead of following him I parked a few houses down. Dying to see what interested him enough to stop. Did he live here now? With Chica? If he did, why didn't he get out? A red Audi sat in front of one of the four garages.

What?

Shrinky drove the same car.

No.

Shrinky? Here? Not nearly as elegant or upscale as Nottingham Lane but still you'd pay a pretty penny to buy this place. Maybe she really did inherit from her stingy mother. Did my father want to talk to her? Was his distress on the phone symptoms of a breakdown? Even Dad had to know Shrinky wasn't a real therapist. What would he want with her?

What about Judge Seward? He was the one sitting next to her at that freak club. What was happening?

Shit on a shingle.

Was Dad making time with this nutcase too? Just how unpacked was his pecker? My mother sure sounded worried about some kind of Shrinky situation. I crept to the first window. Slow as drying paint, I straightened enough to peek in. The sight of the back of Shrinky's head drove me back down. I waited, expected the worst, then got a hold of myself. Unless she had eyes in the back of her ratty head she couldn't see me. Emboldened, I looked again.

Yep, there she sat, cell phone to her ear behind a desk. The chair she sat in swiveled, a little to the left, a little to the right but never enough for me to see anything else or for her to spot me. I didn't want to press my luck so I crabwalked back to where I'd come from. I zipped past Shrinky's Audi. Wait. The trunk looked popped. Dare I look? I'd come this far. Might as well go for broke.

I opened the trunk enough to see several boxes piled in there, tops open. I pushed the trunk up a little farther to see inside a box. A camera? I threw caution to the wind and looked through several more. All cameras. Security cameras. The ones that disappeared from my house? Maybe. They all looked the same. I grabbed a couple of boxes then dumped them in the Rover. When no one chased me down, I made one more trip, closed the trunk as much as it'd been when I found it, open a crack.

Better get the fuck out of Dodge.

****

I hadn't kept track of how I got to Shrinky's house. My GPS took me back by the hidden trail. Walter White sat at the side of the road like he'd been waiting for me to come pick him up. I pulled over.

"Walter White, where have you been?" I flung the door open as wide as it'd go, weak with relief. Walter immediately sank to the dirt on his belly, head on the ground. He only did that after he'd eaten the entire pizza off the counter or chewed the remote in half.

"What's in your mouth, Walter? What'd you do?" I forced his heavy head up. Pulled him by the snout into the light from my car. Walter still wore his collar. I could see some remnants of the wooden stall slat dragged by the end of his leash. Walter spit out whatever he'd carried with him in his mouth, gave me his best pouty face, licked my hand.

"Is that blood?"

The hair around Walter's mouth looked like he'd tried to eat a red Sharpie. He licked my hand again for good measure. I picked up what he'd dropped. A piece of dirty fabric frayed and ripped. A windowpane check summerweight wool.

Chapter Eighty-Four

Isabel

I'd taken it up the ass big time.

How did I not see this coming? Well, I didn't think I'd inherit squat if Mom bit the dust. She'd made a point of letting me know at every opportunity. But I knew Sherman never leveled with me. God only knows what shit he stirred on any given day. If only I'd known about this windfall. I would've never gone to all the trouble with Sherman, or blackmailed Jonathan.

Of course I would've.

To my sad surprise, I wanted my mother. Her death had hit me harder than I thought it would, but I couldn't say I missed her. I missed what she could've been. What *we* could've been.

It came up on me like the rolling tide. Safe to say our wires always crossed, our relationship a morass of complicated feelings. Hard pressed to say who disappointed who the most. No, that's a lie. All things considered I disappointed her more. Yet, she rewarded me in the end in a way she couldn't during her lifetime. Money couldn't love you. But somehow my mom's post-mortem magnanimous gesture felt like love. No matter what I was her child and she'd take care of me in the best way she knew how. Fucked up? Sure. But what relationship didn't ride the razor's edge of fucked up?

I realized my mother thought leaving me her winnings would serve as my Hail Mary. When in fact, it would kill me. Almost had to laugh at that. I'd bet it all and lost. A true gambler, I lived like one and would die like one. I rested my hands on my belly, felt my baby shift underneath. I had to push thoughts of my nesting child out of my brain, or I'd crack. I could call the police, a lawyer, get up and leave. But if I got out of this mess I'd find another and another. The thought exhausted me.

Only way to get rid of the bad in me was to kill it.

I realized knowing when you'll die is a gift not a curse. Wherever my mother was she'd welcome me there. She'd like to know I didn't feel any fear at the end. Only peace.

My ringing phone snapped me to reality.

"Jonathan, Jesus Christ. Can't live without me?"

"You'll get yours you scheming, leeching—"

"I'm in for a treat then." Might as well talk to him, to take my mind off what I knew was coming.

"I told on you." Jonathan laughed like a madman.

"Are you drunk?"

"What if I am?"

"Listen, you weak, pathetic worm of a—"

"I told my wife everything."

I paused to consider whether or not I gave one speck of shit. I didn't.

"Great, good luck to you."

"I told that detective too. That Miley guy. A few minutes ago."

"*Smiley,* you asshole."

"Whatever. Rhonda told him everything about you. At first I denied it like a cringing coward." Jonathan's words tripped over one another, but I understood him.

"Did you?" Why did I entertain this fool? "I'll send you a thank you card later."

"Didn't you hear me? I confessed. Told my wife the whole sad story."

"I'll send her some flowers and an apology note. Okay?"

"You don't get it do you, bitch?"

"I'm sure you'll enlighten me. But do get on with it."

"After I admitted everything to her, I called Miley, oh wait, *Smiley*, of all the asinine names and backed up Rhonda's story. Told him every nasty detail about you. Your bombs, your blackmail scheme. I believe it's called *corroboration*." He snort laughed.

"Old news. No one got hurt. So I started a little fire, BFD."
I could've ended the call but talking to anyone, even jackoff
Jonathan, made me feel alive.

"Brendan Finney got hurt. He got dead."

"You're an idiot."

"You're a bomber. Not a very good one but a bomber
nonetheless."

"I've got to—"

"Quite a coincidence that Brendan Finney's car had a bomb
in it. Is it another coincidence he also bugged a bomber's office?"
He snickered. "I doubt it."

The mechanical sound of one of the garage doors going up
gave me pause. Sherman had arrived. Much as I wanted to delay
the inevitable I knew I couldn't. My bell was about to get rung.

"Sorry, Jonathan. This bomber's about to detonate." I
pressed my phone off.

Chapter Eighty-Five

Preston

Is there anything you can't find on YouTube?

After finding model and serial numbers on the cameras and DVRs, which made searching for how-to videos possible, I set to work in my favorite spot, sitting behind Aunt James's desk. Goddammit. A techno-zero, especially for someone my age, I couldn't figure heads or tails out of the so-easy-anyone-can-do-it YouTube tutorials. Not getting anywhere exhausted my patience. I dashed to the kitchen where I'd dropped the equipment boxes.

I lucked out. The boxes still contained directions—in four languages. Even the ones in English looked like Latin to me. Shit. Fuck. Walter White click-clacked behind me, following me from room to room. In such a hurry to investigate my find I'd freed Walter from his leash but left the broken slat attached. The whole contraption lay on the floor. Water in his dish cleaned some of the blood off his jowls when he took a sloppy drink but not all. He looked a mess.

Now what? Frustrated, I kicked the nearest box over, spilling its innards, more worthless instructions. Walter yelped in support. With my foot I pushed the papers out of the way. What was that? I dropped to the floor to retrieve whatever black, plastic thing had been hiding in the box.

A flash drive.

If the footage on the cameras had been copied to this flash drive, I'd devote my entire life to the church. Once a month at the least. I raced back to my laptop, opened the flash drive.

There batty Isabel stood on my porch ringing the bell, or knocking on the front doors, hard to tell from this angle. She looked less Blanche DuBois than usual. The date at the top of the screen told me the footage was more than a year old. About the time she took over my case from my original therapist. A hand reached out to pull her in. I hit zoom.

Holy Christ on the Cross.

I rewound. Hit pause. Zoomed more. Clear as a summer day, I could see the red scar twisted across the back of Dad's hand. I kept going. For the next half hour, I witnessed Isabel waiting at the door, she and Dad in various intimate embraces, kissing hello or goodbye, over a period of several months up to the week I returned home and relieved them of their love nest.

I hit pause again to absorb the impact.

The man we couldn't make out in the fuzzy stills from the security footage taken in front of the freak club had to have been my father. Not Judge Seward like I'd assumed. Then I remembered the envelope Smiley'd left at the guard gate. I rushed back to the kitchen to grab my purse where I'd dropped it. The manila envelope stuck out the top. I dumped the contents. The photos Smiley's guy had performed his mumbo jumbo on.

Smiley was right, pics weren't much clearer. I brought them nearer to my face for a closer look. The arm coming out of the car reaching toward Shrinky was lit fairly well. Well enough to recognize the cufflinks. Ones I'd seen all my life—on the blingy side, larger than most, with a good-sized ruby in the center. They'd been a gift from my mother. Everything moved at fast-forward now, all coming together. The car in the background had to be the Bentley. So far out of the realm of possibilities at the time, I never considered the car could be his. Nothing about my father should shock me anymore. Back I went to the library, Walter close to my heels, grumbling.

Dad must've taken out the cameras from my house in the middle of the night right after I'd come home. No gate guard back then. He could've easily slipped in and out. They obviously put new locks in after I'd been dragged out, and I'm sure he still had keys.

Not Marcella, or at least not *just* Marcella, two-timed with my father. Shrinky was Dad's side talent and they used my house. I remembered Brendan telling me he'd seen a dark car turn into my driveway when he fled after tripping the alarm.

Probably Shrinky's red Audi.

It all made hideous sense. It's what my mother found out. Shrinky and Dad were the *truth* and the *everything else*. Right under my nose the whole time. Isabel's obsession with me getting out of Haven House, her constant reminders that my mother deserved my hatred, her thinly veiled references to me taking another run at killing her. Isabel had wanted me to get rid of my mother once and for all so my father would marry *her*.

Piqued, I rewound, paused, rewound, paused.

What's this now?

Saw my mother going in and out of my house the months before that night, nothing I didn't already know. Then I saw another flash of my father at my front door. What the—I hit stop. I don't remember seeing Dad at all during those last weeks but that didn't mean anything, considering my state. Something climbed up the back of my brain, a memory, a feeling. A bad prickling feeling. I hit start to keep watching my father.

He picked up a box off my doormat before putting his hand in his pocket. Probably to get the keys that everyone always seemed to have to my place. I stared, bug-eyed while he fiddled with the handle. He couldn't open it, so he rang the bell. I'd changed the locks by that time, I guess. I nearly fell off my chair when I saw myself at the front door, obviously pregnant. My father pushed by me into the house still carrying the box.

Chapter Eighty-Six

Isabel

"So you found it," Sherman said.

"Jesus, what happened to you?" I said. "Your leg—shit, you're bleeding all over the floor."

He limped in carrying towels. Swayed, then half fell, half sat, on the floor. I'd never seen him less than immaculate outside the bedroom. Now his hair smashed every which way, leaves and dirt stuck in, jacket gone, tie stained, barely on, shirt and trousers wrinkled, torn, covered in dirt. He pulled up what was left of his pant leg. Half his calf was torn off. I could see blood, loose flaps of skin, muscle, bone. He pressed a monogrammed towel to the wound, made a sound like an angry snake, leaned his head against the wall.

"You lost the wrestling match," I said casual and calm.

"This. You. It's your doing," Sherman's wound had already taken a toll on him. He struggled to talk and breathe at the same time.

"Mine? I don't even know what *this* is, Sherman."

"Can you please, for the love of fucking Christ, drop Sherman?" He said with more strength than I thought he possessed. "Married you, didn't I? No secrets. No, not anymore." He jutted his chin toward the papers in my hands. "Jesus Christ this thing hurts."

"Looks like it does. *Todd*," I said. His name felt foreign on my tongue. I don't think I'd ever said it out loud even after he started calling me Isabel.

"Why go to the witch's lair, dammit. To Beverley, of all the moronic ideas? Poke around where you don't belong."

"Who cares now? You should go to the hospital."

"Thought about that already, bimbo. Started to go, but shit." He hissed through gritted teeth. "I stopped here first. Needed towels." He grabbed his leg, scowled, made more reptilian-like sounds. "I changed my mind, headed to, to the hospital. Too far. I didn't want to explain to some nosy doctor anyway. So I came back."

"I told you living all the way out here was—"

"Where are they?" He pounded the floor with his open hand.

No point pretending I didn't know he meant the cameras.

"In my trunk. Speaking of the witch's lair. What a stupid place to hide them by the way. The stables at Beverley? Why didn't you destroy them?"

"Marv. Goddamn his stupid ass. He was supposed to destroy the lot of them. But he didn't. Couldn't follow the simplest directions. Found his notepad in his personal shit after he— bastard— blew his head off." He squirmed around like he could out maneuver the pain. "Dumb mick wrote everything down. I might not be the DA anymore but," he said, his face contorted, red. "You can bet I'm still a big, swinging dick who takes what he wants, no matter where or what."

"I'm sure."

Asshole must've forgotten I'd seen his dick on numerous occasions.

"Went to, to, get rid of those stupid, fucking cameras. Some assholes's—somebody's giant ass dog—tied to a post. Damn thing saw me. Broke free. Beast almost, damn near, killed me. 'Cause you, *you* couldn't leave any fucking thing alone. She saw you. *Harrison* saw you."

"When? Today?"

He slapped the floor again. "Does it fucking, fuck all, matter?"

Guess I'd been wrong about the light through the window situation.

"So what?" I said.

He beat the back of his head against the wall, squeezed his

eyes shut, kicked the floor with his uninjured leg. "Do women ever stick to their side of the goddamn street? Mind their own fucking business? Ball-busting bitch got the money back I'd hoarded," he whined.

If the situation hadn't been a matter of my life or death, I'd have laughed. Todd looked ridiculous, like someone out of a campy horror film, and sounded like the squealing, gutless wonder he'd always been.

The gutless wonder squealed on. "Out of the blue she remembered how, and I mean *out of the fucking blue*, she decided to act like a lawyer. Even owns this house now." He went back to beating his head against the wall, this time repeatedly. "Your precious new car? Hers now too. Took everything."

The towel around his calf dripped blood. He threw the bright red terrycloth at me. It landed on the pile of papers I'd found. He pressed another one on then jerked off his belt. Tied the leather above the wound.

"She's got a lot of nerve," I said. "What with a boyfriend half her age."

"What nonsense, I mean bullshit, or whatever, are you talking about?"

"Who's the idiot who didn't know his wife got herself a young stud? Never mind. It's moot now. Besides, you were getting divorced anyway." I shifted my considerable weight around in the chair. My engorged feet and legs throbbed.

Todd's barking laugh echoed around the big, mostly unfurnished room. "Harrison's the original woman scorned. Don't think for a . . . a . . .nano second she didn't see this disaster coming."

"So you stole my money?"

"You didn't even know you had money, you oblivious hag."

His makeshift tourniquet helped him gather strength. It felt strange to hear these insults fly out of Todd's mouth. Todd, who liked to suck his thumb and get paddled 'til his ass bled. Now, at this late date, he dominated. No safe word for this situation.

"How did you know about the money?" I said.

"Well—" He stopped, head hung down. I thought he might've passed out. Then his head popped up like a jack-in-the-box. "If you must know, I went to your apartment to kill you."

That thought energized him for sure.

"*You* were the creeper?"

"Your drunk neighbors, or what not, came out of their apartment in the nick of time. Not before I found uh, um, a business card, lying right in front of your door like the golden ticket." He snapped his fingers a second or two behind the beat.

"Did you kill my mother?" Coroner said natural causes but those could be faked. Todd's connections could've come in handy for him.

"Didn't know a twat like you had a mother. Saw it in the paper. Dropped dead all, yes, all on her own with a prenup, for chrissake. I'm telling you the heavens opened. Everything, and I mean *everything*, the whole kit and kaboodle, went my way. Preordained, ripe for the taking. Didn't even break a goddamn sweat." The belt staunched his blood loss, renewed his sensibilities. His speech bellowed out strong and clear.

"And this?" I held up the copy of the phony driver's license.

He waved his hand like he was batting at flies. "Oh her. Pfft. That's uh, Marcella. Family friend, let's say. Got her to call the attorney. Pretend to be you." Todd threw the second blood-drenched towel in my direction. The stack he'd brought in dwindled. "*That* cost me. After I'd, um, you know, after I'd asked her to babysit Harrison she—bitch—made me buy her annoying mother a condo. You're all, every one of you, money-grubbing whores."

"Says the biggest money-grubbing whore of all time." Didn't care if I pissed him off. Might as well make this worth my while. "I knew I'd heard a woman in the background, guess it was your partner in crime. You're an audacious, money-grubbing whore on your better days."

To my amazement, he chuckled. "Thought you'd caught me when I proposed, but you—no— you actually thought I meant it." He carried on, "Christ, Isabel. Who, no what, moronic twit would marry you unless there was uh, you know what I'm trying to say, um, something to gain? Crazy bitch."

That pained me.

For the first time since I knew this would be my last day on earth, I felt like crying. "I can't believe I killed Brendan because of you," I said.

"You?" Todd tried to sit up straighter, flinched and sucked in air.

"Didn't mean to do more than scare him. But the whole car blew."

"What? Jesus, Isabel. What for?"

"He saw us. Kept showing up everywhere. He even drove up to Preston's house when we were using it. I don't know when he figured it out, but he followed me for days. I worried he might influence Preston. She'd turn you against me if our relationship got out. Or Harrison would find out and make real trouble." I realized how lame and desperate that sounded. "He bugged my office, as it turned out."

"I know. I told him to, to, uh, do that."

"What? Why?"

"Do you think I trusted you—el stupido—for half a second?" The corners of his mouth turned down in pain. His conversation turned more garbled, quieter. He was losing steam. "Brendan. Gullible fool, believed I wanted him to do it for, for, Preston. To make sure you, conniving wretch, were, you know, uh, telling us the truth about her condition. Would've been a loose end but *you* took care of, of, the do-gooder bastard for me." He kicked the floor again with a surprising burst of energy. "How perfect is that?"

The baby I never wanted roiled and kicked, somehow knew we weren't long for this world. Didn't know if I carried a he or a she, never wondered until this second. I felt a deep and painful sorrow. No one would've been a worse mother than me, but I'd changed like you'd never believe in the past few minutes. If given the chance, I might've become a person who could learn to love.

Todd's face wrinkled. "Why'd you push me?"

Drunk from blood loss he started crying. Squeaking little gerbil.

"Sent you clients," he said wiping his nose. "Through family court, my own daughter. You're a fucking traitor. Paid your bills, bought you that primo car. But no, you, you, wanted more. Who the fuck gets knocked up . . . twenty-first century for chrissake?

Whatever happens, well, it's your fault more than mine."

"You won't get away with killing me," I said.

"I'm gonna try." He shook his head from side to side. "Goddamn Marv. Another fucking turncoat."

"Marv Finney? What's he got to do with us? He's dead, didn't you hear?"

"You—you never mind about Marv."

"You'll die first if you don't get to a doctor to get that leg looked at."

"No way, Jose."

The gun surprised me. I hadn't given much thought to the method but thought he'd do something more personal, like strangulation with one of the many restraints we kept around the place. More fitting. Without a thought both my hands wrapped around my stomach, an instinct to protect someone other than me I never knew I had.

I saw Todd shift his glance to his unborn child. He winced.

"We deserved each other," I started to say but never did.

Chapter Eighty-Seven

Preston

Stunned, I stared at the monitor.

My father had known I was pregnant.

In my haze I thought the FedEx guy gave me the box with Cooper's new monogrammed blankets, not Dad. The date stamp on the footage confirmed he'd come the day I delivered. The day I cratered my life for good. How long did he stay? Did he even try to help me? Did I kick him out like I did my mother? I couldn't remember.

Now I needed to find him.

Still crying I hunted for my phone. I could never find my phone. I needed to listen to Dad's messages again. After a fifteen-minute search through the house I found my cell on the floor of the Rover. I thought about his odd-sounding message while I hustled back to the house. Dad must've been near the stables, which is why I thought he was outside when he called. He kept saying, "Preston, where are you?" Sounded infuriated.

The red-stained windowpane check fabric Walter had dropped at my feet belonged to Dad. The rumbling sound at the end of his voicemail wasn't a rumble at all but a growl. Walter broke free to attack my father. The brake lights were his.

Intent on listening to Dad's messages again, I saw I missed another one, this one from Smiley. "Preston. I'm just leaving Judge Seward's. Your dad is the guy in the pictures. He's the one. I'm not sure if he and Isabel are still in, well, whatever they're in, but we know where she lives. I'm headed there with a search warrant to find out what the hell is going on."

I hit redial. Walter interrupted my listening to it ring with a head butt to my thigh. "You want to go out back?" We walked toward the back of the house so I could let him out through the French doors. I'd no more than opened the door when Walter stiffened. I dropped the phone, gripped Walter's collar with all my strength to keep him from lunging.

****

"Dad?"

Walter growled and barked at my father, who stood frozen in the backyard. I couldn't hold him even with both hands. He got away from me. I yelled, "Stop, Walter!" He did, surprising both my father and me, who'd shirked back in expectation. The Greatest Dane dropped to his belly.

"What are you doing here?" I hated myself for the trembling in my voice. For the first time in my life I felt afraid of my father. Walter belly crawled to my side, head down. "How did you get here?"

"You're, you, you." His breath came hard, he couldn't finish his thought. "Not the, uh, the only one who knows secret ways to, to get to, in, places."

A lot of land, dense with trees, surrounded these estates. Anyone who wanted to bad enough could get in just about anyone's backyard on Nottingham Lane.

"What the hell happened?" I pointed to the calf he'd tried to bandage, drenched with and sopping blood, with what looked like his belt tied around his leg, buckle dangling. From the looks of him, it'd taken a herculean act of strength, and will, to propel my dad here through the back ways. "Why aren't you—"

"That, it, him. Fucking dog." He pointed at Walter who stood up, snarled in response. "What the hell was that, that, damn mongrel doing at Beverley?" His face twisted into one I didn't recognize, showing emotions I couldn't even name. Then morphed into something else altogether, something childlike and pitiful. He started to cry. "Can you—you owe me—help out your old dad, Preston? Can you?"

"Help you what?"

Dad held out both bloody hands to show Walter he wasn't planning anything underhanded. He hobbled to the patio, his leg a torn, bloodied mess. "Can I please, pretty please, come in?" He motioned to Walter.

I held firm to my dog, let my father in. "You need to go the hospital," I said.

"I know. You, um, you can take me. Say I was, say I was, yeah, playing with that goddamn dog. He bit me or, or something." He staggered right past the boxes but didn't notice them, then fell into the nearest chair. "Probably can't, I mean *won't*, make the papers. If I ju, ju, just show up this way, that'll be, that'll be, definitely bad. Terrible, awful bad."

My Harvard educated father, attorney, and politician, suddenly inarticulate, meant his injury was serious and getting the best of him. So shocked by his condition, I half expected him to drop dead then and there. Walter crept forward. I jerked on his collar. "Stop it."

Dad looked up, like the command was for him. "Look, I'm serious. I mean, whatever Marv said isn't true. It's, that's why he's, no friend of mine. Dumbass killed himself, you know. Couldn't live with his lies."

Whatever I thought he'd say, it wasn't that.

"Marv? He didn't say anything. Not to me, anyway. What are you talking about?"

"What about the, uh, the whatchacallit? Cameras? Film? Your bitch, I mean, uncorked mother, stole them from Isabel's car. Yeah. Righty-o. I'm sure she did. Made that idiot, duh, duh, driver of hers do it. Who else?"

He struggled with his words. The blood loss was doing his brain no favors.

"You're talking nonsense." I knew very well what film. Mother got the blame for everything. I willed myself not to look toward the empty boxes still in his sight if he turned his head toward the library where the cameras and flash drive sat handily on James's desk.

He looked me over with great care. "Nothing. No, nope nothing," he said senselessly. His face looked white as death. Sweat ran down his forehead from his dyed hairline, his fake blue eyes wet.

"Did you follow me to the stables?" I said.

"No. I, I didn't know you'd be there. I needed—no *had* to— to get the cameras." His lips curled up. "Lived at Beverley for thirty, um, shit this hurts, thirty-some whatever the fuck years. I know that path better than you."

I kept quiet for once. I didn't want to give my father any reason to suspect I knew what was on those cameras.

"I tried to tell," he cried in earnest. "Tell you we'd, uh, no *I* married Isabel. You wouldn't answer. You wouldn't answer the goddamn phone when your own father called."

That came out clear.

He raised his hand, then dropped it, remembering the giant dog who wanted to eat him. "No. One. Respects. Me." If he'd had the strength he would've yelled that last bit. Walter whined dying to attack.

"Marrying Isabel doesn't do much to raise the respect bar. Why didn't I hear? You getting married again would've definitely made the news around here."

"Confi . . . confiden . . . secret marriage license. Yeah, that's it, that's a, a thing. Look it up." Dad's voice had gone cold, hard. "Your mother, Vampira, forced my hand. Didn't have a choice."

"Don't blame Mom because you married a crackpot."

"Wouldn't have if Harrison had let me keep the money."

That came out quick, strong.

"She. Rich crone. Didn't need it. She, *I,* deserved something for all those years." His face turned a deep purple. His words seemed tough to come by. Whatever blood supply he had left fueled his rage. "Strung me along. Let me think our divorce was *friendly.* Smug wretch. She went along with my lies to that cop. Psycho cop. Then bam! What the hell? *She* pulled the rug out."

"You went from one rich wife to another. You married Isabel for the lottery winnings from her dead mother."

"You. Preston. You knew about her mother?"

"Obviously."

"Just like Harrison. Think you know all. Every. Fucking. Thing." He could barely retain his rage even in his sorry state. "You hate that emas . . . emasculate, whatever, bitch as much as I do. You, of all the, *you* tried to kill her. For chrissake. She only loved Cooper. She wished you'd died instead." He leaned far over to emphasize that last bit, hit his elbow on the table. "Godammit," he said to the offending table. Walter jumped up, almost pulled my arm out of the socket but I kept him back. "Do—*don't* you see?" he said. "Me and you." He held up crossed fingers, "We're alike. Twinsies. Both married losers to get even with your mother."

Nothing in my life was what I'd thought. I understood more in five minutes than I had in almost thirty years. So much so that commenting didn't seem necessary, so I didn't.

"You," he said pointing. "Little girl, got to help me get away. Yes, I mean, I mean, you owe me." He wheedled like he used to.

"Get away from who? I don't owe you."

"You sniveling, sweetie, wait. No. I stuck up for you. Made sure you didn't get, mmmm, I mean *go* to prison. Your bitch mother wanted to lock you up and throw away the key."

Almost funny how he could rally when he insulted my mother.

"No, she didn't," I said but balked. I knew she did, at first.

His eyes widened, then narrowed. "Oh, don't tell me you two kissed and, and, made up? Of all the—"

Not exactly but he didn't need to know that. I held my tongue and my dog.

"That's rich," Dad said. "Fuck fucking figures. Well, big shit."

"You killed Aunt James."

Dad looked like I'd punched him in the face.

"James? Wha . . . who, who told you about James?"

"James did."

"How?"

"She left a letter. I burned it."

"I buried your baby, you know."

He couldn't have picked a better way to change the subject. That felt like a mule kick. "What did you do that day, Dad? I know you were there."

It seemed impossible for him to go whiter, but he did.

"How do you know that? You're lying."

Shit. I'd given myself away, so I said the only thing he'd

believe. "I remembered."

With an Oscar winning actor's skill, he turned sober as a preacher. "Damn it, Preston. You know you would've killed that kid eventually."

I gripped Walter to keep from passing out. "Eventually?"

"I couldn't let him live. That kid would've been the messiah. First male in fuck knows how long. He'd have gotten everything. I did it for you. To protect your inheritance."

Another topic that acted like a shot of adrenalin to his failing system and nonsensical speech patterns. I felt my lips open and close like a fish, but no sound came out.

He kept talking, but those last few sensible words about did him in. He sacrificed some strength, and clarity, to eke out his horrifying excuse. "He, he'd have died anyway, already a druggie. Too small. I didn't need to, to do, anything. In fact, that's exactly what I did. Yesirree. I didn't *do anything*. Not a, not a, goddamn thing. Half an hour. Done. Never made a peep."

"Why didn't you call an ambulance? You let me deliver him on the floor?"

"You'd gone. Yes you did—into the bathroom—locked the door. Figured you were taking more drugs. Didn't matter. Kid was a goner."

"So you were there when Mom came?"

"Oh, Bob's your uncle, no. I left. You didn't seem any more dis . . . distressed. Oh, who cares, than usual."

"You left me there? I could've died."

"You didn't though. Oh no, you're a tough little bugger. I do, *did,* worry a little, just a smidge, so I went back. When I got there the front window, you know, was smashed in. I climbed through. Your mother. Naturally, your mother beat me there. She didn't want to let me in to your bedroom. Cunt. So I called Marv. The rest, as you—*they*—say is, uh, history."

I knew in my heart that nothing would've saved my Cooper. My father was right and I hated him more than I could imagine hating anyone at that moment. All I needed to do was let go of Walter. That'd be the end. As if he could read my mind, Walter barked, growled, tried to spring forward. I loosed my grip a little, tightened it again. I couldn't do it. I still hadn't figured out how I tried to do my mother in. Where'd I get the chutzpah for that hideous act?

"See? You do owe me," he said. "You. Filthy, I mean, you're *filthy* rich because of me."

"You're right," I heard myself say. Like I'd separated from my body. I wanted this man out of my house. If I could get him in my car maybe I could drive him to the police station or pull over and boot him out.

"So you'll do it? Help me?"

"Yes, the Rover's got a full tank of gas. I'll take you anywhere you want to go. But there's a price. Tell me where Cooper's buried first or we go nowhere."

"Easy peasy. I'm really, oh, so, you know, very super clever. Underneath the uh, garden thingy. The, the, the, whosit, gazebo."

"What gazebo?"

"The one. You know, that one, in Aunt James's backyard."

Despite the precarious situation I found myself in, I still felt relief, a sense of closure, peace. My son was laid to rest somewhere, not thrown out like garbage. I looked down to see blood pooling around Dad's leg, despite his DIY medical treatment. He might bleed out right here in my house.

"Harri . . . your mother only has herself to blame about, you know, James. It's on her. Isabel too. If your mother hadn't been such a, a, bitch Isabel might still be alive."

"You killed Isabel?" It struck me then. "Brendan. You murdered Brendan too?

He let out a weak chuckle. "What am I? A professional? Ah, no. Isabel beat me to it. Of all the goddamn luck. Brendan decided to, how you say, get with the fucking program. Yeah. Followed us all over the damn place. I'd have done the deed sooner rather than later. No choice."

At that second, I realized I was out of my league. I let Walter go. Dad shot up, pulled a gun out of the back of his pants, a lot faster than I thought he could in the shape he was in. Before he could shoot, or I could run, the front doors slammed. I turned toward the sound, heard Dad cock his pistol behind me.

I'm not sure what actually killed my father. Smiley's bullet or Walter's jaws around his throat.

Chapter Eighty-Eight

Preston

The sun peeked through the early morning clouds as Smiley and I watched the coroner's van and the cop cars finally drive out. We stood on the porch until we couldn't see them anymore and then shut the heavy double doors behind us.

"Glad I blew off the booby hatch for this mess." I led Smiley by the hand to the sofa in the library. We sat. "Makes me miss bars on the windows."

"I'm sorry," Smiley said.

"Your timing was perfect," I said, and quick to shoot when it counts, which I didn't say. "I'd completely forgotten I'd dialed your number right before my father showed up, then I dropped the phone. You heard everything?"

"No, but some. Enough to get an idea of what was happening."

"I could use a stiff drink." Plus some.

"One more thing." He held out a piece of paper. "Marv's suicide note. Colleen wanted you to see it before it got cataloged into evidence."

"You found her?"

"She came to me. He mailed the note to her the day he shot himself."

My heart pitched to see my father-in-law's last scrawled thoughts.

Colleen—

It's my fault our boy is gone. I can't prove it, but I know Todd

Fitzgerald had a hand in his dying. Our son tried to find out the truth. He knew Preston didn't hurt Harrison but couldn't prove it. Well, I knew Todd did it. I saw him. God help me, I did. There's no proof other than my word, but it's true.

Preston and Harrison fought like she-cats over that poor, dead baby. Our grandson. Todd saw his chance and he grabbed the cutter. Sliced Harrison's throat along with his hand. I justified keeping silent because Harrison lived and Preston didn't go to jail. She got help, which we both know she needed.

You and I both know that no one would ever believe me. The Blair Fitzgerald machine would've buried me like they did our son. But with Brendan and you both gone, I can't go on living with the guilt and a secret I can't prove.

I've written everything that happened down in my notepad (you know which one) plus where to find Preston's security cameras. It won't prove what happened inside, but they still might help. I'm sorry for everything.

I'll love you to eternity and back.

Marvin

Smiley held up a blood-smeared notebook. "One of the boys found this on Todd's desk. The one Isabel died behind. Marv's notes."

Hard to say how I felt knowing I was innocent. I didn't jump for joy, sing the hallelujah chorus or shout to the rafters. I didn't move at all. Stillness settled in, down to my bones. I pressed Marv's letter to my face and cried.

I was not a monster.

****

Smiley and I hadn't moved from the sofa. Walter White slept in the corner like he'd died, tired after his superhero antics. I remembered something.

"What on earth did Judge Seward know about any of this?"

"He introduced your father to the fetish club. I guess it's all the rage in the prosecutor's office. He knew Todd and Isabel got together. They both left the scene soon after, so the judge didn't know anything else. But that was enough."

I shook my head. What a world.

"To think I actually loved my father, in my way," I said.

"I'm sure you did," Smiley said.

"His teary visits to Haven House didn't have anything to do with my well being. He wanted to see if and when I'd remember anything."

"Quite the actor, your father."

"I don't know where to go next, what to do." In some ways I felt I'd never seen this room before, or this house, or this man. I'd never see anything the same way again. "For so long I'd tried to piece things together, put my finger on the pulse of what happened. Now that I know, well, now what?"

Smiley said, "Live your life. Sounds ridiculously simple but I find one foot in front of the other is best."

I stared ahead in a daze like my head floated above my body.

"Your Mom's scar always bugged me." Smiley brought me back to earth.

"What?"

"It's the standard ear-to-ear type cut," he said. "That wound had to come from someone standing behind her. When I questioned Harrison about the judge and Isabel I took another look."

I didn't admit I'd overheard his call to her from under the stairs.

"Both you and Harrison remember you fought toe-to-toe," he said. "So unless you'd managed to jump behind her you couldn't have done it."

"I never thought Dad would try to kill his cash supply."

"I don't think he thought about it at all. Crime of opportunity. He saw his chance and took it. Marv nailed that one. No premeditation." He looked thoughtful. "That and he was probably scared shitless you'd remember he was there when Cooper was born."

"I'd never have believed Dad could work up nerve enough." I shifted sideways, draped my legs and feet across Smiley's lap. "I understand the urge." I thought more about the possibility. "I could see maybe something a little more festive, like a shove off a cruise ship. But a box cutter? No."

"Harsh, no doubt." Smiley smoothed my crazy hair.

"Only my dad could fuck up in his own favor. It would've been better if she'd stayed in a coma. He got to do what he pleased with that power of attorney. No one would've ever questioned him."

"I know. Unbelievable."

Smiley lifted his butt off the couch, pulled a cell phone out of his pocket. "Isabel's cell. She recorded her last conversation with your father from under the desk. Right before he shot her." Smiley hit play. We listened to the whole thing. Thought I couldn't feel more horrified than I did a few short hours ago. Wrong.

"I can't believe Dad carried a gun."

"He took it from your mother's bedside drawer when he moved out. Her old school security system."

"Figures. What happened with Marcella?"

"Gone. Probably deep into Mexico by now."

"What on earth was she ever doing at Beverley?"

"Besides pretending to be Isabel, your dad hired her to keep an eye on Harrison. She kept your mother's sedative supply going until Harrison figured it out."

"Dad got it right. He said my mother knew how this would all turn out. She knew he'd sink."

My phone rang. Gate guard.

"Ms. Blair? Your mother's here."

My feet barely touched the floor when Smiley's cell jangled. I'd gotten as far as the library door when Smiley said, "In case you thought this situation couldn't get weirder. Isabel's baby survived. Six weeks premature and struggling. But so far, still alive."

Chapter Eighty-Nine

Preston

All these months I'd wondered how to get myself to show up at my mother's door. Now she showed up at mine. The few minutes it took her driver to cruise up the lane felt like eternity. Smiley and I didn't speak while we waited. I stood by the double front doors like a kid who just found out she was getting everything she ever wanted.

Soon as the Town Car rolled to a stop I flew outside. She met me midway on the stairs. We both froze. When I imagined this moment I assumed we'd find all sorts of new things to say to each other—meaningful, heartfelt things. But the old script sat like a stone at the back of my throat. We'd need time to come up with new material.

While innocent of one crime, I'd inflicted terrible wounds, in so many ways, for so many years. I should've begged forgiveness but my tongue knotted up. Still, I saw in Mom's eyes, blue as the deepest sea, she'd accepted the apology I'd never given. For the first time I felt seen by the most important woman in my life.

She, as always, looked ethereal. Her beauty still a living force. I'd never agreed with those who insisted we were alike. What daughter wants to be a rerun of her mother? Standing there with her, I knew, straight up, we were indeed the same where it counted—not the crumbling kind. Drinking in her presence I couldn't help but notice she seemed free in a way she never did before. When my father cut her throat he cut her loose from a way of life that never suited her.

She touched my face with her delicate hand, the smell of her skin exotic and familiar at the same time. I leaned into her palm—arms limp at my sides. Mom put one arm around my waist, and we walked up the stairs to my house. Like generations of Blair women before us we didn't flag under a torrent of emotions—the strong stand up and carry on, the weak can't. I don't have to tell you which category we fell into.

Chapter Ninety

Preston's Blog

Musings from the Dented Throne

Grey Gardens 2.0

Rumors of my death have been greatly exaggerated. I'm sure you figured I'd been cheating on you with a more amenable, less surly, crowd. Not on your life. I'd never throw you over or close up shop without saying goodbye, my faithful devotees. I must say goodbye for now, but it's not a sad one.

You might've seen our documentary. I don't want to toss too many spoilers in case you DVR'd our fifteen minutes and plan to watch at a later date. Yes, the Queen and I let Jack (our very own commenter, Jack) film his little movie. So, if you prefer surprises, stop reading, because there're things I must tell you, pay-per-view be damned.

I bought my Aunt James's house, unloaded mine. Made the new owners an offer they couldn't refuse. Why? I needed a fresh start for one, and for another, let's just say my heart will forever reside near Aunt James's gazebo, so the rest of me had to follow.

New Detective and I decided to give it a real go. He's left the police force, dabbles in private investigations here and there. My bootylicious beau says I should've been a cop because I closed the case, not him. Says I've got a real nose for finding evidence. If you can call being in the wrong place at the wrong time a skillset then he might be on to something.

Given Jack's Ken Burns imitation and our agreement to

participate, I had to come clean with New Detective regarding this blog. Whatever criticisms or trepidations he might harbor about the Heiress's personality, he's wisely kept them zipped.

As for me, I stay home, write dark, depressing, occasionally humorous stories for little to no money, see to our giant lunk of a dog (you'll need to watch our little film to find out who gave me such a wonderful surprise) and most important, I take care of Ruby James Blair.

I don't like to say Ruby's my sister, which she technically is, but I don't like to say so. Because Jack's film blew my blogger subterfuge, I guess aliases don't matter. I only mention Ruby by name because she's the first Blair girl (she's a Blair as far as we're all concerned) to bear a female moniker. Big improvement, am I right?

New Detective and I think of Ruby as our daughter, our much adored, beautiful, strong daughter. Without giving the whole twisted tale away, I'll tell you this: I didn't intend to acknowledge Ruby's existence, much less take her in. But I did. I felt drawn by a force I couldn't deny or explain. None of us in this terrible story can claim complete innocence except for this sweet baby who could not help the circumstances of her birth. And yes, I'm self-aware enough to know she represents my second chance, however fucked up that might be. I assure you one look at Ruby and I saw the light.

My handsome detective didn't mean to love me. The Queen probably would've liked to stop loving me, my Irishman probably wished he'd never loved me. I'd have preferred to leave love for the saps, but now I know when it comes to love, you've got no say at all.

But the downside to a beating heart is the bleeding.

What of the Jester?

I don't think of him often, even when I catch glimpses of him in Ruby's face or bearing. He's a part of our family's dreadful history and history won't be moved. One thing I've learned from so much death is when all is said and done, and the earth lays its claim to you, no one remembers the beginning, but it matters how things end.

Shrinky?

Well, now that'd give away the farm if I elaborate on her, so I'll leave you to wonder.

What happened to the Queen?

She and Jack's romance cooled, but he remains her close confidant and occasional bodyguard, which is (just my opinion) one small reason why she submitted to his intrusion into her life—to protect her from the press (we're flavor of the day again since we've gone Hollywood) and at the time, the Jester. Our Jack's a giant. The Royal She's decision to commit her life story to film is one I'll never fully understand. Maybe a lifetime of devastating, damaging secrets, her genetically induced requisite to deny the unpleasant, to cover up less than flattering incidents, prompted a need to lay it all on the table. Maybe, like all of us, she wanted to be noticed, *really* noticed. Not for her money, name, or beauty. But for who she really is. And who might she be, you ask? Ah, that my faithful, remains a mystery.

Well, my followers, I couldn't let another day go by without telling you how much you all have meant to me. I know, I know, the Heiress can be one prickly bitch, but you knew all along she didn't mean it.

You saved me before I knew I needed saving. So much water flashed under my bridge I almost didn't survive the flood but for your lifelines. I'll miss you so but will see you all in my dreams and can only hope you remember me fondly.

Try not to gag on my schmaltz.

The Queen and I are off to lunch to discuss Ruby's shit-ton of money. Yes, she's an heiress of blockbuster proportions. Her deceased grandmama's lottery winnings passed right to our little girl. We Blair girls handle our own money, thank you very much, and when the time's right Ruby will know how to take care of it herself.

After lunch we're taking a new doll to Rosalie at the loony bin. You remember Rosie the Ripper? Turns out her endless supply of dolls came from the Queen, whose heart Rosie melted. We visit her often.

We're quite a rag-tag group, me, Rosie and the Queen. All flawed mothers, fatally so, united by our failings and grief, offering one another the tender mercies that no one else can. I think together, we're going to make it through.

BTW, on the way home, I'm going to start teaching the Queen to drive.

The Girl Formerly Known as the Invisible Heiress.

~~ The End ~~

Thank You!

Thank you for reading my book. If you enjoyed it, please take a moment to leave me a review.

Connect with Me

Email: authorkodonnell@gmail.com
Facebook: facebook.com/kodonnellauthor
Web: http://www.authorkathleenodonnell.com
Twitter: twitter.com/authorkodonnell
Instagram: instagram.com/kathleenthewriter
Goodreads: goodreads.com/author/show/7200820
Pinterest: pinterest.com/authorkodonnell

About the Author

Kathleen O'Donnell is a wife, mom, grandmother and a recovering blogger. She currently lives in Nevada with her husband. She is a two time Book of the Year finalist for her debut novel The Last Day for Rob Rhino. You can find short stories and blog posts on her website: www.authorkathleenodonnell.com

Contents